FIRST
THE
THUNDER

OTHER TITLES BY RANDALL SILVIS

FIRST
THE
THUNDER

RANDALL SILVIS

THOMAS & MERCER

Text copyright © 2018 by Randall Silvis
All rights reserved.

Published by Thomas & Mercer, Seattle

www.apub.com

Amazon, the Amazon logo, and Thomas & Mercer are trademarks of Amazon.com, Inc., or its affiliates.

ISBN-13: 9781503905481
ISBN-10: 1503905489

Adapted from an earlier and shorter version of this work originally published as the novella *The Indian*, in *Ellery Queen Mystery Magazine*, no. 139, and reprinted in *The Best American Mystery Stories*, ed. Lisa Scottoline (New York: Houghton Mifflin Harcourt, 2013), 300–49.

Cover design by Shasti O'Leary Soudant

Printed in the United States of America

AUTHOR'S NOTE

This novel began as the novella *The Indian*, originally published in *Ellery Queen Mystery Magazine* and reprinted in Houghton Mifflin Harcourt's annual series *The Best American Mystery Stories*.

For my sons,
Bret and Nathan,
soul of my heart, heart of my soul

I

1

From her car atop the slight rise forty yards from the accident, Laci used the zoom lens of her Nikon to study the wreckage through the darkness and misty rain. And heard herself thinking, *I don't want to do this again.*

A blue pickup truck on its side, its load of old lumber scattered over the pavement. A red Jeep Wrangler, across the drainage ditch and accordioned against a tree, its windshield shattered, front wheels off the ground, one headlight shining into the sky, its beam diffusing in the light fog.

An ambulance was between the two wrecked vehicles, yellow lights flashing, back door swung open to reveal a paramedic leaning over a patient on a gurney. One state police patrol car was parked well beyond the wreckage, another on the near side of it, red and blue roof lights strobing, highway flares burning a deeper red. A trooper stood beside each of the parked cars, flashlight in hand, turning and rerouting any vehicle that approached. The 3:00 a.m. traffic was scarce. Now and then a web of heat lightning cracked through the clouds.

She turned the air-conditioning up a notch higher. The windshield wipers beat back and forth on their slowest setting, swatting at the mist that kept settling over the glass. Between swipes the scene lost focus, blurred like a wet watercolor painting. After each swipe the scene cleared for a few seconds, and the nausea bubbled in her stomach again.

She just wanted to go home to her daughter, Molly. Wanted to hold her and keep her forever safe from this kind of stupidity.

But she couldn't. A hundred dollars wasn't much, but they needed it. The bar was failing and Will had no idea how to turn things around. And now, as of earlier that night, instead of figuring out a way to cut costs and increase business, he was letting himself get involved in some craziness of Harvey's. As if Will was seriously going to lend his brother a revolver so he could shoot Kenny! Why couldn't Will see how his loyalty to Harvey, and to Stevie too, for that matter, was pulling him down? Why did his brothers always have to come to him with their problems? Will needed to pay attention to the things that mattered. Something had to change. She wasn't going to let him take her and Molly down with the rest of them.

She changed lenses on the camera, then adjusted the settings. Fitted a plastic bag over the body, made a small hole for the lens. Then struggled in the small seat to pull a yellow plastic rain slicker over her head and down over her waist. Stuffed her hair under a ball cap. Put her hand on the gearshift and muttered, "Goddamn it, Will." Then drove slowly forward.

On both sides of the road, behind irregularly spaced trees and bushes and sumac, lay wide fields of soybeans, the low green plants nearly invisible in the darkness. Bits of glass and metal on the road and in the dirt along the shoulders caught light from the vehicles and sparkled like shattered stars.

She came abreast of the trooper waving his flashlight beam back and forth, and powered down her window. She didn't recognize him, and thought, *Must be fairly new.*

"Looks bad," she said.

The trooper said, "We can't let anybody through for a while. If you go back about a mile you can take 208 on your left—"

She picked up her camera, showed it to him. "I'm the photographer for the *Clarion*. Any chance I could get a few shots?"

He asked for her identification. She handed him her driver's license. "We don't have press credentials," she said. "I can give you my editor's number if you want. Or you can call the barracks. Ask for Milo, Patterson, Delano—they all know me."

He studied her license for a few moments. "Wait here," he said.

He moved forward a half dozen paces, spoke softly into his radio, held her license to the light and read from it. Then returned to Laci. "Pull over and park right here," he said. "Keep your four-ways on. Leave room for the wrecker to get through. There's a fire truck coming too. To hose off the debris."

Geez, she thought when she climbed out, because without the air conditioner blowing in her face, the air came at her so thick and warm, and lay heavy in her lungs. Then she crossed gingerly toward the ambulance, doing her best to avoid the scattered shrapnel of glass, plastic and metal while also letting the camera do its work, click after click. She would take a hundred photos for every one printed.

Within minutes she was sweating beneath the slicker. The air smelled of fishing worms and wet leaves, but also of gasoline and oil. From time to time she thought she smelled beer too. And the acrid smoke from the flares.

Almost simultaneously she noticed two things invisible from her car, and stopped moving except for subtle turns of her body and the camera. An EMT was hunkered down on the shoulder beyond the tree with the Jeep pinned against it, stretching a large black tarp over a body-size mound. And she now saw that there were three people inside the ambulance, not two: the EMT, the patient on a gurney and, seated near the patient's head, a young man bent double with his face in his hands.

Driver and passenger in the truck, she told herself. *One person in the Jeep. Deceased.*

She took another deep breath to steady herself, to push down the clog of nausea in her chest, and started clicking again, several shots into and outside the ambulance as she continued moving, one cautious step after another. Then a dozen shots of each wrecked vehicle. More of the same from various angles. And then, twenty minutes after she began—

Anything else? she thought. Looked around. Enough.

A heaviness always befell her with the word *enough*. The sadness. With that word she stopped being a photographer and returned to being Laci, mother and wife, sensitive human being. She thought of the victims' families. And felt like an interloper here. An intruder on somebody else's tragedy.

Parasite, a woman had called her once. A grief-stricken woman watching as her house burned down, her husband inside. The woman had been drunk, lashing out, but even so. Grief was grief. Death was death.

The *Clarion* would not print shots of bodies, and she was glad for that. It made her feel a little better about her job. But she took them anyway. In a few days she might show them to Molly and her friends. At fourteen they still felt invincible. Children needed repeated warnings, object lessons, admonitions about the dangers of driving drunk, driving while texting, driving too fast, whatever the police report might finally reveal. Better to frighten her daughter, she always told herself, than to have her daughter appear in one of the photos.

Often the police or the coroner would ask for the body shots, in which case she would get paid twice. Money her family needed.

Now she moved beyond the accident and toward the farther trooper. He stood with his back to her, flashlight held against his waist, beam sliding slowly back and forth above the road even though the highway was dark, no headlights in the distance.

He heard the footsteps, and looked over his shoulder.

In the space of three seconds his face was illuminated three times by the strobing lights. "Trooper Delano?" she said.

He smiled and turned. "I heard you were here."

She continued forward, stood to his left. "So what's it look like to you?"

"You tell me," he said.

"Three victims," she answered. "Driver of the Jeep deceased, driver of the pickup is probably the one on the gurney. The only one I could eyeball was sitting up, but with his face covered. I'm guessing they're all young. And were probably intoxicated. And, considering the location, maybe drag racing?"

"Playing chicken," he said. "The driver of the truck tried to pull out, but not soon enough. He took it from the side instead of head-on. Looks pretty serious. His passenger got the least of it. Banged up pretty good but still mobile and coherent. The deceased exited through his windshield."

Laci shook her head. "And there's still lots of summer left."

The trooper nodded. Then he cocked his head, and a moment later turned to peer into the darkness. Laci heard the siren a few moments later, knew it would be the fire truck or the coroner or another ambulance. The wrecker would not be far behind. An hour from now nothing would remain of this tragedy but for a few bits of glass and a couple of dark stains on the asphalt. Maybe in the next few days somebody would stick a cross into the dirt beside the damaged tree.

"I'll leave you to your work," she said.

"Call the barracks in about an hour," he told her. "We'll be able to release the names by then."

She walked away without saying goodbye.

At her car again she remained steady, waited inside until a second ambulance passed. Then she started the engine, made a two-point U-turn across the highway and headed back toward town. At home she would hold herself together awhile longer, long enough to download the photos onto her computer, clean up the ten best shots and email them to her editor. Then a hot soak with a glass of chardonnay. Then into her bed with Will.

He would be awake by then and would ask what had happened and how she was doing. She would say, "Three boys. One dead." And then she would shiver even though still warm from the bath, and Will would slide an arm under her shoulders and pull her close, and she would lay her head against him and shiver awhile longer and let herself go.

He would say nothing as she sobbed uncontrollably. He would hold her and kiss her forehead. This he was good at. This he could be counted on to do, and it was not an insignificant skill for a husband. In this regard, at least, he never failed her.

And after a while the sobbing would cease. Some of the awful heaviness would melt into the mattress, leaving only the sadness behind. The sadness would be there the next morning too, and for a long while afterward.

2

Eight hours earlier, at twenty minutes before seven on Friday evening, Harvey had shoved open the door to the bar and came striding in the way he always did, walking fast, angry, lips moving as he muttered to himself. Will, standing behind the taps, reached down to the bottom of the well for an icy Schlitz, gave it a wipe with the bar towel, twisted off the cap and set the bottle on the bar just as Harvey got there. Harvey didn't reach for the bottle right away this time, but hooked both hands around the curved edge of the cool wooden counter. His fingers kneaded the scarred mahogany.

Breathing hard, he said, "I swear to God I am going to kill that pasty-faced weasel once and for all."

Will had been standing behind the bar with nothing much to do and thinking about Portugal. In his mind he had been enjoying the view from a bluff overlooking the glittering Atlantic, while behind him on a sun-bleached plain lay a small well-ordered city with wide, clean streets and whitewashed buildings and the dome of a mosque glowing golden in the sun. Everything was bright, clean and spacious and the air was dry and clean and not overly warm.

It took Will a moment to adjust to this sudden migration back to his bar and his brother's anger. Harvey was always bitching about something his brother-in-law Kenny had done or failed to do. Always promising to strangle or shoot or castrate him for one trivial matter or another. Will set Harvey's beer on the counter and then just stood there for a moment, trying to hold on to the Portugal in his head.

The bar had been called Tony's Lounge when he and Laci returned from West Virginia to purchase the building and liquor license. He had wanted to rename it Molly's, after their then-seven-year-old daughter, but Laci had vetoed that.

"How about Molligan's?" he'd suggested. "I'm half-Irish, and there's a golf course just four miles away. We can have golfer specials seven or eight months out of the year. We'll clean up."

"Then call it Mulligan's," she said.

"That's part of it," he told her. "Because this *is* my mulligan. My do-over. But Molligan's is clever, don't you think? To include Molly in all of this?"

She did not think it was clever to have her daughter's name hanging above the door of a bar, and had told him so. Nor had she been happy to give up their spacious rented home for a cramped two-bedroom apartment above the bar. But she agreed to trust her husband. He seemed so happy to be away from the strip mines.

And for two years Will had tried hard to court the golfers. But then an access road had been connected to the interstate just outside of Greenfield, the county seat, less than twenty miles away, and almost immediately the farmland on both sides of the exit and entrance ramps blossomed with new businesses, with hotels and restaurants and a Super Walmart, Home Depot, Starbucks, and a minimall.

Even Will's fellow citizens of Barrowton, though resentful about being relegated to the outskirts, chose lower prices to hometown loyalty. Local mom-and-pop stores closed. The country club went public in Will's third year of business and lowered their restaurant prices. As local employment dropped, his neighbors tightened their belts even further, cut out luxuries such as dining out and playing golf. Now he was lucky to get two or three foursomes a week.

Down near the other end of the bar, Merle, one of his most reliable regulars, cleared his throat, and brought Will back to the present.

Will took a frosted glass out of the other cooler and filled it from the plastic jug of lime daiquiri mix he made twice a week just for Merle. He took away Merle's empty glass and damp napkin and set the fresh napkin and drink in precisely the same place. Merle nodded his thanks and sipped delicately from the fresh drink, his second of the evening.

Three nights a week Merle came in at precisely 6:00 p.m. and sat primly at the far end of the bar, and during the next two hours he would drink precisely four lime daiquiris without ever saying a word unless another customer or Will addressed him directly. But there were few other customers except on game nights and Merle did not come to the bar those nights. At precisely 8:00 p.m. he would lay a twenty-dollar bill on the counter, say "Thank you, Will. Good night," and slide off his stool and walk out the door.

He was a small man who, according to Laci, looked the way Tennessee Williams might have looked had he lived to be seventy-five instead of choking on the bottle cap from a vial of pills. He dressed almost exclusively in tan polyester suits, and on windy days he might wear a brown racing cap to keep what was left of his sandy hair from blowing. For thirty-seven years he had worked at the local driver license center. He failed both Harvey and then Will upon their first attempts many years ago, Harvey for roll-stopping at an intersection and Will for bumping the curb while parallel parking.

Tonight he sat with the heels of his cordovan loafers hooked over the barstool's rung, looking more like a retired jockey than a retired civil servant. It was a steamy Friday night in baseball season but the Pirates were off until Thursday, so the only other customers were four golfers who had come in earlier for burgers and beer. Will was grateful for the golfers because on nights when there wasn't a televised sporting event he didn't sell enough alcohol to cover his electric bill. The big-screen TV at the rear of the room was only two years old but still he could not compete with the motel bars out by the interstate. He could not compete with Comedy Night or Karaoke Night or the spacious dance floors and free munchies tables and the college girls in their short skirts. All he had to offer was a clean, quiet place to spend an hour or so with friends without having to shout to be heard, a place where for twelve dollars a man could quietly submerge himself in enough lime juice and rum to soften the edges on some undisclosed misery.

Not that Merle ever looked miserable. Just the opposite, if contentment is the opposite of misery. Merle was the most contented man Will had ever met. Self-contained, Laci called him. Perfectly happy to sit there quietly sipping his daiquiris, a small smile on his lips as he gazed at the bottles on the shelves or the poster-size photo of Ben Roethlisberger. If not for Merle, Will might not believe that contentment was an achievable state.

Will looked toward the golfers then and asked with a lift of his eyebrows if they were ready for another pitcher. One of the men grinned and nodded, so Will filled a fresh pitcher from the Coors tap and carried it to the table. The TV was tuned to Fox News but nobody was paying any attention to it. The air conditioner was working hard to counteract the sticky August heat. There was something loose inside the air conditioner and every once in a while Will could hear it rattling around in there like a marble in a tin can.

Harvey had both hands around his beer bottle when Will returned to stand in front of him, but the bottle remained full, Harvey hadn't taken a sip. He looked up at his brother and said, only loud enough for Will and maybe Merle to hear, "I swear to God I am going to kill that asshole. You might think I'm kidding but I'm not."

Will filled a small wooden bowl with salted peanuts and set it on the counter. "Stevie's upstairs watching TV with Laci," he said. "Go ahead and go on up if you want."

"I mean it, Will. I am seriously going to do it this time."

Will thought he should say something but he did not know what to say. He was two years younger than Harvey and half an inch taller, and he hadn't been afraid of Harvey since high school, but he didn't want to anger his brother further or add to his troubles. Will wasn't sure exactly what his brother's troubles were and he suspected that Harvey wasn't sure either. All Will knew was that for the past few years Harvey had appeared to be angry most the time. Even in his lighter moods there seemed to be something eating away at him, some worm of bitterness gnawing at his gut. It might have to do with his job as a truck driver for Jimmy Dean Sausage, but Will doubted it; Harvey had a regular route with regular customers, and there couldn't be much stress involved in humping sausage around. It might have had to do with Harvey's marriage but Will doubted that too; Harvey and Jennalee had been married for almost as long as Will and Laci, and Will knew for a fact that his brother was still madly, even desperately, in love with his wife.

Still, Harvey's anger, as nearly as Will could calculate, seemed to be of more or less the same vintage as his marriage. Before that, Harvey never took much of anything seriously. Back when Will was working a dragline fourteen hours a day for the coal company, for example, and socking away every spare nickel for that day when he could become his own boss, Harvey was still jumping from job to job like a teenager and spinning a modified Chevy around the dirt track every weekend. Only after Harvey's honeymoon to the Poconos did he give up racing and take on a regular job.

"I need that .357 for a while," Harvey said, this time lowering his voice so that Merle would not hear. But Merle, if he had overheard anything at all, gave no indication. He stared straight ahead at the bottles on the shelves, he sipped his daiquiri and he waited without complaint for a streetcar that would never arrive.

Will told his brother, "Hold on a minute." He went into the kitchen, checked the deep fryer, lifted out a basket of chicken wings and another of French fries, drained them, dumped each into a separate wicker basket lined with napkins and sprinkled them with salt. He carried these to the bar and handed them to Harvey. "Take these upstairs for me, will you? I'll be right behind soon as I check on those golfers."

Harvey said, "You going to let me have it or not?" When Will didn't answer, Harvey said, "And yes, it will come back to you clean. I'll clean it out with his fucking tongue is what I'll do."

Will said, "Those wings and fries are for Stevie. Laci and me are splitting a pizza, which you're welcome to share. You want anything else?"

Harvey stood there holding the food baskets and his beer.

"Damn it, Will!" he said in an insistent whisper. "I got this damn thunder in my head that just won't quit. I need that .357 of yours. *Tonight.*"

"I'll be up in a minute," Will told him. He turned away then to check on the pizza.

In the kitchen he tried to get back to Portugal but Portugal was lost to him now. It had been burned away in the sizzle and stink of the deep fryer's fat.

3

In the kitchen in the apartment upstairs, Laci poured ranch dressing into a white ramekin, then set the small bowl in the center of a platter filled with celery sticks, baby carrots, broccoli florets, pickles and olives. She knew that Stevie, watching TV in the living room, was typically a quiet man, especially in his brothers' presence, but a noisy eater. If she served the vegetables now, he would have his fill of them by the time the other food was ready, and she, in need of a shower, wouldn't have to listen to him gnawing on raw carrots and celery, a sound that always made her want to scream.

She carried the vegetable tray into the living room and set it down on the coffee table and said, "Help yourself, Stevie. I'm going to grab a quick shower before Will comes up."

She crossed out of the room and turned down the hallway and stuck a finger in each ear until she reached the bathroom. Then quickly stepped inside and closed the door. She did not dislike Stevie, knew he was a kind person, always willing to help out with any task whenever she or Will needed him. But there was also an air of sneakiness surrounding him. Will thought it was because their father had been such a stingy man when it came to doling out compliments. He, like his oldest son, had always seemed angry about something, always simmering with a secret rage. All three sons had tried their best to avoid him.

"I think Dad's the one responsible," Will told her once. "Stevie took the brunt of his anger. He was only five when the old man got cancer. Harvey and me could head outside when we wanted to, but Stevie was more or less stuck at home with Mom. Stevie was an easy target for everybody, I guess."

Ever since hearing that, Laci had tried her best to be kind to Stevie. The truth was, she felt sorry for him. But his noisy eating made her want to jump out of her skin. And she had to admit that a part of her resented both Stevie and Harvey; if not for them, Will would never have wanted to move back to this place. Because of them, she and Molly were trapped here. And Will, too attached to his brothers and this nowhere town, was turning into a nowhere man himself. She needed to find some way to make him realize this before it was too late for all of them.

While in the shower, Laci started thinking about a trooper she used to know. Trooper Alex Wilson. He used to call her Olga because her small body and athleticism in bed reminded him of Olga Korbut, the Belarusian gold medalist who became famous when Laci was still a little girl.

Up until a year ago Laci would sometimes run into Trooper Wilson at the scene of house fires, car accidents, and other photo-worthy events. And, a total of seven times over three months, in a room at the Marriott out along the interstate.

She called it off the night he suggested they pick a specific day and hour to inform their spouses that they wanted a divorce. Because Laci did not want a divorce. She wasn't sure what she *did* want except for something different from what she'd had before the affair started. Something that provided an occasional easement of the heaviness of living in a cramped apartment above a bar that had difficulty staying in the black each month, and of chasing one tragedy after another with her camera, and of watching her daughter growing up in a town that, inch by inch, seemed to be sinking ever deeper into its economic and cultural sinkhole.

In the end, Trooper Wilson left his job with the state police and moved with his children and wife to somewhere in North Carolina. And now Laci stood in her kitchen, wondering about what might have been. A drop of sweat trickled down her spine and made her shiver.

She had changed into a pair of tan shorts and a pale-green tank top, her feet bare and the hair along the back of her neck still damp from the shower. She had towel-dried her hair and run a brush through it, but didn't bother to style it. She leaned against the cool edge of the kitchen sink and sipped from a chilled bottle of Corona. The ceiling fan's hum helped to drown out any crunching noises coming from the living room, but it did little to cool the kitchen or to disperse the scent of grease floating up through the floorboards from the bar's deep fryer.

When she heard the thumps outside the door, her body stiffened.

4

At the top of the stairs, Harvey kicked the door a couple of times. He wasn't even sure why he had bothered to come up the stairs. Or maybe he was. He didn't want to go home, that was why.

A few seconds later, Stevie yanked open the door from inside the apartment, reached for the plastic baskets of wings and fries and said, "About time. I'm starvin' to death here." To Laci he called, "Look who the delivery boy is tonight!"

Laci blew out a breath, took another sip of beer, and stepped into the living room. "Hey, Harvey," she said. "How you doin'? Jennalee come with you?"

Harvey didn't answer. There was a movie on the television, something with Nicolas Cage and Meg Ryan. Laci's police scanner on the mantel was crackling softly with static-filled voices, and a floor fan in the corner of the room made a constant clicking whirr. After a moment Harvey asked, "Molly around?"

"She's at the library with some friends. I'm picking her up around eight. Why do you ask?"

Instead of explaining, Harvey glared at the TV. Even with all the windows open and the fan on high, the room pulsed with a damp, suffocating heat. "It's like trying to breathe through a wet towel in here," he said.

Laci crossed to the end of the sofa, smiled up at him. "You ready for another beer?"

"How do you guys even sleep at night? I can't breathe in here."

"We take the fan into the bedroom. Molly's got a little one of her own."

"Make Will buy you an air conditioner, for chrissakes."

Laci blushed and looked away. "The heat only lasts a couple of weeks."

Stevie said, "You're getting soft, brother. Driving around in a refrigerated truck all day." He finished his first chicken wing, laid the bone in the corner of the basket, sucked his fingertips clean, and reached for another wing.

Harvey stood there at the other end of the sofa and watched the color in Laci's cheeks, saw the way the rubied glow spread down the front of her neck. *What kind of life is this,* Harvey wondered, *when Will has to live in a dump like this, but a jerk like Kenny gets anything he wants?*

Then Stevie said, "You ask around for me yet over at Jimmy Dean?"

"I already told you. Nobody is ever going to hire you as a driver. Not with your record they're not."

"They're mostly just parking violations," Stevie said.

"Because you don't pay attention. You have to stay alert to be a driver."

For most of his adult life Stevie had made his living as the town's handyman, shoveling snow in winter, mowing lawns in the summer, tilling gardens in the spring, raking leaves in the fall. During all seasons he dug graves for the Cemetery Association, hauled away garbage the trash contractor wouldn't accept, painted an occasional house, cleaned out an occasional garage. Every Sunday he helped Will haul in the kegs and other supplies. In return he had his dinner nearly every night compliments of Will, either here in Will and Laci's place or downstairs at the bar. He would have liked to have a girlfriend but understood that he was not anybody's idea of an eligible bachelor, even by local standards.

The accident when he was eight didn't help. Everybody in town knew the story. One day when their parents were absent, the older boys in charge of their little brother, Will and Harvey were taking turns leaping from the front porch roof to the garage roof ten feet away. The trick was to keep running, uphill, when landing on the steeply pitched garage roof, or risk sliding downhill and tumbling to the ground. When they tired of testing each other, they taunted little Stevie to try. Dutifully he climbed out their bedroom window and onto the porch roof, then, after more teasing and cajoling, finally took a fearful run and leaped across the gulf to the garage, where his brothers sat perched at the roof's peak. Stevie landed with one outstretched foot on the shingles, the other foot trailing. He lost his balance, fell onto a knee, and rolled sideways off the edge of the roof.

He lay unconscious for an unknown period of time. Harvey and Will agreed it was "less than a minute," and that Stevie was just fine afterward. But Stevie, who woke up lying on the living room carpet, felt certain he had been out for an hour or more. He remembered wandering around in an immense dark room, walking as if blind with both hands extended before him, the only light coming from tiny flashes of red brilliance popping and fizzing inches from his face. The lights seemed to have an order and purpose, seemed to be trying to convey an important message to him, the way they sometimes came together in small groups, sometimes went careening away from each other, only to return in sinuous, cryptic lines. There had been a comforting familiarity to the lights, a friendliness, which he remembered clearly to this day. He also remembered being very thirsty and tired and wanting only to go home again.

His parents didn't learn of the fall until late that afternoon, when they saw the bruises on Stevie's forehead and shoulder. At first his brothers claimed ignorance, but when Stevie finally said, "I think I fell off the roof," the full story came out. Soon both Will and Harvey had bruises of their own, but theirs were from their father's wide leather belt. And afterward, every time Stevie would forget one of his chores, every time he was sent home from school for fighting or for a smart remark to a teacher, his mother would scold the older brothers and say, "You made him this way. You're the ones who need to be punished."

Consequently, everyone in town now treated Stevie as if he were brain damaged. He knew he wasn't. He was different from his brothers, that's all. But in a small town, being different was its own kind of damage.

"I don't see where it would hurt to ask," Stevie said in response to Harvey's comment about his driving record. "I'd even work in packing, I don't care."

"They have your application on file," Harvey said.

"But that's three or four years old. I don't mind filling out a new one."

Harvey crossed to the police scanner and turned it down. "How can you even hear the TV with this thing blaring all the time?"

"Harvey, please," Laci said. "It's hardly blaring. Turn it up again, please."

"I can't even hear myself think in here."

"Well, how am I supposed to hear if there's a fire or a car wreck or something?"

"You'll hear the siren, same as everybody else in town."

"But I need to get there with my camera *before* everybody else in town. So if you don't mind . . ."

To placate her, Harvey pretended to turn the volume up. Then returned to stand by the open window. Laci crossed to the scanner and turned it to its original volume.

Though nearly forty, Laci was small and still as lithe as a gymnast. Stevie had to deliberately avoid looking at her ass when she passed in front of him. Later tonight, when he was back home at his trailer, he would think about her ass and probably Jennalee's too, which was even better. And sooner or later he would lock his doors and pop a porn

DVD into the player. Afterward he would feel guilty and lonely but he was seldom able to control his thoughts once they began.

Harvey didn't look at Laci at all, didn't see the teasing face she made after turning up the scanner and taking a seat on the sofa. He continued to stare at the TV. Nicolas Cage was standing at the top of a high building, the wings of his trench coat flaring as he peered down at the street far below. *Jump,* Harvey thought. *Go ahead and jump, you idiot.*

Laci said, "So where's Jennalee tonight?"

Harvey squinted hard and stared at the television.

Stevie said, "Another of life's mysteries, I guess," and reached for another chicken wing.

◆ ◆ ◆

Will entered the apartment carrying a pizza, a six-pack, and a handful of napkins. He deposited them all on the coffee table and sat between his wife and Stevie. They opened beers and stole glances at Harvey, who was staring at the window fan now, its blade slowly turning.

Laci said, "Have some pizza, Harvey."

Harvey ran his palms up and down over the knees of his jeans. To Will he said, "I can't believe you still don't have an air conditioner in here."

Laci said, "It's not that bad."

Harvey said, "Buy your family a freakin' air conditioner, Will."

"I already told you we have fans in the bedrooms," Laci said.

Will added, "The electric bill's too high with an air conditioner."

"You run the one downstairs all day long," Harvey said.

Will took a slow breath. Put his hand on Laci's knee. Gave it a little squeeze. He said, "Is this the movie where Nicolas Cage is an angel?"

"That's the one," Laci said, then leaned forward to pick up a slice of pizza.

A minute or so later, Harvey said, "So can somebody tell me the rationale behind the stupid trench coat?"

"To hide his wings," Stevie said.

"Leave it to Hollywood," Harvey said. He turned to face Will. "You going to lend me that .357 or not?"

Will winced at his brother's carelessness. Then said, as if Harvey had made a joke, "Tell me how it would be in either of our best interests for you to shoot your wife's brother."

Laci smiled too. She asked, "What did Kenny do that's got you so fired up?"

Kenny Fulton, Jennalee's brother, used to be Harvey's best friend in junior and senior high school, every bit as wild as Harvey, though circumspect whereas Harvey was overt and bold. At the age of eighteen, however, less than two weeks shy of September, Kenny announced that his father was insisting he attend a college three states away, and that Kenny sell his half of the modified Chevy to Harvey. And just like that, their fledgling painting business dissolved. Six years later Harvey was still churning up dust clouds and scraping paint but Kenny with his brand-new master's degree was hired as the assistant principal at the junior-senior high school from which they had all graduated. By the time he was thirty he was the principal, and five years later he was made the superintendent of schools. Though Kenny and Harvey remained friends through the years, the bond grew ever more tenuous.

Still, it was Kenny who talked his sister, Jennalee, by then a third-grade teacher, into going out on a date with Harvey, who, from skinned knees to sausage truck driver, had been reduced to a shivering puppy whenever in the presence of Kenny's little sister. And against what Harvey thought of as all the laws of probability, she then went out with him a second, a third, and a fourth time—went out with him so many times that he finally asked her to marry him. When she said yes, he had to get away from her as quickly as possible so she would not see him quivering again, this time from the utter wonderment and thrilling mystery of life.

Initially Kenny had been slated to be Harvey's best man, but one day not long before the wedding, Harvey asked Will to be his best man instead. When Will asked why him and not Kenny, all Harvey would say was, "You're my brother. He's not."

Now, in Will's apartment, Harvey stood with his fists hard and pressed against his legs. He ignored Laci's question and spoke directly to his brother. "You think I'm fucking kidding here?"

Then, an instant later, a bit more softly, he said, "I'm sorry for the language, Laci, but I am not kidding. I am seriously going to blow that, that . . ."

"You can say asshole," Laci told him. "I prefer that you avoid the f-bombs, but asshole is okay as long as Molly's not here. Especially in regards to Kenny Fulton."

"I am seriously going to blow that asshole to kingdom come."

Will turned to his wife. "Since when don't you like Kenny?"

"He's tolerable. But he's an asshole all the same."

To Harvey, Will said, "Have some pizza and a beer, why don't you? You're making us all tense standing there like you want to punch one of us."

Harvey opened his fists. Flexed his fingers a few times. "Fine," he said. "All I've got are deer rifles and shotguns at home, but don't you worry about it a bit, little brother. Don't worry at all about me having to jam one of them down into my trousers and hobble across town without anybody suspecting what I'm up to. You don't want to lend me your .357? Fine. I understand. Just because I'm your older brother and by all the laws of the universe you should cut me some slack here, fine, who gives a shit? I'll strangle him with my bare hands if I have to."

With that Harvey turned and strode to the door, yanked it open, strode out, and slammed the door shut. His footsteps pounded down the stairway.

Laci said, in her flat, sarcastic way, "He seems upset about something."

"He's always upset about something." Will wiped his mouth on a paper napkin, dropped it crumpled onto the coffee table. "I better go talk to him," he said as he stood.

Stevie asked, "You want me to come too?"

"Stay and eat your dinner," Will said before going out the door.

Alone in the room now, neither Laci nor Stevie spoke for a while. Both pretended to watch the movie. Then, during a Visa commercial, Stevie asked, "You got any of those little hot peppers left you had last time I was here?"

"The pepperoncinis? Look in the refrigerator. Side shelf."

And she tried not to wonder about this life she had married into, these brothers and the secrets they shared, the secrets they kept to themselves. She wondered instead how many car accidents and other tragedies she would have to photograph before she could squirrel away enough money for an air conditioner. Or, better yet, for an escape.

5

Downstairs, Harvey stood behind the bar and stared down into the beer cooler but otherwise did not move. He could feel his insides quivering but thought that if he stood motionless he could maybe keep his hands from shaking.

Soon Will came up behind him. Will picked a glass off the rack and drew himself a few inches of beer and drank it in one long swallow. He glanced around the bar. Merle sat primly at the end of the bar, but the golfers had departed, leaving several bills beneath an empty glass on their table.

And Harvey said, still staring into the beer cooler, into the cold dark bottom, "I feel like I'm going under, Will."

Will was startled by the unexpected nakedness of this confession.

As was Harvey, who added, with a soft laugh, embarrassed by his admission, "Whatever the hell that means."

Will didn't want the rare intimacy of the moment to slip away. "What do you say we get ourselves a little air."

Harvey remained motionless. Will moved away a couple of steps, and smiled to his only customer. "You doing okay, Merle?"

"Doing fine, thank you. Doing fine."

"I'm going to step out back for a minute or two. If you need a refill, the pitcher is here behind the bar."

Merle looked at the inch or so of liquid in his glass. "I imagine this will do me fine," he said.

Will smiled, returned to stand beside Harvey, and, for just a moment, laid a hand on his brother's shoulder. Then he crossed into the kitchen and out the rear door.

6

Will waited in the middle of the alleyway, breathing the dusky air. He used to love this kind of sultry evening, and wondered when the heat had started to bother him so much, wondered when it became so oppressive and such a chore just to take another breath. The air seemed to pulse with heat like an overpressurized boiler about to blow.

He used to love these summer evenings because they smelled like baseball. All through Little League and Pony League and American Legion ball, that was how every summer night smelled to him. The soft leather of his glove. The cool dirt of the infield. From his position six feet off third base he would watch between batters as the moths flung themselves at the powerful sodium lights, and their passion mirrored what he felt inside but never showed—unbridled life, an exuberance aching to burst free.

These days the town's Little League program could not field nine players and had been forced to merge with a team several miles away. The Pony League and American League divisions had disbanded. Scrub grass grew on the local infield now. People in passing cars tossed bottles at the backstop.

Will stood there in his alleyway and gazed into the narrow space between the buildings, the thick gray clouds overhead. He tried to remember the last time he had looked into a clear blue sky like those of his youth, a sky that seemed endless and bright, just like a twelve-year-old's future. He thought again about how nice it would be to have a house with a yard and a real piece of sky overhead.

Each time he looked at Molly and noticed how tall she was getting, how quickly she was growing up, he wondered again if maybe he should sell the bar and go back to working on a dragline. He could work weekdays in West Virginia and come home on weekends. He liked having the bar and having nobody to answer to but even with Laci working as a photographer for the local paper and the police department, they could barely keep their heads above water.

The door banged open behind him, and Will remembered why he was standing in the alleyway. He didn't turn around, but waited until the door had fallen shut. Then he asked, not loud, "So what's this all about?"

Harvey came forward to stand beside his brother, then put his back to him. "You wouldn't understand."

Will looked at the side of Harvey's face. "What did he do?"

Harvey hooked his thumbs over the pockets of his jeans. Then withdrew his hands and held them below his chest. Then dropped his hands to his side and patted his thighs three times. "You remember that motorcycle Jennalee's father had?" he asked.

"The Indian, sure. You and Jake were restoring it a while back, as I recall."

"We worked on it for most of three years. Turned it into something beautiful again. Then he had that stroke."

"That bike must be what—thirty, forty years old by now?"

"It's a 1948," Harvey said. "Sweeping fenders front and back, a studded leather seat . . . A classic."

Will nodded. He knew to wait now. If he tried to rush things, Harvey would clam up. Would revert to that silent, angry boy who would stand glaring at their father when the belt came off and lashed hard across Harvey's backside.

"I'm the one scrounged the one fender plus the leather for the seat," Harvey said. "I'm the one sanded everything down and laid the five coats of paint on it. Jake mostly just supervised."

"I remember," Will said.

"And when they stuck him in that nursing home, he promised that bike to me. Said he'd put it in his will. Said it would be mine the day he died."

"Which wasn't long after that, as I recall."

"I wish the old guy had lived forever. He's the only one in the family ever treated me like a human being."

"You're not including Jennalee in that, of course. You're talking Kenny and his mother, right? Louise still have that yippy little dog?"

Harvey nodded. "He would've given me that bike back when we finished it, he said, except that he enjoyed just looking at it so much. He kept it covered up and safe in his garage all those years. Told me once how he'd take off the cover sometimes and just sit on it. Pretend he was way out west somewhere, cruising through the hills of South Dakota or some such place."

Will nodded in return. Waited for the rest. When it was not forthcoming, he took a chance and said, "I'm not sure what you're telling me here, Harvey. Was Kenny jealous of the relationship you had with his old man?"

"Kenny hated him. And Jake, I don't know. I don't think he had much fondness for Kenny either. More than once he referred to him as a sissy. Said how he'd never done an honest day's work in his life."

"A lot of people think that."

"It's pretty much true," Harvey said. "On the other hand, why work when you don't have to?"

Will didn't know what to say next. Keep bad-mouthing Kenny, or agree with Harvey? He lifted his gaze to the sky. Saw nothing but a deepening darkness of charcoal gray moving in.

Harvey said, "I guess Jake and Louise used to fight about that a lot, how she spoiled Kenny all the time."

"I wonder what that's like," Will answered. "Getting everything handed to you, I mean."

Harvey responded with a little shrug, a shake of his head. He scuffed his boot atop the dirty pavement. "Ever wish you had a son?" he asked.

"Sure," Will said. "You?"

"All the time. Or a girl. I wouldn't care which."

"You still have time."

Harvey raised both hands to his face now and rubbed his eyes. When he lowered his hands, he said, "You think we'd have screwed them up the way our old man did us?"

"You think he screwed us up?"

Again Harvey shrugged. "You remember any times he'd sit and talk to us about stuff? Lectured, yeah. All the time. But actually sit and talk without getting pissed off about something? That's what I miss about Jake. We talked about everything."

Will looked toward the mouth of the alley. A pickup truck went speeding past, its stereo's bass thumping so loudly that Will winced until the noise eased and finally disappeared. "He taught us to hunt, though," he said.

"And that turned out to be a useful skill, hasn't it?"

"I thought you enjoyed getting out in the woods together."

"I do," Harvey said. "I'm just . . . I don't know."

Will leaned forward just slightly so as to look at his brother's face now. Harvey continued to stare at the pavement, at a spot maybe five feet from where he stood.

Will sensed a deep sadness in his brother and wanted to say something funny to push it away, but his own dissatisfaction with life had rendered him humorless. Only Molly and Laci could bring an honest smile to his face these days, and even then he would be quickly reminded of how he had failed them, how close he was to having to shut down the bar and give it back to the bank. His few regular custom-ers spent barely enough to pay operating costs. If not for Laci running off with her camera at all hours of the day and night, they could never make ends meet. And Molly would be headed off to college in exactly four years. Where was he going to get the money for that? What kind of a father and husband was he if he couldn't even—

Harvey said, "You'd have been good at it, you know?"

"What's that?" Will asked.

"Raising a son. I've watched you with Molly. You just sit there and smile and nod while she goes on and on about something. It makes me feel good just to see it."

"It's easier with girls, I think. I don't know why."

"I know why. We don't try to turn them into miniatures of who we are. We let them be their own person."

And again they both fell silent.

This time Will was the first to speak. "So that bike you fixed up. I'm guessing Kenny won't let you have it now."

Harvey breathed in through his nose. "Turns out it wasn't in the will after all. Or so Kenny says. Says how is he supposed to know whether his dad promised it to me or not?"

"Like that's something you would lie about."

"Exactly."

"What's Jennalee have to say about it?"

"According to her it's up to her mother. And what Louise says is that since Kenny's the oldest child and the only son and all . . ."

"That's bullshit," Will said.

"You got that right."

Will let a little time pass, slow time, as tired as the night. "Somehow I just can't picture Kenny on a motorcycle."

Harvey grunted, an animal sound rich with contempt.

"He never even drove that Chevy you two used to own, did he?"

"Never drove it, never worked on it. All Kenny wanted was to brag about how he owned half it. He still has half the damn trophies I won."

"So maybe he'll sell the bike to you."

"Oh, he'll sell it, all right. Didn't you see the ad in the paper?"

"I don't read the classifieds unless there's something I need."

"Ad says $6,500. Right there in black and white. So okay, that's a fair price. More than fair. So I go on over there today, checkbook in hand. I even had the check made out already."

Will wondered what it would be like to have that much money in his checking account. "The bike's already sold, or what?"

"It's still setting there in the garage! But now he says he wants fifteen thousand for it. Said he did some research, found out it's worth a lot more than he thought. Fifteen thousand dollars for a bike I practically built myself!"

"You think he raised the price just to keep you from getting it?"

"He doesn't care whether I have the bike or not. He just wants to screw me one way or the other. Anybody else shows up, offers him nine, ten thousand for it, you think he's not going to take it? Little pasty-faced weasel. No way I'm going to let this one pass."

This one, Will heard. He studied the tension in his brother's face, the hard line of his jaw. "So what is it about you two anyway? He was supposed to be best man at your wedding, for chrissakes."

Harvey raised his finger in the air, was about to speak, make an important point. But then he backed off, shook his head, bit back his words.

"Okay, so he's a prick," Will said. "Fine. But you're not going to kill him over a motorcycle."

"What'd I tell you already? This thing with the bike is just the last in a long line of things."

"Like what, for instance?"

"Like none of your business, okay?"

"You made it my business when you asked to borrow my gun. Which isn't going to happen. So just tell me what this is really about."

"Just one thing after another," Harvey said.

"Give me a couple of examples."

"Why can't you just trust me on this? Why can't you just believe me when I tell you I have ample cause to despise that slimy asshole with every bone in my body? Am I your brother or not? Doesn't that count for anything anymore?"

To Will's ears there was less anger than desperation in Harvey's words. There was a degree of pain that perhaps even he had never felt.

"Fine," Will said. "I believe you. That still doesn't mean I'm going to help you murder him."

"Then *don't*," Harvey said. "Go on back upstairs to your fucking little sauna and eat your pizza and watch your TV. I don't need your help or anybody else's."

The men stood side by side but did not look at each other now. Will could feel the night simmering. He could smell the stale compressed heat in the long narrow box of the alleyway.

Finally Will said, "How about if we steal the bike?"

"And do what with it? I couldn't ride it anywhere. Besides, he'll just turn it in on his insurance. Probably end up with twenty thousand dollars for all I know."

"So . . . is it the bike you want, or something else?"

"What are you talking about?" Harvey said.

"Sounds to me like what you really want is some kind of revenge. Just to mess him up somehow."

"Maybe I do. Maybe I'm tired of him getting everything he wants. Things that were never his to begin with."

"Okay," Will said after a pause.

"Okay what?"

"Okay, that's maybe something I can help you with."

"Help me how? To do what?"

"We just have to come up with something. Something equal to what he's done to you."

"You have no idea what he's done to me."

"So you've told me. Vaguely." He waited half a minute.

Harvey said nothing more.

"Fine," Will said. "Because I'll tell you what. I don't like him much either. Never have."

"No shit?" Harvey said, and he looked at his brother at last.

"So if you want to teach him a little lesson about fairness and such, then okay. I'm with you all the way. Mainly because I don't think you have the brains to pull something off without getting caught. Especially after asking for my gun in front of Laci and Stevie like you did."

The hint of a smile creased Harvey's mouth. "You never liked him either?"

"What's to like? Back when you two were in school together, you're this big football star, right? And what's he? He's in the freaking band. Plays the piccolo or some such thing."

"Fucking flute."

"Same difference. It's still a girl's instrument no matter how you look at it. So you're the star athlete and all, you're the one set the All-Conference rushing record, he's the one with his little twinky fingers flying up and down. And who gets elected class president? Who gets voted Homecoming King?"

The anger built in him, and it made him feel stronger, more capable. "I was only in ninth grade but, I don't know, that really pissed me off for some reason. There was just something about him I didn't like. What I could never figure out was why you wanted him as a friend."

Only then did Will realize that he had been jealous of Kenny all those years—quiet, soft-spoken Will, the younger brother, a nuisance to be tormented or ignored. Even now the resentment lingered. Even now it burned.

Harvey said, his voice huskier now, "The worst of it is that Jennalee thinks he's like the perfect man or something."

"Yeah, well, she's his sister. That's just loyalty talking."

"She's *my* wife. She should be taking my side on this. On everything."

"Can't argue with you there," Will said. Then, "Maybe she just doesn't want you risking your life on a motorcycle."

"She couldn't care less," Harvey said.

And again Will was too surprised to respond. He'd always thought they were the perfect couple, that theirs was a fairy-tale marriage. He said, "Things okay between the two of you?"

"What did I just tell you?" Harvey said, his voice too loud. "She ought to be taking my side on this. Not his or anybody else's."

So it was a dangerous subject. Will decided to avoid it. He said, "What really pisses me off about Kenny is how easy he's always had it. Jake was right; Kenny's never had to work for anything in his life. What's he make as the superintendent of schools—fifty, sixty thousand?"

"Huh. More like eighty or ninety," Harvey said.

"Whew," Will said. "I used to watch him when you two were painting houses together. You were the one did all the hard work, all the scraping and patching."

Harvey nodded. "We'd come across some dry rot or termite damage, you know what his response would be?"

"Slap some extra paint on it?"

"Slap some paint on it and collect the check."

"Then why in God's name was he your friend?"

Harvey said nothing, but squinted at the dirty pavement as if trying to discern the answer down there, some justification for the choices he'd made a quarter century ago.

Will considered his own resentment, searched all the feelings he had never before examined. Kenny had an easy way with women, that was one thing. He'd been so nonchalant in high school, wore nice clothes that set him apart from all the other kids. And he was a smooth talker, all the teachers loved him. Girls in Will's grade and even younger seemed to melt when Kenny smiled their way. Will's friends had spoken of him with unabashed admiration, said, *I hear he gets laid anytime he wants; I hear he did so-and-so backstage after school yesterday; I heard he's poking the substitute teacher.*

He made Will and his friends feel second-rate. Was that why Harvey now hated him too? *She thinks he's like the perfect man or something*, Harvey had said.

Will and Harvey stood there in the gathering dark, both silently angry. Finally Harvey said, "All right, bright guy. What are we going to do about him?"

"Give me a day or so," Will said. "I'll think of something."

"This better not be a trick of some kind just to get me to cool off."

"No, I want to do this," Will said, and even in the stink and gloom of the alley he felt a kind of malicious glee embolden him. "I could use a little fun in my life."

7

When the movie was over, Stevie picked up his empty baskets, crumpled napkins and the pizza box and carried them into the kitchen. Laci followed with her own plate and napkins. Stevie threw the paper in the trash, then opened a drawer for the plastic wrap and laid out a long sheet on the countertop.

"I'll take care of that," Laci said. "You don't need to hang around to help."

"No problem," he said, then placed the remaining pizza atop the plastic wrap.

"Do two slices separately for Molly," she said. "You can take the rest of it home with you, if you want."

"Okay," he said, then was silent as he carefully wrapped up Molly's pizza, and returned the remaining slices to the pizza box.

"Everything all right?" Laci asked.

He was quiet for a moment, then said, "Same old stuff."

"Meaning what?"

"Just Will. Not wanting me to go along to talk to Harvey."

And with that remark and its wounded intonation, she saw Stevie in a different light, as if the angle of light slanting in through the window had actually changed, had risen to illuminate his features, the softness of his eyes and the slack, frowning mouth. For a moment he reminded her of the pensive subject of Caravaggio's *Boy Peeling Fruit*, half his face in light, the other half in darkness. "I don't think he meant anything by it," she said.

"They say they don't. But they do. Always have."

She moved closer now, laid a hand on his arm and stepped into his field of vision. "What do you mean?"

He shrugged.

"Tell me what you mean," she said.

"They think I'm worthless. You know? Like I've got nothing to contribute to anything."

She moved even closer and laid a hand on his forearm. "I'm sure it's not personal, Stevie. It's just birth order, that's all. You're their little brother."

He nodded and blinked, but he looked so sorrowful standing there that an ache arose in her chest and her eyes began to sting. She was just about to put her arms around him when he turned away and scooped up the pizza box.

"Thanks again," he said, and headed for the door.

"You sure you're okay?"

"Tell Molly I said hi."

8

When Will returned to the bar, he found the room empty, Merle's empty glass on the bar, a twenty-dollar bill folded and wedged beneath the glass. He considered turning the air conditioner off until another customer arrived, but knew how quickly the room would grow stifling, and how quickly a customer might turn on his heel and head back out the door if he stepped in and breathed such heat. Besides, Will could usually count on a customer or two until at least ten. Somebody would show up soon.

In the meantime he wiped the bar and made sure the tables were clean. A part of his mind was still on the conversation in the alley, but a larger part had already returned to his own dilemma. If business didn't pick up soon he would have to think about putting the bar up for sale. But who would buy it after taking a look at the books? *Only an idiot like me,* he thought.

He wondered if Kenny kept any money at home. Maybe he collected gold and silver coins. But they would be in a safe. And Will was no thief. Had never had so much as a traffic violation. Still, the thought was consoling: a man Kenny's age, never married, close to a six-figure income—he surely had a bundle squirreled away somewhere in that big old house. And if he didn't, his mother surely would. Kenny's comings and goings would be easy to track. Even in summer the school board met once a month. But where was Louise during those couple of hours? Probably sipping martinis in front of the TV, half-asleep with that piebald Jack Russell in her lap, ready to erupt into shrill barking at the slightest sound.

Stick to reality, Will told himself. *What can you do to bring in more business?*

Maybe a karaoke night. From what he'd seen on TV, singing off-key with a group of other drunks seemed to be popular.

But that's just one night. You need at least three good nights a week to turn this place around.

Maybe a pizza night. Sell slices at cost, add a little extra garlic salt, keep the cold beer flowing from the taps.

The problem is, he told himself, *who's going to come? Most of my customers are over fifty. Even that bunch of golfers earlier. They don't come here for the beer or food, they come because they are lonely, have nothing else to do, nowhere else to go. Their children, the few who still live around here, are too busy raising their own families to be spending fifty, sixty dollars a week in a bar.*

Will crossed to the cash register, took the little pad and pen he used for orders, and made a calculation. *Fifteen hundred dollars,* he thought, and wrote "$1500" on the pad. Didn't sound like much. But if he could make an extra fifteen hundred a week, he would clear a little bit, start paying down the principal on the mortgage.

He divided the number by fifty. The answer was thirty. He needed an extra thirty people every week to come into the bar and spend fifty dollars each.

Thirty extra people. How the hell was he going to get an extra thirty people a week in there? *Every week.* And at fifty dollars a pop? He couldn't think of a single customer who, over the last few months, had parted with even half that much.

And now he remembered—bitterly, with a burgeoning anger turning his stomach sour—a guy named Rogers he had worked with back in the strip mines. In warm weather the crew would find a patch of shade at noon every day and, often leaning against a pile of dirt or coal, open their lunch boxes and talk about their families, politics, sports, or other employees. They were all making good money then, but they also knew that bituminous strip mining was on its last legs. Too many regulations, too much pollution. The coal burned dirty, went up as smoke, came down as acid rain. The market for soft coal was shrinking.

One day the men took turns revealing their plans for the future. Two of them were taking night and Saturday classes at the community college, one in computer programming, the other in certification as an HVAC technician. A third man joked that he planned to live off his wife, an RN, until she kicked him out. Rogers planned to move his family to North Carolina, where a job in his brother-in-law's furniture factory was promised.

Will was the youngest man in the crew, and so spoke last, and then only when asked. "What about you, Junior?"

"I'd like to have my own business," Will said. "Don't know what kind yet, though."

"Beer joint," Rogers said.

Everybody laughed, because on those few nights when Will joined the others at Enid's after work, Will always limited himself to a single beer, and was always the first man to leave.

"I'm serious," Rogers said. "Think about it. When times are good, people drink to celebrate feeling good. And when times are bad, they drink even more to forget about how miserable they are. And who better to run a bar than a guy who doesn't like beer?"

And, for a short time, Rogers seemed to be right. But then came the new interstate extension. Then came the millennials, craft beer and California wines and organic food, yoga and veganism and Health is Happiness. Will's customer base moved away, died off, joined AA, went low-carb paleo keto whatever.

Will studied his pad. Thirty new customers *every week*. Thirty new Merles spending two and a half times as much as Merle spent per visit.

"Screw you, Rogers," Will said to the empty room. "Screw you and me both."

9

When Harvey returned home that evening, after he unlaced his work boots just inside the back door, then came forward to the kitchen threshold, Jennalee was walking toward him, smiling, on her way out. She was wearing tight blue jeans and a white silk shirt—still, in his opinion, the prettiest woman in town, still slender and naturally blonde and as graceful as a breeze. He could see her nipples through the blouse and sheer bra and something caught in his chest at the sight of her.

"Hi!" she said brightly, and told him that she was going across town to the ten-room Victorian Kenny had lived in, with his mother, all his life. It bothered Harvey that his wife always said she was "having dinner at home with Mom" instead of "over at Mom's place."

He said, "How about staying here for a change and having dinner with me?"

"I had dinner with you last night, didn't I?"

"Most people, you know, when they get to be adults, they're happy not to have to be spending four or five nights a week with their mother and brother."

"You see your brothers practically every day, don't you?" She asked this with a smile, sweetly, then leaned close to him, her hand on his waist. He felt the warmth of her skin through his shirt. Her touch still dizzied him.

She said, "You know, when we lost Daddy last month, the thing I regretted most was not spending enough time with him. And now Mom's getting up there too and—"

"She's barely seventy years old."

"How old was Daddy? Seventy-six. And how old was your dad? It can happen at any moment, just like that."

He took a deep breath to steady his voice, didn't want to sound whiny. "My point, Jennalee—"

She snuggled against him. "I know what your point is, sweetie, and I agree with you. Now you take that casserole out of the oven in about ten minutes, okay? And enjoy a nice quiet dinner by yourself. I'll be home around nine or so and we can make some popcorn and watch TV together."

He knew that the way she held him now, rubbing both hands up and down his back, one knee between his legs, he knew it was a ploy she used, a way to defuse him because she did not like confrontation, did not like voices raised in anger and she especially did not like to be circumvented in any of her choices. He knew that her momentary closeness was a mere device yet he could not resist the smell of her, the vagueness of apricot in her hair still as blonde as a teenager's, still as cornsilk-smooth. And he could not resist the clean scent of her skin either, the subtlety of Obsession in the nape of her neck, the heat of her breasts pressed against him. He breathed her in and closed his arms around her, hands pulling at the tail of her blouse and then sliding underneath, fingers finding the cool smooth wonder of her waist.

"Baby, I'm going to be late," she said, but as he leaned down to lay his mouth against the side of her throat she tilted her head back and exposed her neck to him. Gratitude swelled in his chest but he could not ignore the swift surge of fear that washed through him too, a heat racing up the sides of his face and into his temples, this fear for the loss of her, the only woman he had ever needed, as essential as air, a compulsion as inexplicable as death. Sometimes when he held her he felt himself speeding around the curve of a dirt track at a hundred miles an hour and the rear of the car beginning to slide, but he would hold the speed, unrelenting, correcting with a tiny turn of the steering wheel, and pray that this would not be the last race of his life, that he would not soon roll and lose all control, would not go crashing into the wall and never see the finish line again.

And then his mouth was on hers and his hands fumbled with the snap of her jeans, fingers so thick with dumb desire that she had to take over finally, guiding him into the living room and onto the sofa. And this was the thing that kept him from crying out in the anguish of his desire, that she had never told him no, never pushed him away with a damning look or excuse, had never once denied him. This was what he clung to, how he gauged the truth of her love.

But it was always a temporary affirmation, and as always he was left to deal with his fear and gratitude alone, as weak-legged and hollow as ever, this time with one hand braced against the sofa's back as with the other hand he reached, quivering, for the jeans bunched around his ankles, while Jennalee tucked her blouse in and made her exit through the kitchen, her face as bright and cheerful as ever, her body as graceful as a breeze.

As she headed for the door he called out to her. "Tell your brother for me that what goes around comes around."

A pause; he could picture the way she cocked her head now, smiled in confusion. "Excuse me?"

"Just tell him," he said.

Now he envisioned the way she rolled her eyes before answering. "If you say so."

Then she slipped away and left him standing there in the living room, hollowed out, weak and alone.

Harvey watched television alone, the casserole dish on his lap, bleeding its heat into his skin. He kept the volume low on the TV, wished there were other sounds to hear, something flesh and blood and real. He wished they would have children, that an accident would occur. He'd had himself tested a couple of years ago without telling Jennalee he was going to, then was surprised by her reaction when he told her that everything had checked out okay with him. Instead of being happy she was angry that he had done it. "Why would you do such a thing?" she'd demanded, then immediately turned and stormed into the bedroom and locked the door. Later she explained that she wasn't really angry with him. "It's just that it means it must be me," she said. "I'm the problem."

A few months later he found the birth control pills. He had called in sick that day, a Tuesday, with nausea and a pulsing headache, a rumbling in his head. By noon the sickness passed, and he, thinking it would please her, had seared a sirloin tip roast and put it in the oven to slow-bake through the afternoon. Then he washed two loads of laundry, everything in the hamper. Dried and folded all the clothes and put them away in their drawers. And that was when he found the disk of tiny pills, wrapped inside a camisole too delicate to be crushed beneath the cotton pajamas he was putting away. A disk meant to hold thirty pink pills, twelve spaces empty.

He was in bed when she came home that night.

"Still feeling bad?" she asked, and brought him a glass of ginger ale, and took his temperature, and looked sincerely pained by his discomfort.

She's a good person, he had told himself. *Just doesn't want to be a mother.*

He never mentioned the pills.

And now, sometimes, he would listen to the silence and wish the house did not feel so empty. He wished he could awake some morning and find toys scattered underfoot, a tricycle in the yard. He knew that when he and Jennalee were older, his resentment might grow too strong to suppress. He already resented how much time she spent at her mother's house, and resented that she hadn't taken his side in the Indian argument. What really gnawed at him was that she refused to see what an asshole her brother was, what a smarmy, self-centered dick he had turned into.

Harvey worried now that he was becoming like some of the older men in town, silent, bitter brooders, never smiling. He worried that he might gravitate back to the bottle and his earlier habits, drinking his way toward self-destruction, having conceded at last that love was not his salvation but his undoing.

10

Laci and Stevie came downstairs and into the bar to find Will alone, leaning against the counter, watching TV. "Making money hand over fist, I see," Stevie said with a grin.

Will was just about to say something like *Is that supposed to be funny?* when Laci stepped up close and laid her hand on Will's arm.

"Going to pick up Molly at the library," she said.

Will stared at Stevie a moment or two longer, then finally turned to his wife and nodded. "You think she'll want another salad tonight?"

"We saved her some pizza. But let's go back in the kitchen and see what else you have."

"I can tell you what I have," Will said.

She gave his arm a squeeze. "Let's go look."

He followed her into the kitchen, where she turned at the refrigerator and gave him a smile. "What's up?" he asked.

"Kirby called. He wants to meet me at the Marriott to talk about a new job opportunity."

"On a Friday night? At a hotel bar? Why not at the office?"

"Don't ask me. Maybe that's where he's having dinner first."

"What kind of new job?"

"I have no idea."

"I do," Will said. Laci's boss was barely out of his thirties, a young, good-looking guy who'd inherited the business from his grandfather after working less than a year as the managing editor. He and Will had talked briefly maybe three, four times, and each time Kirby seized Will's hand as if they were long-lost friends, his grip too firm, the handshake lasting too long. "How *are* you?" Kirby would ask. "How's everything *going*?" And something in the young man's inflection, the too-earnest interest, would make Will wince and want to pull away.

"Stop it," Laci told him now. "I thought you and Molly could come along. She can order something there. And we can all spend an hour or so in a nice air-conditioned room."

"Whatever she wants to eat, I can make it here," Will said. "And for a fourth of what we'd pay at the Marriott."

"Come on," she said. "It will be like a little night out for us. And maybe I'll end up making more money after tonight."

"I can't just close up the bar. It's too early yet."

"That's the other thing we need to talk about," she said. "Let Stevie stay and watch the place."

Will raised his eyebrows.

"You hurt his feelings earlier," she said. "You and Harvey."

"What are you talking about?"

"Harvey comes in all ticked off with Kenny over something, which you know and he knows but nobody tells us why. Then you go running after Harvey to calm him down, and I'm left upstairs with Stevie, who is hurt now because you and your brother never include him in anything."

"That's not true," Will said.

"You know it is. And so does Stevie. So here's a chance to show him a little trust. Put him in charge for ninety minutes. What's the big deal?"

"He could start a grease fire, for one thing. Burn the place down."

She grinned. "Are you saying that would be a bad thing?"

The way she was looking at him now with her eyes sparkling, her hands on his waist, he had to smile in spite of himself.

"Plus," Laci continued, "while Kirby's wining and wooing me and promising me the moon, you'll have Molly all to yourself. You're always complaining you don't get enough time with her anymore."

"This is true," Will admitted. "What do you think he wants to talk about?"

"Who knows with him? It's one crazy idea after another. Last week he wanted to add a literary insert. Let local people submit poems and essays and stuff like that. Jerry in layout said, 'Sounds like a high school newspaper to me,' which killed that idea pretty fast."

"So this is all for nothing?"

"Maybe we'll get lucky and he'll have a decent idea for a change. All I know is, I could use a raise. I don't care if he wants me to take photos of old ladies' pets. If I can bring home a few more dollars every week, I'm in."

Will wanted to protest then, wanted to say something to relieve the sting he felt, the suggestion of failure, but he recognized the futility of such a gesture. She was right. She was very nearly always right. They had to seize every opportunity to come their way, no matter how it might dent or damage his self-esteem.

"Pick me up after you get Molly," he told her.

She stood on her toes, leaned close and kissed his mouth. She said, "See you in fifteen." Then turned and exited the kitchen.

He remained in place long enough to hear Laci tell Stevie, "Off to the library. See you later. I think Will wants to talk to you about something."

When Will came back to the bar, Stevie was standing three feet in front of the television screen, clicking through the channels. Will said, "You want a Coke or something?"

Stevie said, "I'd kill for another beer."

"Tell you what," Will said, and now Stevie turned his way. "Would you mind watching the place for maybe an hour? Two at the most?"

"Seriously?" Stevie said.

"Laci has a meeting with her boss out at the Marriott. She wants me to go along. You'll get maybe five people in here while we're gone."

Now Stevie came back to the bar, laid the remote on the counter-top. "I can do that. No problem."

"Anybody wants a mixed drink," Will told him, and pulled a small book from beneath the cash register, "just look it up in here. More likely it will be draft and bottle beer and a few shots here and there."

"It's all cool," Stevie said, and allowed himself a smile now. "I got it covered."

Will nodded but was still uncomfortable. What if, against all odds, a rowdy crowd of college students showed up? What if somebody's bachelor party came stumbling through the door? Stevie would be over-whelmed, get confused, start pouring free drinks for everyone, includ-ing himself.

Stevie said, as if reading the look of concern on Will's face, "I've bartended at parties. This will be a breeze."

"What parties?" Will asked.

"People you don't hang around with. Private parties. Don't sweat it, brother, okay? I got this."

"Okay then," Will said.

And Stevie said, "So what's going on with Harvey and Kenny? Who did what to who?"

Will reached into the well, pulled out a can of Coke, popped the tab and set the can atop a cardboard coaster in front of Stevie. "You remember that old Indian motorcycle Harvey was always working on with Kenny's dad?"

"Absolutely," Stevie said as he reached for the Coke.

"So apparently the old man promised to leave it to Harvey. But now Kenny says there's nothing about that in the will. And every time Harvey makes a fair offer on it, Kenny raises the price."

Stevie shook his head, took a noisy sip. "He's a weasel. Always has been."

"I'm just afraid Harvey's going to go and do something stupid this time."

"He did seem agitated. More than usual, I mean."

Will nodded, but said nothing more. Stevie sipped his Coke, watching and waiting.

"Okay then," Will said, and softly rapped his knuckles on the bar. "I'm going to head upstairs and change my shirt. You're in charge."

"Aye-aye, Captain!" Stevie said. He waited until Will had headed up the stairs, then reached into the well for the house whiskey and poured some into his Coke. Then he stood there grinning for a while, surveying the empty room. Then he picked up the remote again. And clicked through the channels.

11

In the dimly lit room called French Kate's Lounge, named after a woman who ran a brothel in the area in the late 1800s, Laci spotted Kirby looking her way from the corner of the bar. At first his smile was prominent, but the moment Molly and Will entered behind her, his smile faltered—a reaction that gave Laci a shiver of pleasure.

Most of the barstools were occupied, all but one of them by men. Several tables held couples having a late dinner or just drinks and snacks. A flat-screen TV above the bar was playing a golf match somewhere near an ocean, the course impossibly green and the water impossibly blue. Throughout the lounge, soft Motown music played from speakers invisible in the high, dark ceiling.

To her family Laci said, "There's Kirby at the bar. Why don't you guys grab a booth, get something to munch on, and I'll go see what Smiley wants."

"Have fun," Will said, and steered Molly toward a booth against the near wall, a good place from which to keep tabs on the conversation at the bar.

Laci crossed toward Kirby, and, when he attempted to put his arms around her and lean in to kiss her cheek—a greeting he frequently employed with his female employees—she extended her hand. His handshake was less than enthusiastic.

"I see you brought the whole family along," he said.

Laci looked down the bar. "Interesting place for a business meeting, Kirby. In a room named in honor of a prostitute."

"I met some people here a little earlier," he said. "The meeting ended just a few minutes ago. What would you like to drink?"

She smiled at the bartender, who was coming her way. "Iced tea, please," she told him.

The barman was a tall, thin young man with a sparse brown moustache and soul patch. "Long Island?" he said.

"Just plain old iced tea, please. With stevia?"

"I can do Splenda."

"Two, please."

When the barman walked away, Laci said to Kirby, after a glance at his glass, "So you're a whiskey-drinking man?"

"Maker's Mark," he said. "Bourbon." He took a sip and set the glass down atop a napkin. Beside the napkin lay a key card.

Laci nodded toward the card. "You spending the night?"

He glanced toward the booth where Molly and Will sat talking. Then laid his hand over the card, scooped it up and slipped it into his shirt pocket. "It's where we had the meeting earlier," he said.

Laci smiled and said, "I bet it is."

Molly said, "The salads here are at least fifteen dollars each! The steak salad is almost twenty!"

"Get what you want," Will told her.

"The salmon is twenty-two!"

"If that's what you want," he said, and hoped she wouldn't choose it.

She studied the menu a few moments longer. Finally she said, "Is it okay if I get the grilled chicken Caesar salad? It's the cheapest. $14.99."

"Whatever you want, sweetie."

The sadness hit him then like a soft blow to his chest. He had always made a point of never discussing his financial problems in front of Molly. Wanted her to have a happy childhood, free from her parents' fears and worries. But it was clear to him now that he had not been careful enough, and his concerns had infected her.

"Get the salmon," he told her. "I know you love salmon. It's only a few dollars more."

"Really?" she said.

"Absolutely."

"What are you going to get?"

"I had pizza at home. I'm still stuffed."

She smiled. "Actually," she said, "salmon is healthier than chicken. If it's fresh caught. Chicken can be full of antibiotics and hormones."

"Then definitely get the salmon."

"If it's fresh caught," she told him. "I'll ask the server when she comes."

It seemed that every time he looked at her these days, his chest ached and his eyes filled with tears. Something was slipping away from him, and although that thing wasn't precisely Molly, it did have something to do with her. And something to do with Laci. And something to do with who he was and had wanted to be. Funny how a matter as trivial as the cost of a salad could remind him of all that.

"It's all about images these days," Kirby told Laci, leaning close to her now, as if sharing a valuable secret, engaging her in a conspiracy. "The immediate impact. Who has time to read anything? Let the pictures tell the story, right? The photo narrative—the latest and hippest art form. And a girl with your talents, you can be right there at the head of it."

Laci was having a hard time suppressing laughter. "A new art form?" she said. "You talk like this is France in the 1920s."

"Why not?" he said.

"Because all I do is see something interesting and take a picture of it. I don't create anything. Art requires an act of creation, doesn't it?"

"Found art," he said. "Think of photography as found art."

"I've always thought of found art as an oxymoron. An excuse for noncreative people to feel like they've done something creative. To me, found art is a form of plagiarism."

He shook his head. "You're not giving photography, or yourself, enough credit. Probably because you haven't been given the freedom to really explore what you can do with a camera."

"What exactly is it you want me to do?"

"*Explore.* Get playful. Get sexy. Use your camera to make love to the world."

"Kirby, please," she said, and turned to look toward her husband and daughter. "Let's not go there, okay?"

"You don't like my metaphor?"

"I don't like you using this meeting as a way of easing into a discussion we have already had."

"Can I help it if you make me think of sex?"

"What doesn't make you think of sex?"

"Maybe the better question is, what would make *you* think of sex?"

"My husband," she said.

That quieted him for a few moments. He studied the side of her face, took a sip of his drink, then set the glass atop its napkin again. Finally he said, while looking down at the bar, his voice lower and softer now, "Okay, here's the thing. This job I'm proposing is just the beginning. The website, I mean. It will take a while to reach an audience, sure. And then to monetize it. But I'm confident it can be done. From there the picture gets a whole lot bigger. More websites, each one aimed at a different audience. Women, men, millennials, Gen X, even the, uh . . . what are they calling the prepubescent generation these days?"

"I'm a photographer," she joked. "I don't use words."

He nodded, smiling. "This is what I like about you, Laci. You're not just a smartass, you're also very smart. I think I could learn a lot from you."

Her eyebrows went up and she turned to face him. "I know what you want to learn from me, Kirby. And you should learn it from girls your own age."

"So you have no interest in being a part of this project?"

"I still have no idea what the project is. A bunch of websites filled with photographs? How do you monetize something like that?"

"How do you monetize a website filled with cat videos? Do you realize how much money that guy makes?"

She shrugged. "People love cats."

"People love a lot of things. And I plan to capitalize on it. Understand that I'm not talking about just this county. My family has connections everywhere. I've already lined up investors in Pittsburgh, Cleveland, Harrisburg, and Chicago. We'll be on computers, tablets, smartphones, every device imaginable. I intend to be *the* source for visual information everywhere, whether it's news, fashion, food, recreation, whatever. And I am offering you, Laci, the opportunity to get in on the ground floor with me. As this thing grows, we'll hire more staff. And you just might find yourself being the director of photography. You'll get to travel all over the country. Maybe even the world."

For just a moment she felt a shiver of excitement at the prospect. Then her head turned—involuntarily, it seemed—and she looked across the room at her daughter and husband. He was leaning forward over the table, talking to Molly so earnestly, while she sat back against the booth, arms crossed over her chest.

"That could be problematic," she said. "Traveling, I mean."

Kirby said, "Only if you let it be."

Will asked his daughter, "What do you think of your mom's boss?"

Molly looked to the bar. "What do you mean, what do I think of him?"

"He looks kind of, I don't know . . ."

"Skeevy?"

"Is that the same as sleazy?"

"Sort of, but not quite. It's more like creepy. Not to be trusted."

"That pretty much nails him, doesn't it?"

"On the other hand," Molly said, "he might just be a metrosexual."

"And what does that word mean?"

"It's been around awhile, Daddy."

"I'm sorry I'm not as worldly as you. What does it mean?"

"What do you think it means?"

"Something to do with sex and heavy traffic," he said.

She laughed. "It means a guy who dresses well, spends a lot of time self-grooming, and probably likes to go shopping."

"In other words, gay."

"Not necessarily. Or even exclusively."

"Not even exclusively?" Will said. "You're fourteen years old. How is it you know this stuff?"

"You're in your forties," she answered with a grin. "How is it you don't?"

He said, "Do you find guys like that attractive?"

"He's *old*," she told him.

"He's younger than your mom."

"Still ewwww."

"But if he wasn't," Will said. "If he was your age. Is that the kind of guy you would like?"

"Maybe," she said. She gave Kirby another long glance, then looked away. "There's a guy I like now but he's a jock. Mom's boss was never a jock."

The mention of a boyfriend for Molly made something go tight in Will's throat. "What sport does he play?" he asked as casually as he could.

"Basketball and track."

"When did the junior high start a track team?"

Molly looked down at her lap, brushed off an imaginary crumb. "He's varsity."

"Excuse me?" Will said.

"It's no big deal, Daddy. Lots of girls date guys in high school."

"Dating?" he said. "Since when are you dating? And what grade is he in?"

She looked at him but did not answer.

"Sophomore?" he said, and received no reply. "Junior? *Senior*?"

He gave her time to respond, but when she did not, he said, "He'd better not be a senior, Molly."

"It's only four years! You're eight years older than Mom!"

"There is no way you are going to date a senior. Not until you are a senior. *No way.*"

"We were having a nice time talking. Why do you have to be like this all of a sudden?"

"Does your mother know about him?" he asked.

She threw her fork into the wooden salad bowl so hard that the utensil bounced out and onto the table. Then she sat back hard against the booth and clamped both arms over her chest.

Will sat there leaning forward, tense in every muscle. Then realized that he might be frightening her. Slowly leaned back and tried to let his body loosen. But still wanted to strangle someone, wanted to throw some boy up against the wall.

Laci picked up her glass of iced tea, saw there was only an inch of liquid left, most of it melted ice, and drank it all.

"I will be happy to take photographs for your new project," she told him. "Any subject short of pornography. Hourly rate or salary, I don't care which as long as it's fair. But any kind of extensive travel . . . that's not really going to be possible for me."

Again he was silent for a while. Then he said, "I also happen to know about an adjunct position opening up for somebody to teach photography. The art of the camera."

"I'm self-taught," she reminded him. "You know that. Don't you need a degree to teach in college?"

"Most times," he said. "But I happen to have a lot of influence over the people who will do the hiring."

"And how much would something like that pay?"

"Depends on the class load. For a full academic year, two classes per semester, maybe twenty thousand or more."

"Seriously?" she said. "Which college?"

"Well . . . if we're going to keep this discussion on a strictly business level, then there has to be a quid pro quo, right? A benefit for you, a benefit for me."

"Are you always like a dog in heat?" she asked.

"Do you want the job or not?"

It took her a long time to respond. She turned again to face her family. "Exactly what kind of quid are you looking for here?"

"Commensurate," he said. "What's twenty thousand a year worth to you? Plus a significant bump in your pay rate as a stringer."

She looked at her daughter, her husband. Thought *college fund. New clothes. Air-conditioning. A life of my own.*

Then she noticed their postures: Molly sitting huddled up on her side of the booth, as if she had been scolded or insulted; Will slouched back with his head cocked to the side, eyes on the floor. To Kirby she said, "I need to get my daughter home now. She probably has home-work to do. Thanks for the iced tea."

"So you're going to think about it?" he asked.

She paused a moment before answering. "Unfortunately," she said, and crossed to the booth.

12

There were only two customers in the bar when Will and Laci and Molly returned, two divorced men in their sixties, both gone to paunch and self-pity. They had been taking turns riffing on the asexuality of two prominent female senators, making analogies to "prune stew" and "a bowl of cold pudding," when the door sprang open and Molly came striding in. Both men immediately went silent.

"Hey, pumpkin," Stevie said.

Without a word, Molly strode past him, into the kitchen and up the stairs.

Laci said, "Hey, boys," then followed after her daughter.

Will came around the bar and crossed to Stevie and the others. "Gentlemen," he said. "How goes it?"

"Just keeps on going," one of them answered.

Will nodded. Smiled. Turned to Stevie and asked, "Everything okay?"

"Everything but these two nuts," Stevie said, and grinned at his customers.

"Just so you're remembering to take their money," Will said with another tired smile.

Fifteen minutes later, Stevie was walking the long way home with a hand in his pocket, fingers rubbing the twenty-dollar bill Merle had left on the counter, money Will had insisted his brother accept as payment for his two hours of work. And now, in his pocket, it was something more than money, it was Will's gratitude, and Will's trust. Stevie seldom felt like a grown-up when he was with one of his brothers, but tonight he did, and that feeling made everything about the warm summer night look better.

Instead of taking the zigzagging route through back streets that would have gotten him home twenty minutes sooner, Stevie walked the full length of the town, in no hurry to return to his trailer. The town was named Barrowton after its founder, Alfred Barrow, but in recent years its citizens favored another explanation for the word *barrow*, as in a barrow, or castrated, pig.

In the fifties the population had crested at just over four thousand happy souls. The coal companies were busy then gouging money out of the earth and filling one rail car after another with cheap bituminous coal. Then came acid rain and regulations and now the strip mines had been reclaimed and the railroads were out of business.

Until twenty years ago there was a factory that produced soft drink bottles, but plastic is cheaper and lighter and easier to dispose of. There had been a G.C. Murphy's five-and-dime where Will and Harvey bought slingshots and Halloween masks, and where Stevie shoplifted Tootsie Rolls and Superman comic books. The store changed ownership several times but never changed the original sign until the building was converted to a Goodwill store and collection center. The old Western Auto where Harvey and Will and Stevie bought their first hunting licenses was a Dollar General now.

A few small businesses managed to survive the hard times but they too changed ownership frequently, and every few years another shopkeeper would declare bankruptcy. At last count there were eleven hundred and sixty-two citizens in Barrowton. Nearly all of them wished they lived somewhere else.

He liked the town when the shops were dim and the streets quiet. He liked envisioning himself as the sole male survivor of a zombie apocalypse, after the zombies had been exterminated and now only a dozen or so of the sexiest unbitten females remained, having been sequestered during the battle that wiped out everybody else except for them and Stevie. He was sad that Will and Harvey were gone, but glad that the female members of the family were safe. Someday when their grief subsided, even Laci and Jennalee would finally surrender to his charms.

It could happen, Stevie told himself now. Barrowton was ripe for an apocalypse. With its nearest access to the interstate highway some twenty miles away, the town was bleeding a slow death. As more and more businesses crowded into the farmland surrounding Greenfield's exit and entrance ramps, locals kept promising themselves that more people would seek refuge from the noise and traffic by escaping back into the country, back to quiet places like Barrowton. Unemployment would decrease, drug use and domestic violence would dissipate, and real estate values would soar. With each passing year, the promises became weaker, more difficult to sustain. A zombie apocalypse was exactly what the town and Stevie needed.

But until the apocalypse came, he had to satisfy himself with walking past the houses on the northern end of town, those big turn-of-the-century Victorians and sprawling prairie-style homes he envied. He knew where all the prettiest females lived, knew whom they were married to or were dating, how many children they had, whether they were teachers or office managers or stay-at-home MILFs. Those who worked outside the home usually had to drive thirty or forty miles to their jobs, but one in particular, a veterinarian who had converted her basement to an office and clinic, lived only a few blocks ahead. She was an inch or so taller than Stevie, with short reddish hair and lovely breasts and long, delicate fingers. Stevie had once brought her a dog he found along the side of the road, whimpering and bleeding, its back legs useless. "I don't have any money to fix it," he told her as he laid it on the examination table, "but I couldn't just leave it laying there."

She said nothing until she had probed and examined it to her satisfaction. Then told him, "Both hips are shattered. And there's internal bleeding."

Stevie nodded. "I figured it for a hit-and-run."

"The kindest thing would be to euthanize her," she said. "My guess is she's a stray. Poorly fed, her coat's a mess, no collar, no license."

"I could pay you maybe twenty-five dollars," he told her. "More if you don't mind waiting."

"Don't worry about it," she told him. "It was good of you to bring her in."

And now as he approached the house he could see a light in a second-floor window. The same window that was always lit when he walked through town after dark. He imagined her lying up there on her bed, Dr. Victoria Hall, Vicki, wearing maybe a black teddy and matching thong panties, watching a Netflix movie on TV. Sometimes he would see her around town and she was always alone. No wedding ring. No engagement ring. No jewelry of any kind. Her solitude confused and intrigued him. Why was such an attractive woman alone, when nearly everybody else in town, fat and homely, scrawny and skanky, nerd and geek and redneck, male and female alike, were paired up? She was like him, unlucky in love. Maybe that was why he felt a special bond with her.

Frequently, as now, he kept his phone at the ready, hoping for a chance to snap a photo or two. Later he would download the photos onto his laptop, then enlarge and crop them, study her mouth and hands and eyes.

She was one of several local females he liked to photograph whenever opportunity struck. But she was the only unattached female. Sometimes he would see a stray dog or cat wandering the streets, and he would consider grabbing it and inflicting some kind of minor injury.

But then a voice would whisper from the front of his brain, *She would never be with a loser like you*, and he would leave the animal unscathed.

It wasn't fair, though, that he should have to go through life alone. Both of his brothers had wives; why shouldn't he? Sure, Will was a nice-looking man with a business of his own, and Harvey had a steady job with a pension plan, but Harvey was nobody's idea of a dreamboat. His hands were too big and his face rough looking, and there was a meanness in his eyes that intimidated people who didn't know him well. It was a mystery why a beauty like Jennalee would ever fall for him.

Even those two old farts from the bar had once had wives. And if they had been kinder to their women and kept themselves in shape instead of spending all their free time drinking beer and criticizing stupid politicians, they might still be married. Now all they had was each other, which, to Stevie's mind, was worse than being alone.

Stevie didn't want to end up an aging lump on a barstool. He wanted what Will and Harvey had. He didn't really need a dozen wives and a hundred or more children. One of each would be enough. But without a zombie apocalypse, what chance did a guy like him really have?

13

"You mind if I turn this thing off?" Will asked after he came into the bedroom. Some kind of music was emanating from the little TV atop the dresser, a repetitive bass thump that pulsed against the back of his eyes.

Laci peered over the paperback she held open on her chest, a Ludlum thriller. "I didn't even know it was on."

He stood before the TV for a few moments, remote in hand. Two black men in baggy clothes were striding vehemently back and forth across a stage, jabbing their hands at the air, chanting a mostly indecipherable rhyme. "What is this?" he asked. "MTV?"

"Some awards ceremony. Molly was watching it."

He turned at the neck, cocked an eyebrow.

"She was in bed by ten, don't worry. So you can just quit looking at me like that."

He turned off the noise. "Must be a good book if you didn't even know the TV was on for two hours."

"I have amazing powers of concentration," she said, and with her smile he felt some of the heaviness lift away, as if her smile, like the fan in the corner, had blown the day's chaff off his skin.

He came to the bed and sat on the edge of the mattress, removed his shoes, pulled off his socks and then his shirt. Stood again to unbuckle his belt. Hopefully, he asked, "You want maybe I should lock the door?"

"Well," she said, and laid the book flat on her stomach, "I've been staying awake in hopes that Hugh Jackman might show up, but he's usually here by eleven if he's coming. So I guess it's your lucky night, big boy."

He let his trousers slide to the floor. "You want me to get a shower first?"

"How much beer did you spill on yourself tonight?"

"Not a drop, surprisingly."

"So lock the door and get on down here."

She was wearing the short pajamas with the sleeveless top he liked, the powder-blue set he gave her for Christmas last year, and when he slid his hands between her legs he was as grateful for her as on the first time so many years ago. They made love slowly and quietly for a half hour. No woman had ever smelled and tasted as good to him as Laci, and when he pushed deep inside and felt the way her legs trembled as he held them and saw her lovely mouth gasping he knew he would never need any more than this, never want another woman.

Afterward he felt that he had fallen from a great height, but landed softly and without injury. She lay curled against him, her head on his chest, her knees nudging his.

"We're still pretty good together, aren't we?" he asked.

"I think it's better than it ever was. Lasts longer too."

"But we could do it three or four times back in the old days."

"I like it better this way," she said.

He ran a hand up and down her spine, traced the ridges beneath his fingers, the lovely fragile stem beneath her skin, this flower in his hands.

He said, "I meant more than just the sex, though. I mean everything. We work pretty good together, don't we?"

"Mmm," she said. "Fifteen years and going strong."

He winced at the mention of so many years, a decade and a half. The tightness at the back of his skull returned. "I wish I could do better for you and Molly, though. I wish the bar did better."

"It will pick up again," she said. But he did not believe it and knew she didn't either. He was not certain when he had stopped believing it, but now, tired and weak, he knew it for certain. *People drink when times are good*, he had been told, *and when times are bad they drink even more!* But nobody had ever mentioned that nearly all those people would soon be doing their drinking elsewhere.

"We're barely getting by," he said. "After fifteen years, I'd like more for us than just that."

"For instance?" she said.

"I don't know. Portugal maybe."

She laughed softly and rubbed his chest. "Not me, baby. No hablo Portuguese."

But he remembered the way she had looked that Sunday night when they had eaten spaghetti in front of the big-screen TV downstairs. His rule was that Molly could not watch TV during dinner unless it was an educational program, so they had found a travel series on PBS. In this show the host, a lanky New Englander with a mop of brown hair, was visiting the Iberian Peninsula. Molly nearly swooned at the sight of the white beaches.

"Wouldn't it be awesome if we could go there?" she had asked. "Mommy, wouldn't you like to go there?"

"Mmm," Laci had said, and then, "It would be awfully expensive, I'll bet."

Will had felt a heaviness in his chest that night, and now, in bed with the woman he adored, as he inhaled the scent of her hair and absorbed the heat of her skin, the too-familiar heaviness washed over him again.

She said, "You want to hear about my little talk with Kirby?"

"Of course," he said.

"So his idea is to go completely digital with the paper, which will eliminate a lot of the operating expenses."

"I wish I could go digital," Will said.

"He also has some cockamamie idea about starting a kind of visual magazine. Mostly photos and short videos. Hardly any written text at all. Just captions mainly."

Will listened to the fan whirring. Then said, "Okay. Any particular kind of photos?"

"Different categories for different interests. News, fashion, food, sports, et cetera. Whatever the zeitgeist demands, he says."

"And a zeitgeist is . . . ?"

"Whatever's hot and trendy."

"And he expects you to take all these pictures?"

"He wants me to be the director of photography. Said there are tens of thousands of photographers all over the world who will jump at the chance of having their work in an international magazine."

"International?"

"Pictures are a universal language, he says. And the internet goes everywhere."

"He has the money to pay all those photographers? I know his old man is loaded, but . . ."

"According to Kirby, he'll use amateur photographers at first. Thanks to smartphones, everybody's a photographer now. He says he's already getting hundreds of submissions a day, just because of the buzz."

"There's a buzz?" Will said.

"Who knows? With Kirby, everything is seventy percent bullshit and fifty percent lies."

"Does he really think people will pay to look at pictures?"

"The magazine will be free. He says we'll make our money through the advertising."

The words *we'll* and *our* made him wince. "That would be like me giving away drinks and charging Budweiser and Jack Daniels to hang up their signs."

"I know. It sounds crazy to me too."

"So you told him no?"

"I'm going to play along for a while. See if this idea goes anywhere."

He took her hand in his then, interlaced their fingers, and held their hands atop his chest. And wondered if she could feel his heart racing; if she could feel the heavy air settling into his lungs.

"The more interesting thing," she said, "is a college teaching job he says I could get."

"Teaching photography?"

"Apparently he has some connections."

"Which college?" Will asked. "Is it close?"

"He's being a dick about it. Won't tell me which one unless I agree to take the other job too."

A minute passed in silence but for the hum of the fan blades. "I don't know," Will said.

"You don't know what, babe?"

"Molly says he's skeevy. I get the same feeling about him."

"Molly said that? About Kirby?"

"Yeah. Just watching him, you know?"

"Hmm," she said, and Will waited for more, waited for agreement or affirmation, but neither came.

Laci said, "So you heard about Molly's new boyfriend."

"You knew about him?"

"Not till after we got home from the Marriott. I could tell there was something going on between you two."

"There's no way she's going to date a senior," he said.

"Dating to Molly is hanging out at the library."

"If they stay in the library," Will said. "But how long do you think that's going to last?"

"She's growing up, babe. I agree that we have to be cautious with this. But we also have to trust her. She's a sensible girl."

"And he's an eighteen-year-old with his brain swimming in testosterone. He's a loaded revolver. Cocked and loaded."

"Ha ha," she said.

"I'm serious about this," Will told her.

"Don't worry. I'm going to have a nice long talk with her tomorrow."

He said nothing. By now his body was stiff and hot. He could feel how tight his hand was around hers, the stickiness of the sweat on his skin.

"She cares about what you think," Laci said. "You just have to be careful how you talk to her. You frighten her when you get angry."

"She never has any reason to be frightened of me."

"I'll talk to her tomorrow," Laci said.

Will opened his hand and extended his fingers, slid them out from between hers. Then flexed his hand a few times.

"Speaking of anger," Laci said, "what's the story with Harvey and Kenny?"

"Kenny reneged on a deal for that motorcycle Harvey restored. He won't honor the old man's intention to give the bike to Harvey."

"It takes an honorable man to honor something," Laci said.

"This is true."

"Did you talk Harvey down? I hope you're not going to lend him that gun of yours."

"No way," Will said. "He'll cool off in a day or so."

"Are you sure about that?"

"What choice does he have?"

In truth, he wasn't sure about anything. He wasn't sure that just talking to Molly would keep a pretty girl and a horned-up boy apart. He wasn't sure that Kirby hadn't been putting the moves on Laci at the Marriott, or that she had been totally unresponsive to his enticements. And he wasn't sure that his .357 revolver should stay locked in its case, because maybe the world was changing so fast, spinning so out of his control, that the only way to slow it down might be with a few well-placed shots.

14

Stevie stood beside a large trash container at the corner of somebody's driveway, and looked up at the light in the veterinarian's window across the street, saw the way the light sometimes flickered, grew brighter or dimmer, and knew that she was watching television, just as he often did late at night. Then he thought of himself up there with her, beside her on the bed, and then it was too late to stop the other thoughts from coming, the need to slip his left hand down inside his jeans. He could smell the trash in the plastic container, the greasy rotten food odor, and thought about moving away from it, but liked the concealment it provided.

It was only a few minutes later, while leaning against the trash container for support, his knees weakening as he imagined the softness of Dr. Victoria's skin beneath her black panties, that the trash container jerked away under his weight and capsized, spilling its refuse across the driveway. He stumbled and came down on one knee atop the container, said "Shit!" as he caught himself from falling onto his face.

Instantly a large dog inside the nearest house began to bark, and then the porch light snapped on, and Stevie was up and sprinting hard to get into the shadows again. A man's voice from the porch shouted, "What's going on out there?" And Stevie kept running, veering off the street now and into a side yard, across an alley and through a second yard, dodging a swing set and ducking under a clothesline, just running and running, left then right then left again until he was out of breath and far enough from the veterinarian's house to pause and double over, sucking air and listening, listening.

No footsteps following. Nobody in pursuit. His pulse hammered in his head.

He straightened up now so as to better catch his breath. And found himself in the side yard of Kenny Fulton's house.

15

Will had only begun to succumb to sleep when a muted ringtone roused him. Laci lay sleeping on her side, her hand still atop his chest. He slid away, knelt beside the bed and found the phone in the pocket of his khakis. The number was local, but not from his address book.

"Hello?" he said.

"I just caught your asshole brother breaking into my garage," Kenny Fulton said.

"Excuse me?" Will said, and thought, *Harvey. I hope to God he didn't have a gun.*

Will felt himself doubling over, all the strength and air draining out of him. "Put Harvey on," he said.

"It's Stevie. And he's got nothing to say. I have him on my security camera, trying to pick the lock on the side door."

"Jesus," Will said, and felt Laci sitting up in bed now. "Did you call the police?"

"I'm about ready to," Kenny said.

"Can you hold off till I get there?"

"If you weren't my brother-in-law, he'd be in jail already."

"I'll be there in ten minutes. Thanks for calling." Will closed the phone but remained kneeling on the floor, unable to move.

"What's wrong?" Laci asked.

Now he straightened, took hold of the waistband of his khakis, stood and began to dress. "That was Kenny. Apparently Stevie broke into his garage."

"Unbelievable," Laci said.

Will sat on the edge of the bed to pull on his socks and shoes. "Is Kenny my brother-in-law?" he asked. "I thought only the husband of his sister would be his brother-in-law."

"What?" Laci said.

"He called me his brother-in-law. Is that technically correct? I've never thought of myself as his brother-in-law. Jennalee's, but not his."

"Babe," Laci said, and laid her hand on his shoulder, "what difference does it make?"

"It just bothers me," he said.

16

Will had been to the Fulton house more than a few times before, both before and after Harvey's marriage, but he had never felt comfortable there. With its wide covered porch on three sides and its Victorian turret, the house seemed twice as big as the six-room house he'd grown up in.

Behind the main house sat the carriage house, which had been converted into a small apartment where Kenny had stayed during college breaks, but was now stuffed with old furniture and other castoffs Louise refused to give away. Adjacent to the house, where the cement driveway flared into a half circle, sat the three-stall garage. Louise's car, a 2015 Camry she no longer drove, was parked against the far side of the garage, covered by a huge blue tarp now nearly black with years of dust and pollen and decaying leaves.

Kenny sat on a wicker wingchair on the side porch, smoking a cigar, a glass of lemonade on the small wrought iron table beside his chair. Stevie was seated hunched over on the top porch step, looking forlorn and ashamed, his lemonade glass empty against his hip. The only light came through the kitchen window and door and from the bug zapper hanging from the porch ceiling. The air was thick and heavy and smelled like rain. Deep rolls of thunder were moving in from the west.

Will walked in from the darkness beyond the porch, came in as close as Stevie, looked down at him only once, then paused with a foot up on the first step. To Kenny he said, "So what happened here?"

Kenny took a drag from his cigar, then blew out the smoke. "I was down in the game room watching TV. Then the security alarm went off. I came upstairs, looked around, checked the windows, and what do I see but this character trying to jimmy the lock on the side door of the garage."

"I was just checking to see if it was open," Stevie said without looking up.

"You had something in your hand," Kenny said, "which is now, I'm betting, in your pocket."

"There's nothing in my pocket," Stevie said. "I just wanted to have a look at that bike Harvey built."

"My father built," Kenny said.

Stevie started to turn, but Will placed a hand on his shoulder.

Will asked, as calmly as he could, "Do you want to call the police?"

"I should," Kenny said.

"Well, you certainly have that right. But I'm going to ask that you please don't."

"I'm sitting here trying to think of one good reason not to," Kenny said.

"You know the reason. That's why you didn't call already. The strain it would put between our families."

"Our families never have been all that close," Kenny said.

"Between Harvey and Jennalee then," Will said.

Kenny dragged on his cigar. Blew the smoke toward the blue light of the bug zapper. He said, "If I see him skulking around here ever again . . ."

"You won't," Will said.

"I better not."

Will waited a few moments before he spoke. "Then he can go?"

Kenny waved his hand through the air; the cigar glowed red and trailed a wisp of smoke.

Will slid his hand over Stevie's shoulder, pushed forward. "Go home," he said.

Stevie stood, still looking at the sidewalk. Then he lifted his head as if he were about to speak. Will said, "Go to bed. I'll talk to you tomorrow."

Stevie stood motionless for a few seconds, then lurched forward, and hurried away into the darkness, with both men watching after him.

When Stevie was out of sight, Will faced Kenny again. "Thank you," he said.

"If it wasn't for him falling off the garage roof that day," Kenny told him, "I wouldn't even have hesitated to call the police."

Will nodded. "You know we had him tested. There was no neurological damage."

"And how long ago was that? You need to have him tested now."

Will felt in no mood to defend his brother's behavior. He said, "Can we talk about that bike for a minute?"

"So Harvey's been shooting off his mouth to everybody? What's he saying—that I cheated him?"

"He says Jake promised it to him. And we both know that he did ninety percent of the work on that bike."

"And we both know that he didn't pay for the bike in the first place, did he? Or for any of the parts. And if there *had* been a will, Dad must've destroyed it. Because it's nowhere to be found, I can tell you that with absolute certainty."

Will put a hand to the back of his skull, tried to rub away the tightness, keep his anger at bay. "Look at it this way, Kenny. You got everything else Jake ever accumulated. And Harvey wants to pay you a fair price for the bike. It has meaning for him. All the time he spent working on it with your dad, that's what it's all about."

"Well," Kenny said, "maybe if his own father hadn't been such a hard-ass all the time, Harvey would've spent some time with him instead of sucking up to my old man."

And now the anger broke through, too strong to contain. "And maybe if you hadn't egged Stevie on that day, calling him a chicken if he didn't jump over to the garage with us, maybe when he fell you wouldn't have gone running home to hide like a scared little girl."

Kenny stood abruptly then, and Will felt his own body flush hot, felt the eagerness wash through him, the readiness in his fists.

But Kenny came no closer. He took another drag from his cigar, then tossed the cigar into the grass at Will's feet. Then turned away and reached for the door.

Will said, "Any one of us could have ratted you out. Harvey or me or Stevie. But none of us did. Think about that for a while, why don't you?"

Kenny stood with his hand on the door handle, unmoving. Will expected Kenny to say more; Kenny Fulton always had something to say.

But this time he didn't. He opened the screen door, opened the kitchen door, stepped inside and closed both doors behind him.

Will did not move until the kitchen light went dark. And then the bugs that had been clicking against the lighted window came off the glass and toward the bug light, their tiny bodies crackling and snapping from the electrical charge. Will watched the massacre for a full minute before turning away, and then walked blindly toward his car, the bug light's blue afterglow still lingering in his vision.

The sky ripped open during his slow drive home, heat lightning turning into fierce, startling splinters, the thunder so loud that he could feel it booming against his eardrums, could smell the electricity in the air and could feel it on his skin and surging into his blood.

17

An hour later, still wide awake as he lay beside his wife in bed, Will heard Laci's phone ring beneath her pillow, and he shook her awake. She grabbed the phone, said hello, listened for a few seconds, said, "On my way," and ended the call. She rolled away from him, stood, and started pulling on her clothes.

"Two-vehicle accident out on Connor Flats," she whispered. "Sounds bad."

He rolled onto one elbow. "Be careful," he told her. "It's wet outside."

"It finally rained?"

"I'm surprised you didn't hear the thunder."

"I was really out," she said.

He nodded, said nothing more until she headed out of the bedroom. "Be careful," he told her again. "Love you."

"Love you," she said without turning. And a minute later went out of the apartment and softly down the stairs.

He climbed out of bed to sit in his boxers between the fan and the open bedroom window. The night had grown warm again, despite the light rain that continued to fall, and through the screen the scent of the street was even stronger than it had been before the storm, as if the rain had merely stirred up the ugliness instead of washing it away. The air smelled of road oil and dirt, of the garbage in the dumpster in the alley. No stars were visible now, not even a dull smoky glow of moon.

We can't steal the bike, he told himself after a while. *We can't beat up on Kenny. We don't want to do anything that might give Kenny's mother a heart attack. Or anything that Jennalee will find out about and divorce Harvey over. We have to be clever about this,* he thought. *I have to be clever. This is my role in things. I am not bold or fearless but I can think things through. I'm nobody's genius but I can figure this out.*

He turned away from the window then and looked toward the bed. The slight indentations where Laci had lain were still visible. As were his own. For some reason the sight of those indentations filled him with sorrow. She should have been lying there peacefully, not having to scurry away in the middle of the night to take pictures of strangers.

He rose from the chair and walked around the foot of the bed and eased himself down into her space, his head on her pillow. He could smell the scent of her hair, her skin, and those scents aroused him, the image of his wife lying naked beneath him. His erection pressed against the mattress, and he imagined her small hands on his back as they pulled him closer.

He resolved to do better. To be a better husband and provider. Whatever had to be done, he would do it. And this desire somehow conjoined with his desire to help Harvey and to be more considerate of Stevie and to give Molly all the things that such a sweet girl deserved. Only then would there be some relief from the pressure that squeezed at the base of his scalp, the soreness that crept down his neck and into his shoulders at the end of every day. Maybe he wasn't naturally bold like Harvey but he could make himself bold for all the people he loved. He would do whatever he had to do, no matter the consequences.

II

18

Even with his eyes stinging and his body sore from a lack of sufficient sleep, Will found the morning refreshing. Thanks to a cloudy sky, the 7:00 a.m. sun was muted, its heat and glare softened. Jewels of dew still glittered in some of the yards, but the sidewalks were as dry as if last night's rain had never happened.

And what a long, exhausting night it had been. Will had argued with Harvey, argued with his daughter, argued with Kenny. Then, barely asleep after making love to his wife, she had been called out into the rain to photograph an accident at Connor Flats. When she returned home afterward, he was awakened again, and held her until she fell into a hard sleep.

And now, only a few hours later, Laci's story of those three young men was still with him. One boy dead, one severely injured, none of them old enough to buy a beer in his bar. The sadness Will felt for the parents of those boys deepened the resolve he had discovered even before he knew of the accident, a desire for justice, for some small measure of balance to all the unfair, unpredictable blows the world seemed keen to administer.

The mug of hot coffee in his hand steamed into the air. With every sip its warmth spread throughout his body, so that he was sweating after the first five minutes. He told himself that he should try to like iced coffee more, but then the notion of forcing yourself to like something you don't struck him as laughable.

He walked west, the sun at his back for the first six blocks, then turned south for the final two. And there stood Stevie's small trailer home in a narrow lot of dewy, overgrown grass, Stevie's red pickup parked facing the front door. Every time Will visited, a wash of pity flooded over him, and he wished he could do more for Stevie; wished he had done more.

Stevie's neighbor on his right was a Dollar General, and on his left, a small gun shop. Both buildings were still dark, their gravel parking lots empty. Stevie's trailer was dark too. Will finished his coffee, shook the last drops from the cup, and set the cup on the rear bumper of Stevie's truck. Then he walked to the door, pulled open the unlocked storm door, and knocked four sharp raps on the hollow metal door.

Not until the third set of knocks did the lock click and the door come open. Stevie, wearing only a pair of olive drab boxer shorts, squinted out at his brother and said, "You could've waited a couple more hours."

"I have a business to open up," Will said.

Stevie blew out a breath and turned away, leaving the door open. Will followed, came inside and took a seat across from Stevie, who was slouched in one of the orange vinyl bench seats behind a table holding his laptop and an empty Mountain Dew can.

"You don't want to put some clothes on?" Will said.

"It's hot as hell in here."

Will looked around. At least Stevie was keeping the place neat. No dirty dishes in the sink, no crumbs or visible dirt on the carpet. In this heat the slightest invitation would have the place crawling with ants and stinkbugs, cockroaches and mice.

He said, "So what were you doing last night when Kenny stopped you?"

"What do you think I was doing?"

"And what was supposed to happen if you got inside?"

"Wouldn't know until I got there."

The remark sounded truculent, but Will understood. If the bike had not been secured in any way, Stevie might have kicked it into neutral and rolled it outside and down the sidewalk. If the front fork was locked, he wouldn't have been able to move it, and might then have resorted to destruction of some kind; to flattening the tires or scratching the paint job or snipping the brake lines. He might have found a bucket of paint and drenched the bike with it. He might have poured gasoline over it and set the bike aflame. Any of which, Will knew but apparently Stevie hadn't considered, would bring the police to Harvey's door.

Will said, "You know you could be in jail right now."

"I could be dead right now," Stevie said. "I could be asleep right now. I could be anything. So could you. But we're not, are we?"

Will smiled in spite of himself. "We're going to do something, Stevie. I just don't know what yet."

"Do something to Kenny, you mean?"

"Damn straight."

And now Stevie smiled too. He sat up and squared his shoulders. "He ruffle your feathers last night?"

"Arrogant," Will said. "So arrogant I just wanted to smash his face."

Stevie leaned against the table's edge. "Let's burn his house down."

"I think it has to be more subtle than that."

"Where's that going to get us?"

"I know where I don't want it to get us. I don't want it coming back on any of us."

"You got an idea?"

Will shook his head. "It has to be foolproof."

"Nothing's foolproof," Stevie said.

"I'm not saying it has to be perfect. But we have a Deputy Dawg sheriff and two Huckleberry Hound deputies to think about. So whatever we do, it has to seem like an accident."

Stevie, looking a bit surprised, said, "How far are you talking about going here?"

Will too had been surprised by his words. "I guess we should leave that up to Harvey. He's the injured party."

"Yeah, well, he's not the only one with a score to settle, you know."

"I know, brother. I hear you."

They sat still for a while then, each remembering and wondering. Then Will said, "I guess I'll head back."

"You want me to make some coffee?"

"Naw, thanks. Just wanted to see how you were doing this morning."

Stevie said, "I'd be a lot better if this heat would let up."

Will slid across the seat and stood. "Come by later if you want. It's always cool downstairs."

"Cooler maybe. I wouldn't exactly call it cool."

At the door Will paused for a moment, looking out. "Is your lawn mower broke?" he asked.

"I knew you couldn't leave without making some kind of remark."

And Will nodded in acknowledgment: guilty as charged.

19

Despite Will's parting criticism, Stevie felt good after his brother's visit. Of the two brothers, he had always been closer to Will. When they were boys, it was Will who played catch with Stevie, Will who broke him of his habit of throwing like a girl and of flinching when a fastball came his way. Harvey was older, too busy for kid's stuff.

Only at Harvey's wedding, with Stevie standing up front in the church beside Will, both of them dressed in rented black tuxedos while a bloody Jesus peered down at them from a fiberglass cross, had Stevie realized that Harvey loved him too. Harvey, waiting for Jennalee to come down the aisle, had winked at Stevie, and in that moment, Stevie's eyes filled with tears, and he heard a voice that could only belong to Jesus whispering in his ear, *This bond of brothers shalt not be broken.*

That was why Stevie had tried to break into Kenny's garage. And it was why he would do anything either brother ever asked him to do. The bond must never be broken.

20

Harvey had the hoods up on both his Nissan Titan and Jennalee's Infiniti when Will came down the sidewalk. The vehicles were parked side by side on the wide concrete driveway, both newly washed and chamoised dry, the front end of the Infiniti raised up on ramps. Harvey lay on his back beneath the sedan, snugging up the new oil filter. Two five-gallon plastic containers of oil sat unopened along the edge of the driveway, adjacent to a tub of dirty oil he had drained from the vehicles.

The concrete was cool against Harvey's back, the morning sun hot on his feet. He liked the smell of the undercarriage, of metal and rubber and oil and road dirt, the scent of his free-spirited youth. More and more frequently these days he was looking back on his past, remembering that life had once been simple and unencumbered. Neither vehicle had needed an oil change but Harvey had needed to keep himself busy, to distract his thoughts with the simple pleasures he was good at and understood.

"Must be nice," Will said, startling Harvey for a moment.

Harvey ran a finger around the edge of the filter, double-checking the seal. Then he scooted out from beneath the Infiniti and looked up into his brother's face. "What must be?" he said.

"Filling up your driveway with what, sixty thousand dollars' worth of Japanese transportation."

Harvey sat up, wiped his hands on a rag he pulled from a pocket, then rolled onto one knee, and stood. "They're worth maybe half that in trade-in value." He looked around for Will's car. "Did you walk over here? What's going on?"

"Stevie almost got himself arrested last night."

"Doing what?"

"Trying to break into Kenny Fulton's garage."

"Oh for fuck's sake," Harvey said. "What did you do—tell him about that Indian deal?"

"Laci wanted me to start including him in stuff. Said he feels bad because we always leave him out."

Harvey shook his head. "Maybe now she'll understand why." He stared at the front fender for a few moments, then turned to retrieve a container of new oil.

Will said, "Apparently Kenny has a security system with a camera."

"I could've told you that," Harvey said. "Except that it's just on the garage. Somebody broke in last March or April, I forget which it was. They jimmied open the door on his Beemer and set off the car alarm."

"I didn't hear about that."

"A lot of break-ins happening these days. People stealing whatever they can get their hands on."

"Good thing I don't have anything worth stealing," Will said.

Harvey unscrewed the oil filler cap on the Infiniti, then looked around for his funnel. "Be right back," he said, and crossed to the garage. Fifteen seconds later he returned to the Infiniti, stuck the tip of the funnel into the oil reservoir, and carefully poured oil into the funnel.

"So what happened?" Harvey asked. "Kenny call the police or not?"

"He called me. I went over and talked him out of it."

"Shit," Harvey said. "He knew I'd beat his ass if he called the police on my brother. All he wanted was to throw his weight around a little and act like a big shot."

"It was all I could do to keep from smashing in his face."

Harvey checked the oil level, replaced the filler cap, and walked to his own vehicle. He said, "Can you get me the rest of the oil?"

Will retrieved the second container, set it at Harvey's feet while the remainder of the first can was emptied into his truck.

Will watched and said nothing. The sun was hot on the back of his neck.

Harvey finished, then carefully laid the funnel in the grass so as not to stain his driveway with oil. Then he wiped his hands on the rag again. He turned to Will. "So now what?" he said. "Did you come up with a plan or not?"

Will looked toward the house. "I need to know what your parameters are."

"What's that supposed to mean?"

"How far are you willing to go?"

"I want him out of my life."

"Does that mean . . . you know?"

"It means get him to move. Get him to leave town. Make it so he doesn't want anything to do with this place anymore."

Will considered the possibilities, which were scarce. "Do you think he'd move if his mother was out of the picture?"

"I don't know. I don't know why he ever came back here to live after college anyway. I know his old man didn't want him around anymore."

"Is that true?"

"I wouldn't have said it if it wasn't."

"Did Jake actually tell you that?"

"Why would I make it up?"

"So what was going on between those two? What did Jake tell you?"

"He said he wished Kenny would grow up and act like a man. Wished he'd get married and live his own life."

"You think he might be gay?"

"How the hell would I know that, Will?"

"I'm just asking what you think. He was your friend all those years, not mine."

"I thought you said you'd come up with a plan to get rid of him. And you didn't."

"Wait a minute," Will said. "What if we start spreading a rumor about him? Something like . . . being a pedophile maybe. How would that look, what with him being around schoolkids all the time? The trick is in getting people to believe it."

"You get enough people talking, they'll believe it."

"People used to say Merle is a pedophile. He's got that sneaky look to him, you know?"

"He's not a pedophile," Harvey said. "He's not anything."

"What makes you the expert?"

"Jennalee heard it from her mother. Who heard it from Merle's mother. He was born with a condition of some kind. He's got no pecker."

"You mean he's a girl?"

"He's got no pecker, no pussy, no anything. Just a hole he pisses through."

"That's not even possible," Will said.

"Look it up then if you're so smart. It's called genesis something. Or agenesis. Something like that."

"Damn," Will said. "The poor sonofabitch. Life must be hell for him."

"He sure doesn't act like his life is hell. You ask me, life would be a lot simpler without a dick."

Will shook his head. "That's not something I ever want to find out."

Harvey pulled his phone from a pocket, looked at the time. "Don't you have a bar to open up?"

Will leaned down to look at Harvey's phone. "Yeah, I got to get moving. So you want me to start the rumor or not?"

"Why not? All the big mouths in town eventually end up in a bar, don't they?"

"So let's say it's successful," Will said, "and Kenny moves to another school district. Louise will probably go too, right? What's that going to do to Jennalee? I know they're all pretty close."

Harvey said nothing. He stood there motionless for a moment, then remembered the phone in his hand, and slipped it into a pocket. Then put his hands on the front of the Infiniti and leaned into the shade beneath the upraised hood.

"I'm not saying she would ever leave you," Will said, and moved closer to his brother. "She's your wife. She's not going anywhere without you."

Harvey remained silent a few moments longer. Then said, his voice barely above a whisper, "I want him gone. Whatever else happens, happens."

21

Around nine that morning, an hour and a half after Will's visit, while Stevie was washing the plate and skillet he had used for his breakfast of toaster waffles and sausage patties, his cell phone rang.

"Hello?" he said.

"Is this Stevie?"

"You got him."

"This is Kay Miller. Do you remember me?"

He thought for a moment. *Kay Miller? Kay Miller?* Then, suddenly, "Mrs. Miller! Ninth-grade algebra!"

"How have you been, Stevie?"

"I saw you a couple weeks ago at Shop & Save. Anyway I thought it was you."

"It must have been," she said, "because I saw you too. We should have said hello."

"We should have," he said. When he was in ninth grade Mrs. Miller was one of four teachers who gave him an erection nearly every day. None of the teachers was a beauty, especially Mrs. Miller with her short, plump, forty-something hausfrau look, but if he concentrated on her ample bosom he could pass most of the forty-five minutes of each class in a state of aching arousal. When he noticed her recently picking out oranges at the grocery store, he saw her only in profile, and paused—unseen, he thought, at the end of the aisle—to observe that she had put on even more weight since that last time he had seen her in town, and that her neckline was no longer clearly distinct from her sagging chin, and that, from what he could see of her face, she looked to be very unhappy about the oranges, or maybe just unhappy in general. Her breasts, however, were still her most remarkable feature, large and pillowy and inviting even twenty-some years after his initial obsession with them.

"I saw your flyer on the bulletin board as I was leaving," she told him. "And I pulled off one of those little tabs with your phone number on it. In case I ever needed help with anything."

"And do you?" he asked.

"Well, I'm not sure it's something you would want to handle."

"There's not much I'd turn down," he told her. "What's the job?"

"I was out in my garden just a few minutes ago," she said. "In fact that's where I still am. A raccoon ran right past me and into the crawl space under the porch. And it's still there. I'm half-afraid to go inside for fear it will run out and bite me on the ankle or something."

He stifled a laugh. "I doubt that's going to happen," he said. "Not unless you back it into a corner or something."

"But aren't raccoons nocturnal?"

"I think that's true in most cases."

"That's what worries me. If one is out running around in broad daylight, not two feet from where I was weeding, what if it has rabies? I don't want a rabid raccoon living under my back porch."

"Can't say I blame you," he told her. "You want me to come over and get it out of there?"

"That's exactly what I want," she said. "But I don't want you to get bitten either. Do you have the right equipment for it?"

He envisioned the job: crawling into the dark, tight space on his belly, his naked face an easy target. "Do you have any qualms about extermination?" he asked.

"Not in this case I don't. Would fifty dollars be sufficient?"

"Should be," he said. Then, with a little laugh, "I might have to charge a few dollars more if I get my face bitten off."

22

Laci didn't often have the luxury of lying in bed alone in the morning, thinking her own thoughts. Usually the alarm woke both her and Will at seven, and he, still groggy, would roll up close to her, his hand sliding onto her shoulder, then down to her breasts. She would either be sleeping on her back or on her left side, facing the edge of the bed. He always awoke with an erection, and even half-asleep wanted to slide it into her. Sometimes she was in the mood and sometimes not, but if he was patient and took a few minutes of touching and stroking to get her ready, she would accede to his desire and allow him to enter her from behind. His movements were always slow and gentle in the morning, which she found endearing, as if even semiconscious he was aware of their daughter sleeping not far away. Occasionally they made love in the afternoon when Molly was at school or with her friends, and then their lovemaking was more vociferous, with both of them groaning and talking and urging the other on. She would straddle and ride him until she fell moaning and spent atop his chest. He would stroke her back for several minutes, and when she was ready she would slide to the edge of the bed and lay on her left side so that he could stand behind her and finish. It was hard, delicious, delirious work for both of them, and after they showered and Will returned to the bar she would often nap until Molly came home or called for a pickup.

But this morning the alarm had not gone off. Will left early to talk to his brothers.

She could smell the fresh pot of coffee he had made, and hoped he had left enough in the pot so that the bottom didn't burn.

It troubled her a little that he had not awakened her that morning with his erection pressing against her; obviously Stevie's little escapade had him more worried than usual. And Will was a worrier. Every little misfortune became another hole in the dike for him. If he didn't learn to relax once in a while, he was going to drive himself crazy, and drag her along for the ride. Still, she could have used some comforting herself. Some reconnection and grounding.

Last night's job had taken a lot out of her. This morning she felt achy all over. Her eyelids didn't want to open the whole way, and her eyes felt scratchy and red. Images of the crime scene kept flickering through her head, the wet blood and shattered glass on the highway, the boy sitting beside the gurney, his face buried in his hands.

In hopes that sexual arousal would chase the images away and clear her head, she thought about Will touching her, his hand between her legs. But sometimes Will disappeared and Trooper Wilson took his place. And sometimes she saw the black tarp and the form of a body beneath it. She kept jerking her thoughts back to sex but this time it wasn't working. She couldn't make herself aroused and there was nobody around to lend a hand.

She turned her thoughts to her own situation and the possibility of improvement. What if Kirby's plan for a digital magazine really worked? Odds were against it, Kirby being Kirby. But what if? How long could she keep Kirby at arm's length? And was it even worth the effort to try?

She had to be a realist. Had to think in terms of debits and credits. Kirby wasn't Alex Wilson, a man she'd admired and with whom she shared a strong physical attraction. Kirby was just a pampered rich boy with soft hands and a soft body. If she gave him what he wanted, in exchange for what she wanted—a better job, more money, more security for her family—what would that make her? She might as well dress in a miniskirt and boots and parade her pretty little butt all up and down the street.

On the other hand, women had been using their charms for self-promotion since the beginning of humanity. How many housewives despised their husbands yet tolerated their grunts and groans in exchange for food, shelter, college tuition for the kids? Wasn't that prostitution too? *If you stop to think about it,* she told herself, *having sex and getting nothing from it, as she had done with Alex, is way less intelligent than doing it for a better job.*

Heck, she might even enjoy sex with Kirby.

Then she told herself, *Ugh. Don't even think about that.*

Besides, the online photo magazine was probably bullshit. But the teaching job . . . That one just might be legit. Would she really have a shot at it?

Nothing to do but find out.

She slid her legs over the side of the bed, stood, and had a rush of dizziness that made her sit down. She thought about falling back onto her pillow and going back to sleep, letting everything just go to hell and fall apart. But she couldn't.

She pushed herself up slower this time. No dizziness. Then went to her dresser, found a pair of baggy shorts and a T-shirt and pulled them on, and padded lightly into the kitchen. Molly was a sound sleeper, but Laci took no chances. She was careful getting a mug out of the closet, careful getting milk from the refrigerator, even careful opening up her laptop on the coffee table in the living room.

Before starting her search of local college websites, she took a long sip of coffee. So good in the morning. Will always made the coffee too strong for her taste, so she drank it lukewarm with lots of milk. She never complained to Will about his coffee, it was such a tiny thing, not worth mentioning. In every other way he was the perfect husband, a hard worker and attentive father. He just wasn't very good at making coffee. Or making money. That was no reason not to love him. He was doing his best. He always did his best. It was his brothers that were dragging them down right now, not Will himself.

Maybe if she could get the teaching job. Then, with income from that and working for the paper and the police department, she could convince him to sell the bar, find himself another job. Maybe even move to another town. The college town maybe. More opportunities for Molly, for Will, for all of them.

Damn it, she needed that job. But first she had to find out if it was real.

23

Will turned to look when he heard Jennalee coming down off the front porch, moving carefully in her white block-heel sandals. The moment the sun hit her face she slipped her sunglasses on. Still twenty feet from where Harvey and Will stood with their heads under the Infiniti's upraised hood, she said, "What are you boys cooking up this morning?"

Will turned to face her, though Harvey did not. As always, Will felt a little catch in his chest at the sight of his brother's wife: blonde hair perfectly styled, her pretty face and pale red lipstick, white shorts and long legs and red painted toenails, the light-blue silky top against her breasts. If she wasn't the prettiest woman in town, he didn't know who was. "Morning, Jennalee," he said.

She smiled in return, and now, wedging herself between the brothers so that Will had to move aside, she put a hand on each of their backs. "Get me all fixed up?" she said to her husband.

"Good for another three thousand miles," Harvey answered. He stepped back and reached for the hood, waited until Jennalee and Will were clear, and pulled the hood down.

Will said, "Well, I guess I better be on my way."

"Don't leave on my account," Jennalee said. "I left the coffee on for you boys."

Harvey said, "He's got a business to run." Then he turned to Will and said, "Talk to you later."

Will nodded, gave Jennalee a parting smile, and turned away.

Harvey waited until Will was out on the sidewalk. "You be home for lunch?" he asked his wife.

Jennalee said, "Well, I need a new pair of cross-trainers for the classroom, and then I thought I might get my nails done. And then I might stop and chat with Mom awhile."

Harvey turned to face her, but stood looking away, squinting toward the sun. "You just saw her last night, didn't you?"

"Do we have to talk about this again?" she asked.

"How about spending some time with your husband now and then?"

"Such as?" she asked. "Stand here with my head under the hood of your truck?"

"There's lots of things we could do together."

"Okay. Give me a couple of examples. Ones that don't include sex."

He said nothing. Stood breathing shallowly through his nose, his muscles stiff.

"Sweetie," she said, and rubbed her hand against his back, "if you're feeling neglected, just tell me what you want that I'm not giving you."

"Never mind," he said.

"I do mind. I don't like you being this way. Tell me what I'm not doing for you."

He gave her a look, then turned away and crossed to stand in front of his truck. He put his hands up on the edge of the hood but did not pull it down.

She followed to stand beside him. "Really," she said. "What am I not doing? I make all your meals, right? If we don't eat together, your dinner is in the oven or the slow cooker or the refrigerator, isn't it? Have you ever had to make your own dinner? Do I keep the house clean? This house is *immaculate*. Do I neglect my wifely duties in the bedroom? You can't possibly say that."

"You do everything," he said. "You're the perfect wife."

"Now you're going to insult me with sarcasm?"

"The point," he said, "is that you do all that stuff just so you can feel free to take off again. What do you do over there all the time anyway? Do you play cards, watch movies? What do you do?"

"You're lucky you didn't have to watch your parents grow old."

"Oh boy," he said.

"I mean it. She's changing. Getting sad. I think she's becoming aware of her own mortality. Like she knows she's going to die one of these days too. She's being so sweet to me lately."

Harvey grunted. "Your mother sweet? I sure haven't seen any of that."

"Well, you should pay more attention, because she is."

"That still doesn't mean you have to . . . Listen, I get weekends off. Two days a week. We should be spending that time together."

"If there's something you want to do together, just let me know."

"Anything. I don't care what."

"Well, that's just vague enough that we'll sit around all day asking each other, 'What do you want to do? No, what do *you* want to do?'"

"All right," Harvey said. "Let's drive down to Pittsburgh and go to a ball game."

"In this heat? You want to sit out in this heat for four or five hours?"

"Then we'll go to a museum or something."

"You hate museums. You'll just walk around saying, 'That's not art. How is that art?'"

"I don't care what we do! We can go to a movie, for God's sake. Sit in an air-conditioned movie house."

"And listen to you complain about people eating popcorn too loud."

"Then you think of something."

"That's the problem, my love; I already made plans for the day. I told Mom I would stop by. She's expecting me."

"She expects you all prettied up with your makeup and hair all done?"

"Now you know I refuse to leave the house looking like a mess. You know that. So don't start this nonsense, because I know where you're going with it."

"Yeah, well . . . it just seems awfully suspicious to me."

"That I want to look nice walking around the mall?" she said. "You find that suspicious? You want me to throw on some sweatpants and flip-flops from the Dollar Store? Will that make you happier?"

"Just go," he said. "Just go." He pulled the truck hood down partway, waited until she stepped back, then closed it as softly as he could.

She said, "You want us to do something together tomorrow?"

"Yes," he said.

"Okay. You come up with a plan. Anything you want to do, we'll do it."

He said, "We could drive up into the mountains. Take a picnic lunch with us."

"Whatever you want," she said. "Just make sure we have a gallon or so of insect repellant."

"Then forget it," he told her, and pulled away. "Just forget it."

He strode into the garage, into the scent of shade and cool concrete and tools and paint cans and things he understood. He stood facing the workbench and hoped to hear her heels clicking softly as she came up behind him. Instead he heard her car door opening and falling shut. Heard the Infiniti's engine growl to life. Heard the tires whispering across the pavement as she backed out onto the street and drove away.

24

Will pulled out his cell phone to check the time. He had to turn his back to the sun and use his body to shade the screen. Twenty minutes after nine. The bar was fifteen minutes away. He would need another twenty to get everything in place so he could unlock the door. But Harvey's adamancy worried him. Harvey wanted rid of Kenny so badly that he was willing to risk losing Jennalee? Something wasn't right about that. What wasn't Harvey telling him?

Will asked himself, *What if I have another talk with Kenny? See if I can't get this settled somehow.*

Old Ralph and older Eldon, father and son, one in his late sixties, the other ninety-two, would be his only customers until noon or so. They would probably be waiting in their ancient pickup truck when Will arrived, listening to some country-western song with the windows down, the radio so loud Will would hear it from a block away. They had lost their farm back in the eighties and hadn't sobered up since. Not long after the bank's auction of all their farm equipment, Ralph's wife packed two suitcases, and off she went to live with her sister in Myrtle Beach. Less than a year later, Eldon's wife "took the easy way out," in his words, by swallowing a handful of Prozac and half a bottle of chardonnay. Now the men lived together in the old farmhouse, slowly rotting along with the roof and boards, both men as unkempt as their remaining acre of weeds and grass.

They can wait a few extra minutes, Will told himself, and turned left at the corner, returning to the house he had visited only nine hours earlier.

The moment Will knocked on the doorframe, Louise's frenetic terrier started yipping. He raced down the carpeted stairs and into the foyer and up to the screen door, where he stood on his front paws, stubby little claws and blunted snout pushed against the screen. To Will the little dog always reminded him of a big rodent fetus of some kind, looking cartoonishly stupid with its squinty eyes void of lashes, its nose void of whiskers. Every time the dog got excited, as it was now, it sported a bright-red erection.

"Hey, boy," Will said, though he found the dog mildly repulsive.

"Who's there?" Louise said, invisible at the top of the stairs.

"It's Will," he answered. "Is Kenny home?"

How many dozens of times had he said those words? As a child he'd been Harvey's errand boy, always running over to the Fulton house at his brother's behest, fetching Kenny or something Harvey had left behind there the day before, his ball glove or Frisbee, or, when he grew older, a tool of some kind, or the wallet that must have fallen out during Harvey's turn in the back seat with some girl.

Louise's reply was a groan of annoyance. She came heavily down the stairs, one plodding step at a time. Halfway down she came into view. Everything about her seemed soft and bloated to Will, from her fat swollen feet in their translucent compression stockings to the corpulent body beneath a brightly flowered muumuu to her flabby arms and thick crepey neck and broad, scowling face.

She was unrecognizable from the attractive Louise Will had known as a boy. Never a small woman, she had played a lot of tennis in her younger years to maintain what was then called "a statuesque figure." She had been flirtatious with all of Kenny's friends, even on occasion with Will once he entered pubescence. But now, Will noticed, she seemed as asexual as a flatulent cow.

She came to the door and silenced Tippy by shoving him aside with her foot. "What do you want with him?" she asked through the screen.

"Just want to talk to him about a couple of things."

"That idiot brother of yours should be in jail right now," she said. "If it was up to me, he would be."

"He, uh," Will said. "He made a mistake, that's for sure. And he's very sorry for what he did."

"What good is that supposed to do?"

Will blew out a breath; looked off to the side. Through the foyer he could see part of the spacious living room, the long red sofa, the stuffed chairs and paintings and expensive tables and lamps.

He said, "Is Kenny around?"

"That's bullshit what Harvey's saying about a will," she said. "Pure unadulterated bullshit. I don't appreciate him going around lying about that."

"Harvey doesn't lie," he said quietly, straining to remain calm. "Mrs. Fulton, that's your son-in-law you're talking about."

"Don't try blaming that on me," she said. "I was against that marriage from the start."

Will felt his eyes begin to sting; felt the skin of his face tighten. "We need to get something worked out here," he told her. "Jake promised that motorcycle to Harvey. Harvey did all the work on it. He deserves some consideration."

"Jake made a lot of promises he never intended to keep. What's done is done. And it's going to stay done."

"Could you tell Kenny I would like to speak with him?"

"I already told you he isn't here."

"No, you didn't tell me that."

"Well how many times do you have to be told?"

Again Will released a slow breath. It was the only way to keep himself under control. Talking to her was useless.

"I believe my brother," he told her. "If he says Jake promised it to him, then that's what happened."

She leaned closer to the screen, almost touched it with her nose. "It's a Goddamn motorcycle!" she said. "Your brother needs to grow up and get over it. You all do."

"I guess that would apply to Kenny too, wouldn't it?"

She gave him a long, glowering look. Then jerked away for a moment, reached to the side, and reappeared with a broom in her hand. She banged the straws against the screen. "You get off my porch right now!" she bellowed. Tippy broke into a fury of barking as he jumped and clawed at the screen.

25

The urge to break things, to just start smashing and destroying everything in sight, was strong in Harvey after Jennalee drove away. But little in the garage belonged to her. He scanned his tools, the wrenches and hammers and saws, the screwdrivers and shovels, the axe and machete. Even the plastic containers holding oil, transmission fluid, and windshield fluid felt off-limits to his rage—none of them belonged to her but were extensions of his own hands. He had always thought of himself as the kind of guy who fixed things when they broke. This urge to destroy was new to him.

Then his gaze landed on Jennalee's golf bag. Pink and white and filled with expensive Ping clubs. Some of the clubs had animal-head covers. A tiger, an elephant, a silly-looking squirrel. Those clubs infuriated him.

Five or six Sundays every summer Jennalee would play eighteen holes with her brother and mother. Louise couldn't play anymore but she liked to ride around in the cart, a thermos full of martinis in the cup holder, while her children played. Once, several years back, when Harvey had complained about losing Jennalee on yet another Sunday morning, she had talked him into coming along, but he was no golfer. His body was too stiff for golf; it didn't flex and turn the right ways. By the fourth hole Kenny was calling him "Shankster."

"You're up, Shankster," he would say, and everybody, including Jennalee, would grin. That made him even stiffer. He had walked off the fairway after only eight holes. Sat in the clubhouse drinking beer and watching a ball game.

He fucking hated golf. "Stupid game," Jake had told him afterward. "Tell you what. Hang around with me on Sundays, okay? I've got my eye on a beat-up old Indian bike. What say you and me restore it together? Leave golf to the girlies."

And now, standing there in his garage, remembering how Kenny and Jennalee and their mother had embarrassed him, had made him feel stupid and small, the distant rumble in his head took on a low but steady beat. He knew it was probably just the sound of his own pulse, his blood pressure rising, but it was annoying as hell all the same.

He eyed Jennalee's golf clubs. He could break one or two, but she would just go out and buy more. So instead he walked up to the bag, lifted the silly squirrel-head cover away. Putter. A very important club for a golfer. So what if he maybe bent the shaft a little? Not enough that she would notice, but enough to make the ball roll cockeyed?

He drew the club from the bag, carried it to his workbench, fitted the club into his vise. A little push here. A nudge there.

The work was delicate but forceful. Very satisfying.

He did the same to the driver and the four wood. Slipped them back into the bag and replaced the head covers. "Who's the shankster now?" he said.

It had felt good, but also wrong. Satisfaction was followed by guilt. The drumbeat in his head grew louder. He asked himself, *What the hell is going on with you?*

He didn't want to go back inside the house. Didn't want to sit there stewing in his resentment, simmering with anger. He walked to the mouth of the garage, looked up and down the street. Yards full of sunlight. Flowerbeds and driveways.

Maybe he should take a walk. Walk off this uncomfortable mix of feelings. Maybe even jog for a while if the mood seized him. He could walk to the high school, six blocks away, and trot around the track for a while, sweat all the toxins out. But what if Kenny was in his office, catching up on work? He might look out a window and see Harvey plodding around in circles. Knowing Kenny, he would come to the rear door, out onto the parking lot, and call out when Harvey trudged past. "Twenty-six more miles, Shankster, and you will burn off a whole pound of that sausage! Only a hundred and three more laps to go!"

Fuck Kenny. Fuck the whole fucking family. I'll walk around town, Harvey told himself. *Take my own fucking time.*

Within a couple of minutes he was short of breath. Felt as if he had run two miles. Yet he was moving. Maybe the only thing in the entire neighborhood moving this morning. Where were all the kids that should be outside playing? Back when he was a kid, the yards were full of noise and motion. Now all he could hear was somebody's lawn mower a street or two away. Sure, it was hot today, eighty-plus degrees already. But was that any reason to hide inside?

His chest was heavy, skull tight. He could hear his pulse thumping in his ears. Felt a low fire burning his lungs.

You're going to give yourself a heart attack, he thought, but not without some pleasure. He didn't think he would mind being dead. Dead meant either something better, or, more likely, nothing at all. He didn't believe in Hell, saw too much Hell all around him every day while driving his route from store to store, stocking shelves with microwavable breakfast sandwiches, with eggs and sausage patties and biscuits waiting to be irradiated in the little black boxes in everybody's kitchens. One hundred and seventeen million pigs consumed every year. Thirty-one pigs per American over the course of a lifetime. Nearly eleven steers and calves. Over two thousand chickens.

People eat, he told himself. *That's what they do mostly. They eat and shit and sleep and screw. They work too, but only so they can eat and shit and sleep and screw.*

Every weekday he drove over four hundred miles to feed his little slice of America, through neighborhoods filled with every kind of misery, with violence poverty crack heroin homelessness and craziness of every flavor. So why would there be a Hell in the Afterlife? Another Hell would be redundant.

He used to be happy in this town. Not so much as a kid, when nearly every day brought a smack or two from somebody. But around seventeen or so, when he was big enough to defend himself, that's when life improved. When he was big enough to get hold of a little money now and then. Enough for him and Kenny to go partners on a car. He did all the work, made all the engine modifications and drove all the races on Friday and Saturday nights. Even won his fair share of them. And afterward, the girls. Kenny had a knack for drawing them in. Those years were the best Harvey had ever experienced.

He never should have let himself fall in love. That was when all the trouble started. Not right away, though. The first few years were good. Full of promise. Big expectations.

Then the economy tanked. The town was dying. Friends moved away. Boredom set in. And the resentment with Jennalee festered. Some things could not be forgotten.

And now he stopped walking. Out of breath, heart thumping hard, a stitch in his side, he realized he'd been staring at nothing but hot concrete as he walked. A stench of melted tar was stinging his nostrils, little bubbles of black oozing up from the street.

He had walked the whole way across town without knowing it. And now felt like a complete stranger to this town. This miserable little town in Hell.

Had there ever been a place, or a life, more pointless?

26

Not long after Will opened up the bar for the day and served Ralph and Eldon their first cold drafts of the morning, on the house because he had kept them waiting so long, Molly and Laci came downstairs and into the kitchen. Molly, wearing a bulky PINK backpack containing her inline skating gear, grabbed a bottle of water from the cooler and, from one of the cardboard boxes against the wall, a bag of nacho tortilla chips.

"Whoa there," Laci said, and shifted her camera bag to the other shoulder. "How about a bag of pretzels instead?"

"What makes you think they're any healthier?" Molly asked.

"I don't know. They just sound healthier."

Molly turned back to the boxes and rummaged through them until she came up with a bag of pretzels. She read silently from the tables of contents. Then held out the bag of chips. "Corn," she said. Then the bag of pretzels. "Flour, sugar, and lots of salt." Then the chips. "Vegetable." The pretzels. "Tiny loaves of white bread. Almost seven hundred milligrams of sodium in every ounce."

"Fine," Laci said. "Eat the vegetables."

Molly tossed the pretzels back into the box, then turned to cross toward the door into the bar, where Will stood watching and smiling. "Good morning," he told her.

"You think?" she said, and strode past him to the front door, which she flung open before marching out into the brightness.

Laci came forward to stand behind the counter with Will, whose smile had gone lopsided. "She's still mad at you," she said.

"So I see."

"I'm dropping her off at school for a couple hours while I take some shots around town. We should be back by noon. I was thinking that, if you want, I can watch the bar for a while so you can try to patch things up with your daughter."

"Is that possible," he said, "since there's still no way she's going to be dating a senior?"

"She understands," Laci said.

"Does she? Guys like that have a permanent hard-on."

"We had a little mother-daughter talk."

"What did you tell her?"

"Same thing you did, but without going postal on her."

"Don't exaggerate."

"She said she thought you were going to hit her."

"She did not. She knows better than that."

"Just talk to her, okay? Don't get angry. Keep your voice low. Pretend she's one of your customers."

"That's not fair, Laci."

She stood there at the corner of the bar, watching out the open door. Why was she so irritated with Will this morning? Where had that sudden annoyance come from? Heat washed in from the street, poured over her face and made her eyes sting. Even diluted by the halfhearted air-conditioning, the air felt thick and dirty on her skin. "Okay," she said.

Will waited a moment for more, but she said nothing else. "What kind of shots?" he asked. "For the paper?"

Now she turned his way again; gave him a smile. "Remember that teaching job Kirby mentioned?"

"Sure," he said.

"Turns out it's for real."

"He called you?"

She shook her head. "I did a search online. Every college within fifty miles."

"And?"

"Venango County Community College."

"That's only, what, twenty-five miles from here?"

"Twenty-six point eight," she said. "So I called them. Talked to the chair of the communications department. Two sections, an hour and a half per section every Saturday and Sunday morning. It's called Weekend College."

"Sounds good," he said.

"That's not the best of it. They have two requirements. First, you have to be a working professional photographer."

"Which you are," he said.

"And have a strong portfolio."

"You must have years and years of photos by now."

"Except that they're top-heavy with tragedy. So I figure I'll wander around awhile today, take some human-interest shots. Laughing babies, puppies licking themselves, things like that."

He said, "Take some in here if you want."

Laci glanced down the bar at the two old men leaning over their beers. One was grumbling under his breath; the other stared blankly at the large photo of Ben Roethlisberger releasing a pass while three Ravens hung from his waist and back.

She said, "Call me when somebody smiles."

Will blinked, bit his bottom lip. Then he said, "So Kirby wasn't full of it after all. You think he can really get you the job?"

"Screw Kirby," she said. "I'm qualified. The chair even said he's seen my photos in the paper. Remember the one from the county fair a few years back? When I caught the knockout blow in the boxing match at the very second it happened?"

Will nodded. "With one of the ring lights shining like a star right under his arm when his fist connected."

"He said he's used that photo in his classes."

"Wow," Will said.

"So if I make the short list, I have to teach a one-hour class in front of a few students and the rest of the department, which consists of three other people."

"You think you can do that?" Will asked.

She gave him a long look, and wondered what frightened him more—that she would fail, or that she would succeed.

Will said, "I just mean . . . it's not something you've done before, is it?"

"I talk to people all the time. Without drooling or slurring my words."

"Then you'll be great," he said, and laid a hand on the small of her back.

"I've already planned out a PowerPoint presentation."

He smiled. "I wish I could be there to see it."

"They might let you. I can ask."

"That would be great," he said. "My wife the professor."

"Well, let's not get ahead of ourselves. I still have to apply and make the short list."

"What about that other job," he asked, "for the online magazine?"

"I'm ninety-nine percent sure it's bullshit. I'll just have to wait and see."

He held his smile, nodded, and rubbed his hand against her back. She thought he really did look happy for her, sincerely happy. Why would she have thought otherwise?

Then Will told her, "Somebody's getting impatient," and nodded toward the entrance. Molly stood on the threshold, frowning, hands gripping the backpack straps, her body sagging as if from the pack's enormous weight.

"Later," she told him, and kissed his cheek.

"Have fun," he said.

27

When Stevie came crawling out from underneath his former teacher's back porch, wriggling feet first into the heat and light, he was so out of breath, less from the physical exertion than from awaiting a guerrilla attack by tiny claws and rabies-dripping teeth, that as soon as his head cleared the last board, he rolled onto his back in the grass and, laying the pistol atop his chest, sucked in a lungful of hot air.

"You didn't see him?" Mrs. Miller asked.

"Nothing in there but dirt and cobwebs." Then he sat up, flicked the safety on his 9mm Taurus, and ejected the full clip.

"I don't see how he could have gotten past me without being seen."

"They're clever little buggers," he said.

"I'm so sorry you went to all that trouble for nothing. It was very brave of you to crawl in there."

He rolled onto his side, then pushed himself to his feet, and used his free hand to brush the dirt off his clothing. "I couldn't see any signs of a den," he said. "He was probably just looking for a quick place to hide."

"Well," she said, "as long as he's gone. Why don't you come on in and wash up and I'll get your money for you."

"I can wash up at home. No use tracking this dirt into your house."

"Don't be silly," she said. "You can use the downstairs powder room."

Without waiting for his reply she strode past him, onto the porch and inside.

Stevie went to his pickup truck and placed the pistol in the glove box. Then he spent another minute brushing the dirt from his arms, then again slapped at the front of his jeans and knocked his work boots together. Then he walked up onto the porch, and was relieved to feel the breeze of air-conditioning wafting toward him through the screen door.

The moment he stepped inside, she handed him a tall glass of iced tea. "You must surely be thirsty after all that."

"I am," he said. "Thank you." He reached for the glass but saw how dirty his palms were. "Maybe I should wash my hands first."

"Straight through the kitchen and on your right," she said. "I'll put the tea on the kitchen table while I look for my purse."

Stevie bent to unlace his boots, pull them off, and set them beside the back door. Then he checked his socks. Dingy but no holes. Thank God for small favors.

When he returned to the kitchen from the powder room after washing his hands and forearms, then rinsing out the sink three times to flush all the grime down the drain, he found Mrs. Miller seated with her own glass of tea across the table from his glass. Beside his glass was a folded fifty-dollar bill, and beside it a plate of snickerdoodle cookies.

"Sit down and drink your tea," she told him. "And help yourself to the cookies. Let's get reacquainted again."

Awkwardly, he took his seat. Scraped the money off the table and shoved it into a pocket. Then lifted the glass to his mouth and drank.

She asked him then if he'd heard of the accident earlier that morning, and when he said no, she filled him in. "It's all so senseless," she said. "I had every one of them in my class. Makes you wonder, doesn't it?"

"About . . . playing chicken, you mean?"

"About how precious our time is. How we should make the most of every minute of life we have."

"That's for sure," he answered.

"I've seen you driving around from time to time. But how long has it been since we actually had a conversation?"

He picked a cookie off the plate. "I don't know if we ever had one. Unless you count all the time you scolded me for not having my homework done."

"You were a time waster," she told him. "But you seem industrious enough now."

"I try to keep busy," he said.

She nodded. Smiled. Took a sip of her tea. "I lost my Eddie eight months ago," she said. "I don't know if you knew that or not."

"I think I heard about that. I'm sorry for your loss."

"Thank you. It's not easy losing somebody you spent your entire adult life with."

"I imagine it's not."

"You lost your father a good while back."

"Yep. That's true."

"And your mother?"

"Living in Florida now."

"Well good for her."

"I guess so," he said.

"But you and your brothers are still here. Harvey and Will. How are they doing?"

"Good, good," he said. "They seem to be doing all right."

"Both married," she said. "And how many nieces and nephews do you have now?"

"Just the one. Molly. Will and Laci's."

"Molly is a smart girl. Very smart, from what I hear. All the teachers like her."

"She gets that from Laci. Obviously not from my side of the family."

"There's nothing wrong with your side of the family, Stevie. Boys are boys, that's all. Especially in junior high. They have other things on their mind."

Hearing this, Stevie blushed. Was she aware of all the times he had stared at her breasts, envisioned them unmasked, full and heavy and warm against his face?

"But you've never married," she said. "Never settled down."

"I guess not," he said.

"Do you have a girlfriend?"

"Not right now," he told her. "Used to, sort of. A while back."

"You had a sort-of girlfriend?" she asked with a smile.

"More or less," he said.

She took another sip of tea. Looked at the bare tabletop. Ran her finger across a tiny nick in the wood. "What's the term young people use these days for a relationship like that? Friends with benefits?"

Again he blushed, but smiled, amused. "I guess that's right."

"In my day we called them fuck buddies," she said.

Startled, he looked up at her. She was holding the glass of tea between her breasts, head lowered just a bit, but still smiling and meeting his gaze.

"We still say that too," he told her.

"So we're not really that different after all, are we?"

"I guess we're not," he said.

They sat quietly then for a few moments, long enough for Stevie to think this might be a good time to leave. He ate the last bite of his cookie, then washed it down with the rest of his tea.

She said, "Do you not mind being alone? Without somebody close to you? I'm finding it very hard to live that way."

"It takes some getting used to, I guess."

"What do you miss most?" she asked.

"You mean . . . from high school?"

"From not having a girlfriend."

"Oh. Well . . ." He thought for a moment, then grinned. "That's probably not something I should talk about here."

"I know what I miss most," she said. "The touching. The intimacy. Eddie was a beast, you know."

"You mean . . . he hit you?"

"Oh my no. I mean in bed. Four nights a week minimum. Almost forty-six years, and he never once slowed down. Even the night before his heart attack. And now it's been eight long months without him."

"Wow," Stevie said, and could think of nothing else to say, and so said it again. "Wow."

Again a silence. He hoped she wouldn't start crying. She looked as if she might. He lifted his empty glass to his mouth, though there was nothing to drink.

She said, "You're welcome to take a shower if you'd like."

Again he was startled. Where did that statement come from? "I washed my hands and arms already," he told her.

"Even so. Crawling around in the dirt like I had you doing. All those cobwebs and who knows what else. It would feel good, wouldn't it? A nice cool shower?"

"I guess so," he said, but he could not look at her now, was studying the cookies, trying to puzzle out the direction of this conversation.

"It's a nice big shower," she told him. "Marble tiles, one of those showerheads that feels like rain falling down. There's even a bench seat if you feel like sitting. Eddie installed it a couple years before he passed."

"Sounds nice," Stevie said.

She nodded. "It's more than big enough for two people."

"Oh yeah?" he said.

"I could wash your hair and your back for you. The way I always did for Eddie."

And now, because he could not help himself, he lifted his gaze off the cookies.

"I would do his back and he would do my breasts," she said. "Eddie loved my breasts. He really, really loved them."

And Stevie found himself nodding, returning her smile. "I can understand that," he said.

28

Laci walked away from the elementary school playground, where she had photographed empty swings, an empty jungle gym and sliding board, and was standing at the intersection with Main Street, wondering which way to walk next, when Jennalee's Infiniti pulled up to the curb.

Jennalee powered down her tinted window and said, "Hey, lady. You lost?"

Laci turned, saw her sister-in-law's pretty, smiling face, and, instead of answering, raised her camera and clicked off a couple of shots. Jennalee pulled off her sunglasses and widened her smile, so Laci clicked three more shots.

Then Jennalee asked, "So what's the haps, girl? You look like a woman in search of something."

Laci said, "Just fattening up my portfolio. There wasn't a single child in the playground. Where have all the children gone?"

"Didn't you hear? We had an auction the other day. Sold them off to a textile mill in Bangladesh."

Laci smiled, though she didn't find the joke very funny, especially coming from a third-grade teacher. "So what are you up to this morning?"

"Shoe sale at the mall."

"I heard they're going out of business."

"They are! Fifty percent off everything. I'm stocking up. Why don't you come along? We'll get a couple of frozen mocha cappuccinos and catch up."

"A frozen cappuccino sounds good. Unfortunately, I really do need to take some photos."

"Of what in particular?"

"Nothing in particular. Just human-interest stuff."

"So come to the mall and take pictures of the mall walkers in their pink velour jogging suits."

"That's not a bad idea," Laci said. "But I promised Will I'd be home around noon."

Jennalee glanced up the street, then in the opposite direction. "Are you walking?"

"Car's around the corner."

"So go jump in it and meet me in the food court. Coffee's on me."

Laci considered the offer.

"Come on. We haven't gotten together since Christmas. The boys see each other all the time. Why should they have all the fun?"

Laci sensed that Jennalee had something more she wanted to talk about. As did Laci. "Okay," she said. "See you in fifteen."

Jennalee blew a kiss out the window, then pulled away from the curb and drove off. Laci stepped back into the shade of a storefront, quickly reviewed the photos she had taken of Jennalee, and deleted them.

29

The morning was slower than usual in the bar. Halfway through his second beer, Eldon rose from his stool without a word, turned and trudged to the door, pulled it open and walked outside. Ralph finished off his own beer, then reached for his father's glass.

Will walked down behind the bar. "Was he not feeling well?" he asked.

Ralph sipped his father's beer. "He'll nap in the truck awhile."

"It's awfully warm out there, though. If he's not feeling well . . ."

"Worn down," Ralph said. Another sip. "Winding down's more like it."

"How do you mean?"

"He's been talking about joining Mom," Ralph said.

"Jeez," said Will. He took the empty glass off the bar and placed it in the basin filled with sudsy water.

"Yep," Ralph said. "We all wind down sooner or later."

Will said, "You think you should maybe get him to a doctor? Get him some antidepressants or something?"

"Nope," Ralph said. "He's lived too long and so have I. We've both outlived our usefulness."

"Hell," Will told him, "you're describing sixty, seventy percent of this town."

"I think your figures are a little low," Ralph said.

Three beers later Ralph ambled off, and Will was left alone in an empty bar. He checked the time. Ten fifty-eight. Another sixty minutes at least until Molly and Laci came home for lunch.

He spent half a minute wiping down the bar again, then four minutes more with his hand flat on the damp surface, thumb going up and down beating out a slow, dull thump while he stared at the opposite wall. Then he shook his head, blinked, and dug around beneath the bar until he found a small tablet and pen. On a blank sheet of paper he printed **OPEN AT NOON**. Then tore the sheet from the notebook, did another search under the bar and came up with a thumbtack, went to the door, stepped outside and pulled it shut, locked it, and tacked the note to the door.

He told himself that he would take a nice leisurely stroll to the school, watch Molly and her friends skating for a while, then walk her back home. Maybe while walking he would come up with a plan for dealing with Kenny Fulton. The important thing was that nobody should get physically hurt, and that neither he nor Harvey would be implicated. What could they do that would so embarrass or humiliate Kenny that he would never live it down? Something that would make his life in this town as unpleasant as everybody else's?

As far as Will was concerned, Kenny's comeuppance was long overdue. He and his mother, and even, in Will's opinion, Jennalee, had always looked down their noses at Will's family. And Will would never forget or forgive the way Kenny had hightailed it home after taunting Stevie to jump onto the garage roof. Would never forget those sickening moments on the roof when, before jumping down, he and Harvey had stood side by side, looking at their little brother motionless on the ground.

The more he thought about those times, the faster Will walked, and the angrier he became. He soon found himself a hundred yards from the high school. Just in case Kenny was in there in his office, Will took a side street and circled around toward the rear of the building. He didn't want Molly to see him approaching either, lest she accuse him of spying on her, which, he admitted, was exactly what he was doing.

He walked past the long rows of windows on the side of the building, three empty classrooms in a row. How many hours had he wasted in those rooms? What good had his third-rate education ever done him? He had enjoyed music class, listening to and singing along with old folk songs. And he had enjoyed phys ed, was a fair athlete compared to most of the other kids, but nothing exceptional, just a smidgeon better than the rest of the lunkheads. Football had been fun now and then, but not when his coach mistakenly called him Harvey instead of Will, or when he said things like "Your brother never would have missed that tackle." Or "Your brother would have intercepted that pass."

Will came to the corner of the building then. Beyond lay the parking lot, wide and flat and empty but for two cars parked at the far end, plus five boys and three girls skating back and forth from one end of the lot to the other, chasing and grabbing at each other, the boys showing off by skating fast and making hard, quick turns, the girls pretending to be unimpressed.

Will watched them, smiling, and tried to spot Laci among the moving bodies. But she wasn't there. He looked beyond the parking lot to the football field and bleachers. All empty. Then to the parked cars. The sun was glinting off the windshields but he thought he could detect movement inside the black Civic, shadows behind the reflected sunlight. And suddenly his stomach felt strange, hollow yet heavy, a peculiar kind of nausea.

He crossed quickly toward the cars, walking in the shade close to the building, and was halfway there before the skaters noticed him. One by one they came to a stop and looked his way. They spoke softly to one another, looked toward the Civic, looked back at him. One of them reached into her pocket for a cell phone.

Will cut directly toward the group. And they skated away quickly, one after the other, leaving him a clear path to the car.

He yanked open the driver's door, his body bent low, leaning in. For an instant he did not recognize the girl lying up against the passenger door with the boy atop her. But then she slid to the side to look his way. A moment later he was reaching inside, seizing the boy's leg, dragging him over the console.

"Daddy, don't!" Molly cried.

And he froze. Saw himself as she must be seeing him, his face tight and full of malice. He released the boy, pulled back his own hand, three quick breaths and exhalations. "Go home," he told her.

She twisted toward the door, popped it open, climbed out. She looked at him only once over the top of the car, her own eyes full of tears and anger, and then hurried away.

He watched her for a few moments before looking inside the car again. "Move over," he told the boy. He waited while the boy pulled his legs over the console and sat upright against the passenger door. Then Will climbed into the driver's seat.

For a while he did nothing but stare at the boy. *Maybe it's not him,* he told himself. *Maybe this is a boy her own age.*

But boys her age would have peach fuzz on their faces, and this one had black stubble above his lip, sparser stubble on his cheeks. Boys her age would be terrified, nearly pissing their pants with fear. This one sat with his body tense, fists held close to his belly.

Boys her own age don't drive, he told himself.

The boy was at least as tall as Will but slender, arms tanned and muscled, stomach flat, jawline firm, eyes clear and body tensed; ready not to run but to defend itself.

Will's voice when he spoke sounded strange to him, deeper and softer than he intended, and came from low in the throat, less like words than a growl. "If you ever touch her again," he said, "if you ever, at any time, come near her again, do you know what I will do to you?"

At first the boy said nothing. Then, "All we did was to kiss and make out a—"

Will jerked toward him and the boy flinched, pulled back so quick that his head banged the glass. Will said, "Do you *know* what I will do to you?"

A few seconds ticked by. "Yes," the boy said.

"No you don't. You have no idea of the many ways I will mess up your life."

Will continued to glare at the boy until he looked away, out the windshield, into the glare. Then Will swung his legs out the door and stood. All the other kids were near the far wall of the building, clustered together, watching him. He was ashamed of himself, but was also glad for the confrontation. *It's what any father would do,* he told himself. And regretted only that he had almost gone too far. And knew that, if not for Molly's cry, he would have pulverized the boy.

30

Harvey's walk across town and back was so exhausting, his neck and back so slick with sweat, that he didn't even wait to get back inside the house, but jumped into his truck, started it up, turned the air conditioner on full blast, and held his face close to the vent. *It's a pitiful thing,* he told himself, *when air-conditioned air smells better than natural air. This town stinks.*

When his face was cool Harvey leaned back in his seat and let the blowing air wash over him. He had thought it would reenergize him, but the effect was the opposite. His body was too heavy and tired to move, even just to walk fifty steps into the house so that he could collapse on the bed.

Great way to spend a Saturday, he told himself.

And then he started thinking about previous Saturdays, all the good ones he had had back in the early days. He had loved the noise and dusty, smoky air at the tracks. Loved flying around the oval at triple-digit speed. Loved how all the easy, drunken girls swarmed around him when he walked away with the trophy.

And then came the early times with Jennalee. Those Saturdays were good too. Getting up early to wash and detail his car. He drove a vintage Eldorado back in those days, always had a thing for the old land yachts, the way they filled up the lane on the highway and commanded everybody's attention and respect. Then hanging out with a few buds to learn who was doing what that night, where the good bands or movies were playing. Then grab a piece of shade somewhere, anywhere but home, and nap for a while, charge up the batteries for the long night ahead. Then sneaking back home as quietly as he could, hoping the old man was asleep in his ratty old chair and wouldn't have some shit-brain job for Harvey to do. Picking out his clothes for the evening—his newest jeans and whitest shirt—and ironing them in the kitchen without waking up the old fart, then getting a long, cool shower, slapping on an abundance of deodorant and aftershave, getting dressed and slipping out of the house.

What he liked best with Jennalee was being alone with her, and that usually meant the drive-in. Kenny had never wanted to double-date when Harvey was with his sister, and that was just fine with Harvey. There was nothing worse than being cock-blocked by another couple watching from the back seat when you were trying to put the moves on a girl.

And now Harvey sat up in his truck, leaned over the steering wheel and looked through the windshield at the glaring day. Jesus, he had been so deep in his reverie that he could still smell the drive-in—that mashed-up scent of weed and pizza and carbon monoxide—and the perfume Jennalee used to wear.

And now the emptiness returned. God, how he missed those days. How long ago they seemed!

Drive, he heard himself think, and, for a moment, wondered why that thought had come to him. Then decided, *Why the hell not? What else do you have to do?*

And as he pulled out of the driveway he told himself, *Anyway, this is what you do best, isn't it? You drive. It's all you've ever done, really. It's all you're good for.*

Seventeen miles to the drive-in. Now it was overgrown with weeds, was used from time to time for a flea market, and for that goofy Civil

War encampment during the last week of September. But now it was as silent and still as a cemetery. He drove slowly, reverently, past the dilapidated booth where he used to hand over a ten-dollar bill for entry. Then up and down over the low mounds until he came to their favorite spot, four rows from the back and just left of center. It was their favorite only because it had been where he parked the first time he brought Jennalee there, the first date he had with her.

He pulled up close to the rusty post that used to hold the speaker. Now it was just an old metal pole growing out of the weeds, paint flaked and corroded, its blunt, rounded top looking somehow naked and exposed.

He remembered his first night there with Jennalee. Even then the drive-in was a rarity, one of only two in the entire county. This one played nothing but old movies from the last half of the century. The movies that night were *Conquest of the Planet of the Apes* and *Battle for the Planet of the Apes*, both starring Roddy McDowall and Natalie Trundy. The good thing about watching old movies was that you had probably already seen them a dozen times, and didn't feel that you were missing anything by making out.

That first time, Harvey, who had already been with dozens of girls, was awkward and unsure of himself, and did nothing more than take Jennalee's hand in his for the first hour. Then, halfway through the first movie, she snuggled up close to him, and after kissing for a while she took his hand and placed it under her shirt. He could still remember how warm her belly felt, how soft her skin. He kept his hand there through five more minutes of kissing, fingers spread so as to encompass as much of her as he could, but never sliding his hand up or down, afraid to offend her and end the wonder of this night.

Then she said, "You don't have to keep your hand in one place, you know. What if it gets stuck there?"

"You think it might?" he said.

"Unless you don't *want* to move it anywhere else."

"I do," he said. "Up or down?"

"I don't think it matters," she said, "seeing as how I'm not wearing anything underneath in either direction."

"Sweet Jesus," he said.

She laughed softly and flicked her tongue against his ear.

"I think I better go up," he said. "I'm likely to have a heart attack if I go the other way."

"You're a big strong boy," she told him. "Why don't you take a chance and see what happens?"

Fifteen minutes later her top was off and her shorts were down on the floor mat. He had already given her an orgasm with his hand, yet he was still surprised when she unbuckled his belt and unsnapped his jeans, then squished down to the floor, kneeling atop her shorts, and worked his jeans down over his thighs. He said, "You don't have to do that if you don't want to," and she told him, "I never do anything I don't want to."

He had had sex on first dates before but this was Jennalee Fulton, a third-grade teacher, for chrissakes. Until two minutes before she took his penis into her mouth, he had never once believed he could have sex with her. He had fantasized about it a thousand times but never imagined it actually happening. The mere realization that it *was* happening made him come hard and fast, and though afterward he recognized a disappointment that she had been so easy and skillful, by the time he took her home he was already longing for the next time, which took place the following night on a blanket on the seventeenth green of what used to be the country club course before it went public in an attempt to stave off bankruptcy.

And now after years of marriage, they still had sex at least twice a week. He had begun to want it most when she was on her way to have dinner with her mother. Then it was always rushed and usually in an awkward position, such as leaning her over the sofa or kitchen counter. It felt fast and desperate to him and he did not ask how it felt for her. She always smiled and kissed him afterward and promised to be home by nine but seldom was. On weekdays he had to be on the road by 5:00 a.m., so he was usually asleep when she got home.

Now and then he would awaken before the alarm buzzed at 4:00 a.m. and his erection would be so hard that it hurt. He would slide over against her, and if she were sleeping on her back he would gently roll her onto her side. She would wake just enough to cooperate and turn her back to him. Even in winter she slept naked, and soon she would be wet and he would slide inside. Sometimes he tried to fuck her so hard that she would cry out for him to slow down, but she never did. She lay there with his left hand pressed against the small patch of trimmed pubic hair, his middle finger on her clitoris, his right hand under her neck and sometimes squeezing so hard he thought for sure he must be hurting her.

Afterward he would lie very still, his mouth pressed between her shoulder blades. Sometimes he would whisper "Sorry," and sometimes "Thank you," but she never answered and continued to pretend to sleep. When he saw her again twelve hours later, she would smile and kiss his mouth and ask, "How was your day, baby?" as if he had never been rough or selfish with her.

No matter how he behaved, she remained unchanged. And maybe that was why there seemed—to him, at least—to be a distance between them. When he tried to talk about it, she denied a distance existed.

"Don't be silly, baby. We're as close as we ever were."

"That's what I mean," he'd once said.

"Then what are you worrying about? Everything's fine."

Had he been better with words he might have been able to make himself understood. He was good with his hands but could never find the right words to express himself clearly. His senior English teacher had repeatedly admonished the class to expand their vocabularies, because "words are tools for shaping your thoughts," but the only word tools he could call forth seemed to be the blunt and cumbersome ones, the mallets and sledgehammers fit for little but demolition.

And now, sitting there in the desolation of a place that had brought him such joy and wonder, he realized, sadly, that he no longer liked his wife. He still loved her desperately, and was afraid of losing her and living the rest of his life alone, but he resented the desperation, and resented her for invoking it in him. He resented himself as well, and disliked himself even more than he disliked her. But what could he do about it? What could he do about anything?

The thunder in his head, always there as a distant rumble, now grew louder, became a low, muted roar. He turned the ignition key on and turned the radio up loud. The sounds of the Allman Brothers' "One Way Out" filled the cab, the rapid-fire guitar licks kicking against Harvey's eardrums, the beat hammering sonic nails into his eyes. He could feel something building inside him, music or madness, he did not know which. And when the song's chorus began the second time, he acted without thinking; he turned the volume up high, yanked the gear-shift into first, and floored the accelerator. The tires spun and whined, turning the weeds to gel and throwing up clouds of dirt. Up and over the mounds he flew, bouncing in his seat, cranking the steering wheel this way and that, wheeling around in a huge circle until he careened over the side of a mound and lost control for an instant, and barely managed to keep the vehicle from flipping onto its side.

And then, hands shaking, breath coming in shallow, shivering gasps, he punched the Off button and silenced the radio. Then guided the truck to the exit, where he waited for an opening in the traffic, then pulled out onto the highway. He wanted to pull over and hug the steering wheel but was afraid to. Afraid that if he stopped driving, he would lose the last and only thing over which he had any control.

31

Even at 50 percent off, the shoes were too expensive for Laci. She could never justify spending ninety dollars for a pair of heels she might never wear, even though they did look spectacular on her feet. Reluctantly she sat down beside Jennalee on the padded bench, pulled off the heels and replaced them in the box.

"Normally there are people here to do this for you," Jennalee said as she admired herself in the mirror, her feet in a pair of white suede sandals with four-inch heels. "Putting them on and taking them off. I can't believe how fast this place has gone downhill."

Laci slipped her feet back into her Skechers. She'd had to wait for a sale and a 30 percent off coupon in her email to buy these shoes for thirty-nine dollars. The most expensive shoes she owned were the black high-top skate shoes she wore when taking photographs for the police. They were sturdy and washable and provided good ankle support for all the crouching and squatting the job required. With a pair of gel soles, they were nearly as comfortable as the Skechers.

"Do you always buy such expensive shoes?" Laci asked.

"Expensive? Honey, Stuart Weitzman for under a hundred dollars is the opposite of expensive."

Laci watched her try on eight more pairs of shoes before settling on the sandals and a pair of Schutz sneakers with a leopard-skin pattern.

Jennalee paid with a platinum card, then turned to Laci and said, "Now let's celebrate with another cappuccino!"

"I should get busy taking some shots."

"You should have taken some of me trying on shoes. Just the feet, I mean. For a series. Like Warhol."

"I should have."

"We can still do it," Jennalee said.

"Let's just grab that coffee," Laci said, "and then I need to get to work."

On their way to the food court, Jennalee asked, "What's the job?"

"Excuse me?"

"You said earlier that you need to take some shots to fill out your portfolio. Are you applying for another job?"

"Maybe. We'll see."

"Something local?"

"One's a part-time teaching position at a community college. The other one is, I don't know, probably never going to happen."

At the Starbucks counter, Jennalee ordered for both of them. They carried their cups to a small table overlooking the parking lot.

"Mmm, this is so good." Jennalee said after a sip. "I deserve this. I was both practical and sensible today."

"Cheers," Laci said, and toasted with her plastic cup.

"So how's the family?" Jennalee asked. "Molly? And Will?"

"All good," Laci said. "Molly's skating with her friends today."

"And Will? How's the bar doing these days?"

"Slow as always. The bar, I mean. Not Will."

Jennalee chuckled, sipped her cappuccino. "I saw Will this morning when he was talking to Harvey. He looks good. Looks like he's lost a couple of pounds. Is he working out?"

"Will was talking to Harvey this morning?"

"At our place. Out in the driveway. Harvey was changing the oil or something in our vehicles."

"He must have walked over while I was still in bed."

"You're sure everything's okay?" Jennalee asked.

"With Will?"

"I only ask because Harvey seemed in a bad mood afterward. For a couple of days now, in fact."

"Well," Laci said, and wondered how much she should say. "I do know that Harvey's been upset about that motorcycle thing. About Kenny not letting him have it."

"The bike is for sale," Jennalee said. "Anybody can buy it."

"Well, Will said that Harvey told him that Jake wanted Harvey to have it. Because he'd done all the work on it."

"I don't know anything about any of that," Jennalee said. "All I know is that Kenny has the bike up for sale."

"I wish they could work things out. It's not like Will doesn't have enough to worry about already."

"You want me to talk to Kenny about it?"

"Could you?" Laci said. "It would make life a whole lot easier for us. Will is half-crazy already just worrying about the bar."

"Yeah, well, men are born half-crazy, if you ask me. The trick is to keep them from getting worse. Fortunately, it's not all that hard to do."

"It's not?" Laci said. "What's your secret?"

"It's no secret, sweetie. Give it to them whenever they want it. Keeps them happy and dopey, just the way I like them."

Laci realized then that in all their years of acquaintance, she had never before spent time alone with Jennalee, time without their husbands sitting nearby or at least in an adjacent room. In truth they had little in common, Laci from a blue-collar family, daughter of factory workers, Jennalee a country club kid. Yet Jennalee worked as a teacher, even though she didn't have to. Before her father died he had sold off his business, three car dealerships and half ownership of four Cinnabons, her father's weakness. So she was set for life. Still, she taught. She went to work five days a week. There was obviously good in her.

"So this teaching job," Jennalee said.

"Just part-time. Teaching basic photography skills. It's no big deal."

"It is for the people you teach," Jennalee said.

"I guess so."

"I hope you get it."

"Me too. Thank you."

"And the other job?" Jennalee asked.

"Hmm. Yeah. I'm not even sure it's a real job. Besides, it comes with strings attached."

"Ah, intrigue! What kind of strings?"

"Well, the guy who offered me the job is a man. So I'm sure you can imagine what the strings are."

"So predictable," Jennalee said. "On the other hand, how badly do you want the job?"

"If it's real? I think it would be amazing. I'd travel, meet lots of interesting people, probably get lots of great opportunities."

"Then why are you hesitating?"

"Because I'm married."

"Is the guy repulsive?"

"Not entirely. A little boyish for my tastes."

"Variety is the spice of life, you know."

"Are you, uh . . . speaking from experience?"

Jennalee smiled. "All I'm saying is this: you deserve to be happy. Would this new job make you happy?"

"If it's everything it's supposed to be. However . . ."

"You would feel soooo guilty."

"Wouldn't you?"

Jennalee looked out the window, watched an old woman in a hatchback trying to back into a parking space. She said, "You know how marriage got started, right?"

"Not really."

"For strictly economic reasons. So that a man's property would stay with his family when he died."

Now she turned away from the window and leaned across the table. "It wasn't about who you could or couldn't have sex with," she said.

She leaned back in her chair again, took a languorous sip of coffee. "Men used to marry their own mothers, their sisters, their brothers' wives. Just to protect their assets. The men had a dozen wives, and their wives all had lovers. This whole monogamy thing, it goes against human nature. Our bodies tell us to fuck and enjoy it; they don't tell us to hold off, suppress your desires, be good little girls and boys. That's what *society* tells us. It's not sex that's wrong, Laci, but society's attitude toward it. We can thank the screwed-up Puritans for that."

"So you're saying . . ."

"I'm saying make yourself happy. I mean, think about it. What's the best thing you've ever felt? Can you think of a single thing that feels better than having every cell in your body blasted by a level-ten orgasm?"

Laci smiled, was about to say *There's some truth to that*, then shuddered at her own thoughts. She looked down at the coffee cup, the glint of gold on her finger. Then she said, "The best feeling in the world is seeing my child happy."

"Well," Jennalee said, "I guess they ran out of that gene when they got around to me. Besides, I'm not talking about procreation here. I'm talking about physical pleasure. And if your man is falling a little bit short in that department . . ."

"Will is a good, good man. Everything he does is for us."

Laci heard her own words and felt the shift in the atmosphere, a subtle increase in the conversation's barometric pressure. She noticed too the nuanced change in Jennalee's smile and the dimming of her eyes, as if she felt insulted by Laci's comment.

"Sure," Jennalee said. "Of course. The same goes for Harvey. We're both very lucky; we have good, happy marriages. I'm just talking theoretically here."

"I know," Laci said. Then, a few moments later, "Okay, two cups of coffee and now I have to pee. And I really do have to get busy with this camera."

"Let's get together like this again sometime," Jennalee said, her voice flat now, void of its earlier excitement.

"It's been fun," Laci told her, and stood. "Thanks again for the coffee."

"Anytime," Jennalee said.

32

Will leaned against the side of the building, invisible from the school's parking lot, and tried to calm his breathing, to command his stiff muscles to release their tension. He had come so close to attacking the kid. *A boy,* he told himself. *He's still just a boy.*

Would Molly ever speak to him again?

He should have handled it differently. Should have been the same old imperturbable Will he always was. Except that *always* no longer applied. What was wrong with him?

For one thing, he told himself, *the bar. The money pit. And then Harvey dragging me into his misery. And Stevie nearly getting himself arrested. And then my sweet baby girl, my all and my everything.*

It didn't help that Laci was about to spread her wings too. He wanted her to have opportunities, wanted her to soar, but what if she soared away from him? What if, surrounded by college kids and professors, she started to see him differently? He knew he was a plodder; he knew he was boring. And had always prayed that she wouldn't realize it too.

He leaned his head against the rough brick and closed his eyes. Concentrated on his breath going in, going out. Let his shoulders droop and his arms go slack.

So okay, he thought. *You can't fix everything. You can't control the world. Just try to control yourself.*

He should apologize to the boy. Not because the boy deserved it, but because Molly did. His and Molly's relationship deserved it.

He rolled onto his left shoulder, looked toward the boy's car. Thought the boy might still be sitting inside, too worked up to climb out yet. But no, there he was half-sitting against the hood. Another girl, one of the skaters, had joined him. Stood leaning up against him, her legs between his. She had one hand on his thigh, his hand on her hip. The girl's other hand held a cigarette, which she then passed to him. Except that it wasn't a regular cigarette. Too skinny. And the way they inhaled . . .

The other kids were twenty yards away, skating in single file up a small concrete ramp used for loading and unloading from the handicap van. They skated across a short covered walkway, then down another ramp, then circled back to do it again and again, all of them singing some song he could not identify.

Will reached into his pocket, pulled out his cell phone. Touched the video icon. Aimed the camera at the older boy's car.

The camera ran for thirty seconds before one of the boys in the group shouted, "Hirsch! Hey!"

The boy at the car looked toward the other boy, who now pointed toward Will. Hirsch turned, saw Will with his phone extended, still recording. Will smiled, raised his other hand, and waved to the couple against the car.

33

When Will returned to the bar, no customers were waiting. Maybe they had come, found the door locked, and hustled off to get their burger and beer somewhere else. He hadn't expected anybody to wait. In fact he was relieved to have a few minutes alone before calling upstairs.

Laci had parked their car down the block, so he knew she was home. Molly should be too. They were probably in the kitchen, or maybe Laci's bedroom, both of them blasting him for his crude behavior, for humiliating his daughter so that she could never show her face in public again.

He sent a text to Laci: I'm downstairs if you need me to come up.

No reply. Then, several minutes later, footsteps thumping down the back stairs. He went into the kitchen area and waited for the door to open.

Laci came through the door, scowled at him for a moment, then strode up to stand just two feet away. "What the hell were you thinking?" she said.

He had the cell phone ready. Touched Play, and held the screen up so she could watch the short video.

"They're smoking weed?" she whispered.

"That's how it looks to me."

"This is the boy?"

"Same one. Name's Hirsch. Last name probably."

When the video ended, she looked up at Will. "When did you shoot this?"

"Couldn't have been five minutes after Molly left his car. The kid's not only a senior, he's a hound *and* a pothead."

She took in a deep breath, then blew it out. "Do you plan to show this to her?"

"I'm not sure what to do. What do you think?"

She took a long time to answer. "Your daughter despises you right now. I assume you're aware of that."

"Well aware."

"The question is, Will this video make her despise you more or less?"

"I wish I knew the answer to that," Will said. "What I do know is that Hirschy boy saw me recording this. So did a bunch of other kids."

"Which means Molly will know about it too."

"Sooner or later," he said.

Laci shook her head. "God, Will."

"I know," he said.

Again she paused before speaking. "I assume you read him the riot act without breaking any bones?"

"Not so much as a fingerprint."

She nodded. "So your talk, plus this video . . . should be enough to keep his hands off her from now on."

"It better be," Will said.

"You know this is just the beginning. If it's not him, it will be another boy. This is going to go on for years and years. Do you think you can survive it?"

"Are you saying a convent is out of the question?"

She raised a fist, and thumped it lightly against his chest. Then leaned against him, her fist caught between them.

She said, "I heard you were over at Harvey's place this morning."

He drew back a little. "Where did you hear that?"

"Jennalee stopped to talk to me on her way to the mall. While I was out taking photos. I ended up having coffee with her."

"And?" he said.

"And what?"

"The whole motorcycle thing. I'm sure you must have talked about it."

"She acts like it's none of her business. Said she'd talk to Kenny about it, though."

"Really? That's good."

"She also hinted that maybe there's some tension in the marriage. Not necessarily related to the motorcycle."

"What did she say?"

"Nothing specific," Laci said. "But she went into this weird little speech about monogamy. About how it's against human nature."

Will's neck straightened; his eyes opened wider.

"I know," Laci said. "I got the distinct feeling that she's cheating on him."

"Shit," Will said. "No wonder he's so ticked off all the time. When you can't trust the person you love, every other problem seems a whole lot bigger than it is."

"I could be wrong," Laci told him. "I hope I am."

"He'd fall apart without her. I know he would. The same way I would without you and Molly."

She leaned against him again, wrapped her arms around his waist. He kissed the side of her head.

When she pulled away, she said, "Why'd you walk over there this morning?"

"Just to check on him. See if he'd cooled off any."

"Has he?"

Will thought about what to tell her. "It's not really about the motorcycle, you know. It's about Jake."

"I know that."

"I think he realizes he can't be doing something stupid, putting his whole life in jeopardy. He's just frustrated is all. I wish I'd known about Jennalee before I went over there. It puts a different slant on things. You have any idea who she might be seeing?"

"If I had to guess," Laci said, "it would be one of the other teachers. The workplace is the number-one location for infidelity."

"Seriously?" he said.

"It's where people spend most of their time."

"It's sad," he said, and stroked her hair. "Nobody is honest anymore. Everybody lies. Everybody cheats."

"I know," she said, and buried her face against his chest.

Business was better for Will later in the day. A group of three thirsty guys, then two couples, all in their twenties. A pair of senior citizens, regular customers, sat at the bar and kept the Iron City tap busy.

Around six Laci brought down a salad to go with the lasagna she had baked in the bar's kitchen. She fixed a plate for him and carried it out to the bar. While he ate, she pulled an occasional draft or refilled pitchers. Molly, she told him, had chosen to stay home and in her room instead of hanging out with friends.

"I guess I'm still in the doghouse," he said.

"She won't even answer her phone. She's too embarrassed to talk to anybody."

"Should I talk to her maybe? After things slow down here?"

"Of course you should. Just don't expect any miracles."

He ate a little more lasagna, despite having no appetite all day long.

Laci watched the small crowd for a while, listened to the easy laughter, the clink of glasses and animated talk. "Thank God for these kids," she said.

Will nodded. "I'm thinking of getting one of those Jägermeister cold shot dispensers."

"How much?"

"The chiller-tappers are about three-fifty."

"Couldn't you just keep the bottles in the cooler?"

"I do. It's just for looks, you know. Make the place a little hipper."

"Oh, honey," she said, but she did not finish the sentence.

34

Not long after 9:00 p.m., Laci came briskly down the back stairs and into the bar, which now had only two customers, an older man and woman having a quiet nightcap before heading home. Will turned to see Laci standing at the end of the bar, her camera bag slung from a shoulder. He left the couple to cross to her.

"Garage fire out past where that old dragline used to sit," she told him. "They think it was a meth lab. Dispatch put out a call for HazMat and two ambulances. And somebody from Children and Youth."

"Jesus," he said.

She kissed his cheek. "Molly's still awake. Watching Netflix on her laptop. One of her friends gave her a password."

"Be safe," he told her.

Twenty minutes later he finished cleaning the couple's glasses and wiping the bar. Then stood against the bar for another five minutes, motionless, before deciding to close early. He shut off the TV and was reaching for the air conditioner switch when the door swung open and a man in a gray suit, white shirt and blue tie walked in. He was bald and cleanly shaven, late fifties, and paused just inside the door to survey the room. To Will he said, "Closing time already?"

"Doesn't have to be," Will said.

The man smiled and approached the bar. "I won't keep you long," He swung his leg over a stool and eased down. "Wild Turkey rocks. Make it a double and you won't have to pour twice," the man said.

Will poured two ounces and a little more.

"Is it always this slow on a Saturday night?" the man asked after a sip.

"Unfortunately," Will said.

"The death of small-town America. I see it all over the place."

"You do a lot of traveling?" Will asked.

"Sales rep. Mid-Atlantic region. Sort of a Willy Loman of the text-book industry."

Before Will could think of an intelligent question to ask, the man held his glass out toward the photograph on the wall. "Now there's a guy who has it nailed," he said.

"This could be his last year, though. The Steelers won't be the same without him."

Will kept looking at the photo, Roethlisberger standing tall, eyes downfield despite the three defenders pulling him down.

"Who do you think was the better quarterback?" Will asked. "Bradshaw or Big Ben? I never saw Bradshaw play except in the high-light reels."

"Well, Ben has the edge on all the stats. But he's playing under a different set of rules—rules that protect the quarterback and his receivers."

"You think he's as good as Brady?"

The man shrugged. "Sure, Brady has the arm, but he also has a front line that keeps his uniform clean. You notice how he whines to the ref every time he gets knocked down? He wouldn't last four quarters if he had to take the kind of beating Ben does. To me, that's what a champion is."

Now he raised his glass to the photo, then drank off the rest of his bourbon.

"Refill?" Will asked.

"Thank you just the same," the man said. He slid off the stool and stood with both hands against the curved edge of the bar. "I need to find a bed for the night. Just had to get off the interstate for a while, you know? I'm glad I picked your little town to do it in. I bet it used to be nice here."

Will smiled. "I guess so. Before we were old enough to know any better."

"Good luck with the place. I hope business picks up for you."

"I'm trying to hold on to that hope myself," Will said.

The man nodded and offered his own sad smile in reply. Then he turned and headed toward the door.

Halfway there, he paused. "A man once told me," he said, "that each of us is born with three things: your name, your family, and your inherent limitations. You learn your name fairly quickly in life. You never really know your family. And most of us will never have a clue of how much, or how little, we are truly capable."

He raised his hand in farewell. "May the Force be with you," he said, then pulled open the door and stepped into the darkness.

35

When Will walked upstairs after closing the bar for the night, his legs felt like water-soaked logs, nearly too heavy to lift from one step to the next. The stranger's words continued to weigh on him. Was the stranger suggesting that Will was capable of less than he imagined, or more than he imagined? Was he merely confirming what Will had been taught to suspect, that he lacked the wits and gumption to ever rise above his own mediocrity?

Harvey had always been the bold one, the risk-taker. He was no smarter than Will but fearless, the kind of man who, had their circumstances been different, had they come across a mentor as boys, just one caring, attentive guide, might have excelled as a professional athlete, a businessman with a string of car dealerships, maybe even as an actor in action movies like *Lethal Weapon* or *Fast & Furious*. He would have made a great Jack Reacher, a thousand times better than Tom Cruise, who in real life would have a hard time punching out an inflatable clown.

Even Stevie, who had grown up more or less on his own, seemed to have greater resources than Will. Like Will he flew under everybody's radar, but like Harvey he was unconcerned with living what others thought of as a normal life. He lived as he pleased, and had a knack for making a lot out of a little. Did he lust for a house like Harvey's or

Kenny's? Did he lie in bed at night and dream about making a hundred grand a year? At most times Stevie seemed perfectly content with a beer and a slice of pizza, especially when they were free.

Will could never live so nonchalantly. He was the practical one, the fair and reasonable one. If somebody bought him a beer, he would insist, absolutely insist, on buying the next round.

The truth, Will told himself, *is that Harvey and Stevie make their own decisions. You just react. A guy says, "Buy a bar," and you buy a bar. A pretty woman walks up to you at the community picnic and says, "Hey there, good-lookin'," and you marry her. Every important decision you've ever made really hasn't been a decision at all, but a reaction to somebody else's decision.*

And now, considering all this as he removed his shoes just inside the apartment and then quietly closed the door behind him, he realized that what he had previously thought of as virtues were, in fact, liabilities—facets of his personality that had always held him back. Only men as fearless and aggressive as Harvey thrived. Only men as adaptable and carefree as Stevie enjoyed more than fleeting moments of happiness.

They were, all three, men of the same blood. Will must have possessed, somewhere deep inside, the same possibilities. Why couldn't he too be bold and carefree? Maybe he was nobody's genius, but what difference did that make? The world was full of successful, happy men of average intelligence. All Will had to do was call up the potential that lay sleeping inside him.

He eased open the door to Molly's bedroom, and peeked inside. She was sleeping on her side, fully dressed but for her shoes, earphones still plugged in, the small light burning on the end table.

He moved closer and gently removed the earphones. She stirred just a little when he pulled one earphone from beneath her head. Then he closed the laptop and set it on the end table, and turned out the light.

And then, with only the light from the hallway illuminating Molly's face, he bent down and kissed her forehead and felt something catch in his chest. *My child,* he thought.

It was then the idea came to him. Startling. Horrifying. And brilliant.

Quickly he tiptoed out of the bedroom, eased the door shut, then hurried to his own bedroom. He undressed as if in a hurry, his body flushed with an inner heat. He turned on the fan, pulled a chair close to it, facing the open window, and tried to contain his excitement long enough to order his thoughts. *We do this, and then this,* he thought, *and then this will happen. It has to. It has to.*

He got up, lifted his khakis off the floor, pulled his cell phone from a pocket, and returned to the chair by the window. Laci would be home any time now. He had to get things in motion *now*.

Stevie answered on the fourth ring, just before Will's call went to voice mail. "What's up?" he said in a whisper.

"I have an idea," Will told him. "A great idea. Why are you whispering?"

"Not alone," Stevie said.

"Who's with you?"

"Never mind."

"All right then, just listen," Will said. "I have an idea for dealing with Kenny. But I need to ask a favor of you. I need you to get something for us."

"Like what?"

Will told him what he needed, and why he needed it.

"Are you crazy?" Stevie whispered. "I don't want the FBI pounding on my door!"

"Can you do it or not?" Will asked.

"Look. Will," Stevie said.

"Harvey would do it for you. You know he would."

"Over some stupid motorcycle? I could go to jail!"

"It's for your brother, Stevie. For family. You wanted to be a part of things, right? Well this is your chance."

Stevie went silent. Will leaned toward the window screen, breathed in the warm darkness, felt it embolden and strengthen him. "You're either in or you're out," he said.

"Jesus, Will."

"We're brothers," Will told him. "We're all we have left. Don't forget that."

"Okay," Stevie finally said. "Okay. I know a guy I can call."

"Do it now. We're going to get this thing done."

Will ended the call, smiling. It was all coming together. He had promised a plan, and now he had delivered. He sent Harvey a text. Have great idea. Will come by in morning.

36

Laci returned home that night after shooting photos for the police, plus a handful for the newspaper, the scent of the smoldering ruins of a two-stall garage still in her nostrils. In her mind's eye she continued to see the charred bodies of the husband and wife secured in body bags. Their little girl, a crying toddler in a filthy T-shirt, had been recovered from the mobile home and was comforted by a woman from Children & Youth Services, but Laci couldn't stop worrying about the fate of the child, her probable seventeen years of negligent and abusive foster care. What were the odds that she would grow into a healthy, stable young woman?

Molly was sleeping soundly when Laci looked in on her. Will was asleep in their bedroom, spread-eagle atop the covers, wearing only his boxers. He mumbled as he slept, his fingers twitching. Laci went to the kitchen and took a cold bottle of beer out of the refrigerator and sat on the sofa and stared at the black screen of the TV.

The mobile home where the child had been found was a pigpen. A skillet full of cold, dried-out spaghetti and sauce on the stove. The sink full of dirty dishes. A half-gallon plastic jug of milk, a quarter full and soured, on the sticky counter. The trash can overflowing with dirty diapers. The child, when the officer discovered her, sat huddled behind a safety gate in a closet, her bed of filthy blankets soiled with urine and fragments of potato chips, a dirty gray cat huddled up close to the gate like a loyal but useless sentry.

The stink of the place was still with Laci, still in her nostrils with every breath. She needed a shower. A hosing down. But was too exhausted at the moment to move. First she would finish the beer.

Jesus, how she hated this life. Not specifically her life with Will and Molly but this human life of struggle and misery. What kind of psychopathic god would create such a place?

Again she thought of two people dead, horribly burned. The fire had erupted between them and the garage doors. How long had they screamed and clawed at the walls before they fell to the ground? How long had they raced back and forth in their shrinking space before their skin began to tighten from the heat, the fine hairs on their arms curling, eyeballs stinging, lungs filling with toxic smoke? And in their wake, how many dozens of addicted individuals had they left behind? Plus the little girl. Wholly innocent. Yet the one who would suffer most in the years ahead.

And that was when she started crying, sobbing, her body shaking. She huddled into a ball and pulled her shirt over her mouth so that no one would hear.

37

A few minutes before seven the next morning, Sunday, while most people were sleeping in or making their groggy ablutions prior to having their souls scalded clean by a fire-and-brimstone sermon, Harvey, standing barefoot in his dew-wet yard, wearing old cargo shorts and a sleeveless black T-shirt, stared down the empty street. He could not remember why he had stepped out into his yard. Behind him, the house was quiet, Jennalee still sound asleep.

A few hours earlier he had awakened with a rock-hard erection and a need to touch his wife, so he had rolled against her, run his hand down her naked back and over a hip, then let his hand slide across her buttock and between her legs. "Mmm," she had said, but nothing more. His hand moved gently until she grew wet, and then he slid up tight against her and slipped inside, thinking *This is all we have left* as his body rocked harder and harder against her. His orgasm came fast and hard and there was something jagged about it as it pulsed out of him, yet he held her tightly afterward, fighting back the need for additional expiation, a need to weep or cry out in pain, until she moved her hand to pat the top of his hip. Then he rolled away and gazed deep into the darkness as it hovered above them.

He remembered all that but he could not remember why he had come outside, and now stood gazing into the distance, truck key in hand.

His testicles ached. He slipped his free hand down his shorts, squeezed his balls, pulled them away from his body but could not release the ache.

He turned and walked to the front of the garage, punched in the four-letter code on the door opener, *JLEE*, and watched the door slide up. Then he went to his truck and climbed in behind the wheel. The cab was cooler than the morning, but its air not as fresh, the light dim and uninspiring.

Where to? he asked himself. Then he remembered the text last night from Will. He put the key in the ignition, turned it to the right but did not start the engine. Told his OnStar system, "Text Will. Sheetz for coffee. Meet there."

He sat waiting, finger and thumb still holding the ignition key. He was ready to turn the key to the left, lean back and close his eyes, when the reply appeared on the screen, and a female machine voice said, "New text message from Will. On my way."

Harvey started the truck, pulled out onto the driveway, forgot to hit the remote to close the garage door, and drove away. Everything he looked at along the street appeared somehow peculiar to him, familiar but changed in a way he could not discern, as if the colors were slightly off, as before a damaging thunderstorm, when a pale wash of yellow paints everything with a kind of dread tinged with excitement. But the sky was not overcast, no heavy dark clouds, only blue firmament and golden light. Yet something was different. Maybe it was the muscle twitching in his bare foot on the accelerator. Maybe the way his balls ached. Or the seat belt signal beeping its warning.

"Doesn't matter," he said.

38

Will pulled up alongside Harvey's truck and saw him sitting alone at one of the red patio tables, bare feet on the dirty concrete. Will climbed out and approached him and said, "Where are your shoes?"

"You mind getting the coffee?" Harvey said. "I forgot my wallet."

Will looked at his brother for a moment, then turned and went inside. When he returned to the table four minutes later, Harvey was sitting in exactly the same position as before, hunched forward with his elbows on his thighs, hands clasped between his knees. Will nudged him on the shoulder and handed him the cardboard cup of coffee. Then sat next to him.

"You look a little out of it," Will said.

"Didn't get much sleep last night. Or did but . . . I don't know. Not the good kind."

Will nodded. Took a sip of coffee. "I don't know why they have to make it so damn hot."

"It's always hot this time of year. Dog days. That's what Mom used to call them."

Will considered telling Harvey he had been referring to the coffee, not the weather, but decided to let it go. Obviously Harvey had other things on his mind. "Dog days," Will repeated. "Why do you think they're called that?"

"I always thought it was when dogs go crazy with the heat. Like in that song 'Mad Dogs and Englishmen.'"

"That was an album, wasn't it?" Will asked. "Not a single. A Joe Cocker album."

"I thought it was a single," Harvey said.

They sipped their coffee, said nothing for half a minute.

"Rabies," Will finally said. "The time of year when dogs get rabies."

"Okay," Harvey said. He drank his coffee in quick little sips, three or four in a row, then a pause. He said, his voice flat, Will thought, almost robotic, "What's the idea?"

Will glanced around to see if anybody was close enough to hear their conversation. A guy in a white SUV and a young woman in a red compact were at the pumps. The other tables were empty. Only then did Will become aware of music oozing from speakers somewhere. He thought it sounded like a Fleetwood Mac song.

Traffic was light out on the street. The whole scene felt odd to Will, like a scene from a movie, the camera focused on him and Harvey. He wondered if the convenience store's security cameras could pick up their conversation.

He leaned across the table and asked, in a voice barely loud enough for his brother to hear, "You still set on doing this thing?"

"Depends on which thing you're talking about," Harvey said.

Will brought his coffee up from between his legs and set it on the table, but held the cup in both hands, and leaned over it as he spoke. "You said you wanted him out of town. Out of your life."

"That hasn't changed," Harvey said.

"So what's the worst thing a guy in his position could do?" Will asked. "Something to make the whole town want rid of him?"

Harvey looked off into the distance for a moment, his body very still, as if he might be watching a bird soaring off, watching something beautiful fly away from him. Then his body sagged a little and he said, "I'm too tired for guessing games."

"Kiddie porn," Will said. "But instead of me just starting a rumor about it, we plant the porn on his office computer."

Harvey was still for a moment, then he turned just his head toward Will. "How are we supposed to do that?"

"We're going to have to break in. I have Stevie working on getting some DVDs. We get into the school, load the stuff onto Kenny's computer."

"What if the computer is locked?" Harvey asked. "Needs a password we don't know."

"I guess in that case we just leave the DVDs in his desk."

"So he sits down at his desk Monday morning, sees the DVDs, and tosses them in the incinerator. Good plan, Will. Foolproof." He turned away and looked at the tabletop, the braided mesh of thick strands of metal, the smooth coat of plasticized red paint.

"Don't worry," Will said. "Stevie's good with computers. He'll get the shit loaded. Because that's school property, see? It makes everything that much worse for Kenny."

Harvey sat motionless but for his head going back and forth. Then he said, "Let's stick with the plan to start a rumor. Get people talking."

"So what if people talk?" Will asked. "What does that accomplish?"

"Your plan's no better."

"I'm not done yet," Will said. "We mess the place up, trash it like a bunch of kids would do, and on our way out we set off the alarm. The police are first on the scene. They find the DVDs before Kenny even gets there."

Harvey listened while running a finger along the tabletop pattern, in and out of the triangular holes. "I don't see it," he finally said. "What's to guarantee the police even find them? Why would they turn on the computer in the first place?"

"So we ransack the place. Pull out all the drawers. Leave the DVDs in plain sight in one of the drawers."

Harvey shook his head. "And our Keystone Cops are going to be bright enough to know what they're looking at?"

"I told Stevie to get some magazines too if he can. Something eye-catching."

Harvey leaned back in his seat. Looked out at the street. Watched a couple vehicles go by.

"Well?" his brother asked.

"It's a stupid idea."

"Then let me hear a better one."

A full minute passed before Harvey spoke. "What the fuck," he said.

"And that means?"

"It means fine. It either works or it doesn't. When are we doing it?"

"I say tonight. Figure we could meet at eleven. That old house of Earl Bigley's has been sitting empty since last winter. Plus there are no streetlights there. We meet behind his house, then walk across the practice field to the rear of the school."

"You want me to bring anything?"

"Stevie said there's no security cameras on that side of the building, but I figure we better wear ski masks and gloves anyway. Wear dark clothes."

"And how are we supposed to get inside without setting off the alarms?"

"Stevie said he has that covered."

"Stevie does."

"He's done some work there more than a few times, Harv. The tar and gravel roof this past spring. Helped refinish the basketball court a couple summers ago. Says he's the go-to guy whenever the maintenance supervisor needs an extra hand."

"Jack of all trades," Harvey said.

Will waited a few moments, then said, "Just meet us at eleven. Behind Bigley's place. I'll walk over; Stevie will bring the stuff we need. You want him to swing by and pick you up?"

"I'll meet you there," Harvey said.

Now Will leaned back in his seat. Drank off the rest of his coffee while he watched a young mother fill her tank. As she did so, she leaned close to the rear window and made baby talk through the glass. *Wouldn't it be funny,* he thought, *if there's no baby inside? Just some crazy girl talking like there is.*

And there was something about the harmless banality of his situation—of sitting there outside a convenience store with an empty coffee cup and smiling as he imagined a movie scene—that reminded him suddenly that his life was not a movie, and that plotting to destroy a man's life did not come without possible consequences. They could all get arrested. Their own reputations destroyed. Families ripped asunder.

A wave of dizziness swept through him then, and his field of vision shrank and darkened, and he thought he might pass out. To keep himself from falling he pressed a hand to the mesh tabletop and stuck three fingers through the holes.

When, half a minute later, his vision cleared and the dizziness passed, his first thought was of how quiet the morning was, and how still. No music from the store's speakers, no soundtrack. No actors rehearsing their lines. No chance for a second take.

39

Eleven hours later Harvey ladled a plateful of pot roast out of the pressure cooker but didn't really want any of it. He'd had no appetite all day long, couldn't remember the last time he'd paid enough attention to a meal to actually enjoy it.

Before lifting the lid off the pressure cooker he looked again at the note Jennalee had left on his plate.

Taking Mom to the mall. See you around 9. Love you.

And again he told himself that she had been at the mall yesterday. Spent half the day there. Came home with two pairs of shoes. Two pairs for half a fucking day.

Now he sat in his chair in the living room, faced the TV, the plate balanced on his knees. He stared at his reflection for a while in the blackened screen.

The room was too warm and he considered climbing out of his chair to turn the air conditioner's thermostat lower. But Jennalee liked to keep it set at seventy-two. She liked to sleep without a blanket, with only the slowly throbbing ceiling fan to stir the air. That was why, when they were married, he had the central air-conditioning installed, because she promised to sleep naked and uncovered every night, as natural as an animal in its burrow, as long as the house wasn't too warm or too cold. But the nakedness, he soon discovered, was an exaggeration. From the very beginning she wore lingerie to bed.

Another deceit, he told himself. He felt them accumulating all around him, stacking up in the corners. One of these days they were going to crush him to death.

Around ten-thirty that night, Jennalee's entrance into the kitchen woke him out of a dream of hunting, a dream in which he had gotten separated from his father and brothers in the oak woods. He was awakened by a click that, in his dream, was the snapping of a twig, followed by the sound of something crashing toward him from behind. He awoke with a start, looked around, momentarily disoriented. Then he saw the kitchen light on, heard Jennalee tearing off a strip of cellophane to stretch over the leftover pot roast, sliding the bowl into the refrigerator. He closed his eyes again before she came into the living room, didn't want to talk just yet, wanted the smell of the woods awhile longer.

Jennalee stood there looking down at him. Then, before she made her way upstairs, she spread an afghan across him, a knitted blanket of a dozen bright colors, one of many her grandmother had made. It was an act of tenderness that almost brought his eyes open, almost caused him to look up at her and smile, except that he recognized other scents now too, the odors of food from another house, wine on her breath, and a vague, fleeting fragrance he could identify only as neither his nor her own.

Upstairs she showered and brushed her teeth, changed into satiny panties and a matching teddy, turned on the ceiling fan, climbed into bed, turned on the TV. He followed her through the sounds she made, envisioned her careful movements, always so feminine and precise. He felt something like hunger in his belly but maybe it was the nausea again, that strange hollow hunger that earlier in the evening had made him afraid to eat anything.

At ten forty-five he mounted the stairs as quietly as he could, wincing with each creaking step. He peeked around the doorjamb, saw her asleep, curled on her side, her back to the flickering images on the screen. The ceiling fan made a barely audible thumping sound as it spun. By the time he turned away from her, his arms were pimpled with goose bumps.

Downstairs he recovered the black khakis and black T-shirt he had stowed in the hall closet, changed into them and left his other clothes on the closet shelf. Then he wrote a note on the pad Jennalee used for her grocery lists:

Went over to Will's for a beer or two.

He knew that even if she woke up and wandered downstairs, she would not call to check on him. She never questioned his whereabouts.

Outside, Harvey walked at a pace he recognized as too slow to get him to the Bigley house on time, but the heaviness in his legs and the emptiness in his stomach and the steam-room heat of the night all worked to weaken him further, conspiring with the stifling darkness to weigh him down. Most of the houses he passed were already dark, though here and there a window dully glowed with the pale light from a flickering screen. He remembered that when he was a boy on a night like this the streets would be full of people. Kids chasing fireflies or playing kick the can. Adults scraping back and forth on their porch swings and gliders. Old folks rocking. These days everybody stayed inside breathing air blown out of a box while they stared at another box until narcotized enough to sleep.

Eventually he came to the right street and walked as silently as he could to the empty Bigley house two blocks away. He had known old man Bigley and his emaciated wife, who had died five years before her husband, but, for as long as Harvey could remember, both had seemed ancient, withered and frail. Harvey as a boy had mowed their lawn now and then, five dollars an hour. Will and Stevie had done the same, each brother taking over for the one before him.

Harvey stepped into the yard and felt the weeds brushing against his trousers. Apparently Stevie, he figured, was the last person to mow the yard. The house had been boarded shut ever since Bigley's suicide three or four years ago. Harvey could not remember exactly when the old man had died; the years had flown by too quickly, the days flying off in the wind like pages from a book with a broken binding. All he remembered was that a pistol had been used. A Mauser C96 Bigley had brought home from Korea. Harvey had held that pistol when the contents of the house were auctioned off. Wanted to buy it but was afraid it might be haunted. Wished now he had bought it anyway.

He walked along the side of the house, his hand trailing lightly over the rough, weathered clapboards. He half expected to find that Will and Stevie had chickened out, that nobody was waiting for him. They weren't really going to do this thing anyway. It was a chickenshit plan to begin with. Nothing ever works out the way you want it to.

But then he turned the corner and saw two silhouettes sitting on the back porch steps, odd shapes of gray against the darker gray of the building. Harvey could see well enough to distinguish the silhouettes as two men, and he pushed his sudden heave of disappointment away.

And that was when he thought, *Maybe we are going to do it. Breaking and entering and who knows what else.* He would have liked to back out and return to his life but he despised his life and everyone who had made it what it was, not least of all himself.

And what is it? he asked himself, and paused for just a moment before walking up to his brothers. *What is your life?*

A joke, he answered. *Just one big fucking joke.*

40

"You're ten minutes late," Stevie said, his voice too loud to Harvey's ears, startling in the darkness. Both Stevie and Will were clad in black from head to toe, only their faces from eyebrows to chin visible beneath black ski caps.

Harvey thought of his wife at home in bed, curled on her side. Who was she dreaming about right now?

Inside his head a distant thunder rumbled, and he hoped that this night's action and whatever followed would quiet the noise, would release the band of metal ever tightening around his skull. He asked, "So what's the plan?"

Will flicked on a small flashlight and shone the light toward the ground, illuminating a duffel bag and a telescoping aluminum ladder. Stevie zipped open the bag and held the sides apart so that Harvey, leaning forward, could see two cans of neon-orange spray paint, a long-handled screwdriver, a loop of new nylon rope still in its plastic bag, and several magazines. Stevie pulled one of the magazines and a DVD out of the bag and held them in the flashlight's beam, just long enough for Harvey to see the glossy photos of half-naked boys on the covers.

Then Will flicked the flashlight beam off the covers. "Did you bring gloves and a ski mask?" he said.

"I don't have a ski mask," Harvey said.

Stevie reached into the bag, pulled out a pair of dark-brown cotton work gloves and a black ski mask, and handed them to Harvey. "Now you do," he said.

Harvey stuffed the gloves into a hip pocket, and pulled the ski mask over his head, but left his face exposed.

Stevie snickered. "I had to drive almost fifty miles to get those magazines and DVDs. Clear to the adult bookstore at the truck stop on Exit 41. Jesus, I was so nervous I thought I was going to piss my pants before I could get back outside."

Harvey looked at Will's face but could make nothing of his brother's expression in the darkness. Harvey asked, "Who's watching the bar for you?"

"It's Sunday night," Will said. "Remember?" He closed the bar at nine on Sunday evenings. Laci, years ago, had insisted. *Family time*, she had said. *At least one night a week, Will. Please.*

Their plan as new bar owners had been to eventually hire a couple of bartenders as soon as business took off. Maybe even a short-order cook. They would buy a house and rent out the apartment upstairs to one or more of their employees. They would have plenty of time for vacations and family outings, while every night the cash register would sing like a fat soprano. That's what the previous owner had said on the day they closed the deal. *A couple of tweaks and you'll have that cash register singing like a fat soprano.*

But not a single song had ever issued from that cash register. It never even hummed.

"I close early on Sunday nights," Will said.

Harvey nodded. For some reason this did not feel like a Sunday night. He remembered Sunday morning, remembered meeting Will at the convenience store, but that seemed too distant to be the same day as this one. His mouth tasted chalky. He worked up some spit, swallowed, but his throat did not clear. It felt tight, as if a hand, his own or somebody else's, was gripped around his neck.

"The plan," Will whispered, "is so simple it's brilliant. We use the ladder to get onto the roof, then get inside through one of the skylights over the cafeteria. Using the rope, of course. Then to the administrative offices, where Stevie will plant the magazines in Kenny's desk and load the porn onto his computer. We're thinking maybe—"

"Wait a minute," Stevie said. "I just thought of something. Any uploads will be time-stamped."

Harvey asked, "What does that mean?"

Will said, "Shit!"

"What?" Harvey asked.

"So we just leave them in a drawer," Stevie suggested. "Maybe one in the disk drive."

"Okay," Will said. "Okay. Then we trash the office, spray graffiti all over the walls. Then we get out of there the same way we got in. Once we're all home again, Stevie uses a burner to place an anonymous call to the police to report suspicious noises and lights at the school. The police get there, find the porn, and within twenty-four hours everyone in town is going to want to run Kenny out of town on a rail. Hell, he'll probably be tarred and feathered before it's all over and done with."

"This could work," Stevie offered. "It really could."

Harvey's head was spinning. "I know for a fact that Stevie can't climb twenty feet *up* a rope."

"Speak for yourself, fat ass," Stevie said with a grin.

"Okay, me too. I doubt like hell I can do it."

"Then we'll find some other way out," Will said. "We'll open a window. They open from the inside, you know. Every classroom's got them."

"What about janitors?" Harvey asked.

Stevie said, "Last summer when I helped do the roof, everybody went home by six at night, didn't show up again until six the next morning. The place is empty for twelve hours."

"You sure we can get in through a skylight?"

"We replaced all the flashing for the roof job, had to take the skylights off to do it. All it takes is a Phillips screwdriver."

"What about security cameras?"

"Only place that isn't covered is the rear wall of the boy's locker room. 'Cause there aren't any windows there."

"Where'd you buy the paint?" he asked, and felt a sour swell of panic in his stomach. "Stores have security cameras, you know. And the rope. And everything. Shit, Stevie, we're as good as caught already."

"The rope's old," Stevie told him. "I've had it for years, just never used it. I got the gloves at Dollar General along with six packs of flower seeds. I got the ski masks at Burton's at the mall. Five-finger discount. They were having a going-out-of-business sale. The place was so busy, no one will even remember I was there."

"Somebody's going to remember two cans of orange spray paint," Harvey said.

"Harvey, come on," Will said. "He bought them at the Walmart in Gallatin. Used the self-checkout scanner."

Stevie said, "You can't for once in your life give me any credit at all, can you?"

Harvey stood there shaking his head, looking at the ground. How could he describe the feeling washing through him, the dark heaviness of foreboding, the bubble of panic inflating his chest?

"What?" Will said.

"If any one thing goes wrong," Harvey said.

"Nothing's going to go wrong."

"Famous last words."

"What's with you?" Will asked. "Now you don't want to do this?"

"I'm just saying," Harvey answered. "There are way too many variables."

"You know, this is how it's always been with us, hasn't it? You get some wild hair up your ass and come running to me about it. I lie awake all night trying to figure out how to help you out with it, and next day you're like, 'Oh, I guess it's not so bad after all.'"

"Did I say that?"

"I don't know; did you? Truth is, I don't think you even know what you're saying half the time."

"I can still beat the shit out of you."

"Still? You never could. Not since I was sixteen anyway."

Harvey tried without success to suppress the small smile that, despite his discomfort, came to his lips. He remembered well the time Will first took a swing at him, how after all those years of torment from his big brother, all those knuckle thumps and punches on the arm, how Will, instead of running away as he always had, threw a short, unexpected punch that bloodied Harvey's lip, then stood there waiting for the rest of the fight, stood his ground like a man, ready to take another beating if necessary. Harvey should have told him then that he was proud of his little brother, glad to see that the boy's balls had finally dropped. But he hadn't. He had sneered, as if the blow stung no worse than a mosquito bite. And then he had walked away wordless, still seeing stars.

"Come on," Will said. "Haven't you wanted to trash the place ever since you went there? I know I have."

Stevie said, "Yeah but don't do anything to Mrs. Miller's room."

Both brothers looked at him.

"She was nice to me," Stevie said. "I liked her."

In the distance a car horn sounded. It was answered by a barking dog.

Harvey said, "Part of me hates this town and everything in it. I sometimes wonder if we all wouldn't be better off getting the hell out of here."

"Tell you what," Will said. "Let's concentrate on getting Kenny out first. Then we'll see how it looks to you."

"The thing is," Stevie said, "if Kenny goes, he might take the motorcycle with him."

Harvey said, "Screw the motorcycle."

"Good," Will told him. "Because this isn't about the motorcycle anymore."

"It never was."

"Yeah?" Will said. "In that case, it might be good for us to get some specifics about what this really is about."

Harvey replied without inflection. "You don't need any specifics."

Fifteen seconds of silence passed. Then Stevie bent down, grabbed a rail of the ladder and lifted it up. "So are we going to do this?" he asked. "Or do I need to drag this thing back to my truck?"

Will studied his older brother for a moment. That moment stretched into thirty more seconds. Harvey remained motionless, staring off into the darkness. Then he lifted his head, raised his eyes to the dark sky.

"I can't remember a time in my adult life," he said quietly, "when I didn't feel alone. Maybe the first few years with Jennalee, I don't know. But even then . . ."

Will waited for him to continue. When he did not, Will said, "Everybody feels alone sometimes."

"It's different for you," Harvey said. "I've seen you with Laci and Molly. You're a family. You're tight. With me, there's Jennalee and Kenny and Louise. Then there's Harvey. I'm just a sidenote to them. Always an outsider."

Another long silence surrounded them.

Then Stevie said, "You guys don't know the first thing about being alone."

"Everybody," Will said, "and I mean everybody, feels alone at one time or another. I mean sure, Laci and Molly and me, we all love each other. A lot. And we couldn't make it—financially, I mean—without Laci's help. But I'm the *man* in the equation. I'm the one who's expected to come through. But I can't. There's a lot of aloneness in that too."

"Okay," Harvey said. "But let me ask you something. Have you ever felt as if you really *belong* in this place? The way you did when we were kids? Dad was rough on us, yeah, but we were his kids. We were his family. And we knew it."

Will nodded. "Thing is, we're not anybody's kids anymore. We're the adults."

Stevie shook his head back and forth. "You guys have no idea."

Harvey said, "What are you talking about?"

"You both *have* a family."

"Are you saying you don't?" Will asked. "What the hell are we?"

"It's hard to tell sometimes."

Harvey said, "We're your family, asshole."

"Since when?" Stevie asked. "'Cause as long as I can remember, you've both treated me like a leper or something. Like I've got a contagious disease you don't want to catch."

"You do," Harvey told him. "It's called stupidity."

"There you go. That's exactly what I mean."

"What's exactly what you mean?" Harvey asked. "*What?*"

"You treat me like I don't matter. You always have."

Will put his hand on Stevie's shoulder. "I'm sorry you feel that way," he told him. "But we never *saw* you that way. You're our little brother. We just . . . and I know Harvey will agree with me on this. We always held ourselves responsible for your accident. So we did our best to keep you out of, you know . . ."

"Stuff like this?" Stevie said, and gave the ladder a little shake.

"Yeah," Will said. "Stuff like this."

"First of all," Stevie told him. "I came here tonight to bail *your* asses out when one of *you* screws up. I'm good at this kind of stuff. Secondly, it wasn't you two who told me to jump. It was Kenny. And I still owe him. So if you two pussies want to chicken out on tonight, adios. I'm still going in, even if I have to do it alone."

Will smiled. Then turned to Harvey and asked, "Satisfied?"

Harvey stared into the darkness, felt the warm, thick air engulf him. Then he leaned over, feeling like he was going to throw up, but instead picked up the duffel bag, and said, "I'm not sure I know the meaning of the word."

41

Will was the first man down the rope, sliding into the stale-scented coolness, the cafeteria a cavern. At the bottom he quickly adjusted the ski mask to improve his vision through the eyeholes, then stood motionless, catching his breath. He could see reasonably well in the large room, one long wall lined with tall windows overlooking the practice field where, for three years as a boy, he had run wind sprints every August until he thought his lungs would explode. Dim red exit lights glowed over every cafeteria doorway, and even softer white lights shone from the kitchen.

Though no lunches had been served in this room since the first week of June, the familiar smell was unmistakable, Meatloaf Thursday, and for a moment he heard the clamor of a hundred hungry kids all jabbering at once, the scrape of chairs, clack of plastic trays, clink of forks attacking plates.

"Hey!" Harvey whispered from above.

Will aimed his flashlight at the heavens, flashed an "all clear."

Harvey came down an inch at a time, grunting. He lost his grip while still eight feet above the tile floor, dropped with another grunt and the smack of his tennis shoes. The duffel bag's strap slipped over his shoulder and the bag thudded to the floor.

"For chrissakes," Will whispered.

Harvey blew on his hands through the ski mask. "I forgot to put my gloves on. I got a rope burn."

Stevie surprised both of them by coming down quickly, sliding in full control with one leg wrapped around the rope. Harvey asked him, "When did you get so agile?"

"You should see me on the climbing wall at the Y."

"The YMCA? In Gallatin? What the hell are you doing at a YMCA?"

"Tae Bo classes every Tuesday night. Lots of tits and asses in spandex."

"Any chance we can get on with this?" Will said. He grabbed the duffel bag and headed for the exit into the hallway.

Out the double doorway, a right turn down a short hall, then into the spacious lobby, where, every school-day morning, a half dozen buses spill out their charges, hundreds of adolescents loud and eager, groggy and grumbling, carrying with them their scents of bed or shower or breakfast or barn. Then a hard right past the lighted trophy case, up the four steps, administrative offices on the left, faculty lounge, boys' and girls' restrooms on the right.

The hallways were dark but navigable, one or more small equipment lights glowing in every room, illumination bleeding through the glass or under the solid wooden doors. Will's eyes quickly adjusted to the dimness, and his memory flooded with details.

The door to Kenny's office was locked. The glass panel in the door was opaque, rippled and thick. Will said, "We're going to have to pry the hinges off."

But Harvey pointed to their brother at work four feet away, leaning close to the door that opened into the front office. Stevie had stuck a small suction cup to the clear glass and was now dragging a glass cutter around it in a slow circle.

"He's just one surprise after another," Will whispered.

Stevie grinned beneath his mask but said nothing. Finally he pocketed the glass cutter, tapped his knuckle around the circle he had cut, wiggled the suction cup until the circle of glass snapped free. Then he inched a gloved hand into the opening, felt for the door lock on the other side and gave it a twist. He swung the door open wide and said to Harvey, "*Now* will you ask around for me over at Jimmy Dean?"

And Harvey said, "I guess maybe I will."

Just inside the front office Harvey set the duffel bag on the floor. The moment he zipped it open, Stevie reached inside for the spray paint. He handed one can to Will, gave the other to Harvey.

"I'll take the porn," Stevie said. "You guys decorate the walls."

Will said, "Tell him what else you're going to do in there."

Stevie turned to Harvey and said, "That was Big-Ass Bobbert's desk before it was Kenny's, and I've been drinking water and saving up for this all day."

Harvey remembered Conrad Bobbert too, the pear-shaped guidance counselor who told each of the brothers in turn to forget about college, don't even consider it. He had recommended the army for Harvey, a two-year business school for Will. And he had recommended that Stevie—then in his junior year and a talented cartoonist, a boy who had covered his bedroom walls with pen-and-ink caricatures of movie stars and famous singers but was too shy to show his work to anyone outside the family—that Stevie drop out of school and fill the school's new vacancy for a janitor. None of the boys took Bobbert's advice.

"Have fun," Harvey told him. The bubble of fear was still there in his chest, and his body still felt unresponsive and heavy, as if he were being chased in a dream, but there was something else also making itself known in him now, a warming current of satisfaction, electric and invigorating.

He and Will watched as Stevie crossed behind the front desk and made his way to the door in the rear of the room. There Stevie paused, put a hand on the doorknob, gave it a slow turn. The latch clicked. He swung the door open, turned back to his brothers, gave them a thumbs-up, and swaggered into Kenny's office.

"Piece of cake," Will said.

With their cans of paint he and Harvey scrawled neon-orange epithets in three-foot letters on the corridor walls, their backs to one another. Will wrote DEATH TO TEACHERS! and SCHOOL SUCKS! Harvey wrote FULTON SUCKS DICK! Both men chuckled to themselves as they wielded the cans in looping flourishes. Will painted in an evenhanded script, Harvey in thick, angry letters.

Harvey had finished his first composition and was contemplating his second, trying to envision FULTON IS A PERVERT! emblazoned across the tile floor, when he heard Stevie's hoarse whisper. "Hey Harv! Harvey! You might want to come have a look at this!"

Harvey half turned to see Stevie leaning out the door to Kenny's office.

Will asked, "What wrong?"

And Stevie said, "You're not gonna believe this."

Will was closest to Kenny's office and soon disappeared inside. By the time Harvey crossed the threshold, Will was already coming toward him, hands outstretched to stop Harvey's progress as he shouted back at Stevie, "Get that shit off there!"

But Stevie, seated behind Kenny's desk, unsure of what to do, looked from the glowing computer monitor to Harvey, and Harvey knew in an instant he could not let Will keep him out, and he shoved his brother aside, pushed past him, and all but lunged forward to stand beside Stevie.

"I was just going through the drawers," Stevie told him, his words spilling out in a nervous torrent, "when I came across one that was locked, that one on the bottom there. I figured if it was locked there must be something good in there, so I jimmied it open. At first all I saw was that bag of caramels there on the desk, but after I pulled the bag out I noticed this flash drive stuck clear in the back of the drawer, and I was just curious, you know? I swear I had no idea what was on it till I booted it up."

Harvey stood beside the chair and leaned close to Kenny's desk. The can of spray paint dropped from his hand, and with both hands Harvey gripped the metal edge of the desk. He'd needed only one glance at the screen, and all the air had rushed out of his lungs. The bubble in his chest exploded, filling his stomach and chest and throat and brain with nausea. He kept staring at the screen, eyes moving from one thumbnail photo to the next. He was aware of Stevie's voice but discerned no words, heard it only as a buzz growing louder and louder, and the tug of Will's hand on his arm just a meaningless pressure, Will's voice like that of a distant barking dog.

Tiled across the twenty-seven-inch monitor were the photos Stevie had found on the flash drive, pictures he opened one by one, working in stunned amazement until horror set in, three rows of six photos each, all featuring Jennalee, Harvey's wife, Kenny's sister, photographed from every angle, gorgeous but appalling. Sometimes Kenny was in the photo with her. Sometimes other men were. Sometimes two or three men with her at the same time.

It was Will's hand gripping Harvey's shoulder that started the fulmination, the slow explosion in Harvey's brain. He jerked away as if shocked, shoved the desk with such force that it was jarred several inches across the thick carpet. The monitor wobbled on its pedestal but didn't fall, so Harvey seized it in both hands and ripped it into the air, only to have the cable jerk it out of his hands again. It came down with a loud crack atop the desk, the screen and plastic housing shattering. The screen crackled and went black.

Then Harvey seized the desk itself and drove it hard across the floor, pushed it crashing into a wall. Will grabbed him by the arm but again Harvey jerked away, lunged for the door, arms swinging blindly at everything in his way.

Will turned to Stevie now, who had pushed his chair backward, up against the large dark window. "You get that flash drive!" Will told him. "Get everything. Everything we brought with us. And then you get the hell out of here!"

Stevie nodded in response but Will didn't see it, already in pursuit of his brother.

A shattering of glass—a trash can hurled into the trophy case. Trophies heaved one by one against the cement-block wall.

This time Will did not merely take hold of his brother's arm or lay a hand upon his shoulder. This time Will ran at Harvey and tackled him around the waist, drove him away from the broken glass and ringing metal, and slammed them both against a wall, Harvey's knee in Will's stomach as they crashed to the floor.

"Listen to me!" Will shouted, gasping for air, his face two inches from his brother's. "We have to get out of here. You understand? First we get out. *Then* we kill the sonofabitch!"

Now Harvey faced him, eyes flooded with furious tears. "Those were new ones," he said.

"What?" Will asked, confused, unsure of what he had heard.

Harvey shoved him aside, pushed himself up and started jogging down the hallway, a strange lumbering gait that looked apelike to Will, elbows hooked, fists closed, Harvey's heels thudding hard against the floor as he ran toward a door marked EMERGENCY EXIT ONLY.

Will rolled over onto his hands and knees. "No! Come this way!"

But Harvey continued on, and when he was close to the exit he kicked the lever bar across the middle of it and the door popped open and the alarm shrieked.

Will scrambled to his feet. Still short of breath, he chased after his brother, followed him out the open door and caught up to Harvey standing outside in the grass, turning in an awkward circle, pivoting around his left foot while breathing loudly through his mouth, head thrown back, eyes on the heavens.

Will seized Harvey's arm just above the elbow and yanked him out of his pivot, tried to drag him stumbling toward the Bigley house. "Let me go," Harvey pleaded. "Let me go."

But Will could not let go, could not surrender his brother to whatever emotion was rendering him impotent. "Run, damn it!" he shouted while the alarm shrieked and echoed down the empty hallways. "Goddamn it, Harvey . . . Run!"

42

Stevie, with no monitor to guide him, had no choice but to yank the flash drive out of its port. For a few moments he wondered what to do with the computer; should he grab the tower too? But then he wouldn't be able to carry the duffel bag and ladder.

Things were breaking down the hall, glass shattering, Will's voice calling out to Harvey. Stevie pocketed the pink flash drive and took a last look around Kenny's office—*what else? What else?*

He patted his pockets. Glass cutter and suction cup secure. The duffel bag. He zipped it shut, grabbed it and went to the door.

Silence down the hall. Stevie listened, waited. Will's voice again . . . and then the alarm screaming. Stevie turned toward the windows, glanced out, saw only darkness, no strobing lights. Then told himself, *You have three, four minutes at most.*

He turned and sprinted out the door, down the short hallway, leaped down into the lobby before encountering the glass and broken trophies scattered everywhere. His feet slid through the glass but he did not fall. He looked down at the floor, all those smiling faces peering up at him.

He knew many of the faces in those photos, kids he had seen around town, and in the older photos kids he had gone to school with, kids who had bullied him, made fun of him, ignored him. And there was a picture of Harvey's football team the year they had won the conference championship, a youthful, thin-faced Harvey grinning in the front row, a football in his hands.

For some reason Stevie wanted that photo, needed to take it. He leaned down, picked it out of the broken frame, shook off the dusting of glass, rolled the photo, opened the duffel bag, slipped the photo inside.

Then quickly to the cafeteria. He slipped one arm through the duffel bag's handles, then grabbed hold of the rope and pulled himself up. In a series of ten vertical lunges he scaled the rope, dragged himself up onto the roof. Stood in the warm tar-scented darkness and looked toward the front of the building. No headlights yet, the street still dark.

He untied the rope and quickly retrieved and coiled it, threw the loop around his neck and scurried down the ladder. As his feet hit the ground he yanked the ladder toward him, let it fall with a loud clank onto the grass. Grabbed the top section by the bottom rung, lifted it free of the hooks, doubled it over the bottom section. Then grabbed the rails in his left hand, took the duffel bag in his right, and ran. He knew then that he would make it. They would all get away free and clear.

He smiled. Grinned. Felt smart and competent and agile.

Then he remembered the photos on the flash drive. The look on Harvey's face. And felt all the lightness and grace go out of him. Whoosh and it was gone. Because this was the end of something. He did not know what. Only knew that now, with the school's alarm fading behind him, the ladder clanking against his leg as he ran, sweat tickling down his spine and the rope scraping his neck and the patrol car with its strobing lights only a minute or two away, something crucial to his happiness had ended. He knew that after this night, after all those damn photos in his pocket, nothing would ever be the same, and that the cascade of damage to his family and his world had only just begun.

43

It took Will and Harvey a minute and a half to cut across the practice field to the yard behind Bigley's house. Stevie's pickup was parked farther down the unlighted street, in front of other houses not much better maintained than Bigley's. They slowed to a walk on their way to the truck, Will taking the lead, Harvey behind, neither man speaking, both still trying to catch and silence their breath.

At the rear of the truck, Will turned, sat down lightly on the rusted bumper. Harvey bent forward over the tailgate.

Not long afterward, Will said, "Listen," and they held their breaths. In the distance a soft clanking noise, as rhythmic as footsteps.

"Go ahead and get in the truck," Will said. "I'll be right back." And he disappeared into the darkness at the side of the nearest house.

Will met Stevie coming across the practice field, the extension ladder clanking with each step. Will snatched the duffel bag from Stevie's other hand and turned back toward the street, matching Stevie's gait.

"Did you get the rope?" Will whispered.

"It's around my freaking neck," Stevie said.

"You get the flash drive?"

"I got everything."

"Harvey didn't have his gloves on when he came down the rope. I can't remember if he ever put them on."

"It's too late now to worry about it."

"What about the paint cans?" Will said.

"You didn't grab them?"

"You said you got everything!"

"Everything there was to get," Stevie said. "I figured you guys were bright enough to take your own paint cans."

With every clank of the ladder, Will winced. Behind them the alarm still whined inside the school. Will calculated that the police had probably pulled up in front of the school by now. But only one deputy would be on duty this late on a Sunday night, either Ronnie Walters, all two hundred pounds of him and as lugubrious as a black bear in January, or his polar opposite, skinny Chris Landers, the one folks called Barney Fife because he was always patting his pockets, checking for his keys, a nervous talker always adjusting or fiddling with his belt. In either case the deputy at this hour would have been watching TV at the fire station, maybe playing euchre with a couple of volunteers who preferred to spend their nights away from home. Too far from the school to actually hear the alarm, they wouldn't be alerted to the break-in until called by the county dispatcher.

He's probably climbing out of his car right now, Will thought. He and Stevie approached the pickup as quietly as they could, then gingerly slid the extension ladder over the tailgate and into the bed.

"We'll be fine," Will said aloud, and Stevie chose not to answer. He went to the driver's side of the truck, climbed in and eased shut the door. Harvey, seated close beside him, leaning forward with hands clasped between his knees, neither spoke nor looked Stevie's way, and remained just as motionless when Will opened the passenger door and squeezed in beside him.

Four long minutes later Stevie slowed to make the turn toward Will's bar. "Just pull over and let us out," Will said. "You better keep going. Get your stuff back home."

Stevie pulled close to the curb, kept his foot on the brake. Will slid out first and held the door wide for Harvey, who walked straight to the bar's door.

Will leaned into the truck. "You sure you got everything?"

"Everything but the paint cans," Stevie said.

Will nodded. "I'll call you tomorrow." Then he closed the door as softly as he could, and turned away.

He was surprised to find Harvey hunkered down against the bar's front door, sitting exactly as he had in the truck but with his butt braced against the wood. He was doubled over his clasped hands, and was making a groaning sound with each exhalation, a soft "Hunh" that Will thought might be from crying or hyperventilating.

Will stood beside him, his own back to the wall, and laid a hand on Harvey's shoulder. He could feel the rigidity of Harvey's clavicle, the way his shoulder quivered. Will had never before felt so helpless, so foolish. The air was thick and warm and stank of dirty pavement.

A few minutes later Harvey unclasped his hands, placed both hands against the wall at his back and pushed himself upright. Yet he remained slumped over, his head moving slowly back and forth.

Will said, "We better get inside."

Will took the key from his pocket and unlocked the door, then followed his brother inside. For some reason the scent of the place, the stale air and lingering food scents, made his throat tighten, made his stomach turn. Even the soft security light in the kitchen seemed too bright.

He closed the door and locked it, then slid his hand over the light switch, but paused. "Lights or no lights?" he asked.

"No," Harvey said. He walked straight to the bar then and sat heavily on a stool. Will could not remember another time when Harvey had sat at his bar; he always stood at the open end; never sat.

Will went behind the bar, reached into the cooler and brought out two bottles of beer. He wiped them with a clean bar rag and twisted off the caps and set one in front of Harvey. Will tilted up his bottle and drank, surprised at how thirsty he was and how good the beer felt on his throat. Harvey held his bottle in both hands but did not drink from it.

Will told him, "I don't know what to say, brother. I'm sorry we ever went over to that damn school. I'm sorry I talked you into it."

Harvey was silent for a while. Then he said, "I should have taken that flash drive."

"I'm pretty sure Stevie grabbed it."

"You think he did?"

"I'm pretty sure."

"I hope so."

Will leaned back against the cash register, the hard metal edge against his spine. He sipped his beer. He thought he could hear a police siren across town but wasn't certain; it might be nothing more than the residue of the school's alarm still ringing in his brain. He thought of other things he might say to his brother but discarded them all. What good would they do? Clumsy phrases. Useless. There was no magic in words.

It was Harvey who broke the silence. "The two of us were over at the Marriott one night," he said. He picked at the label on his beer bottle as he talked, tore off tiny pieces and left them on the bar. He spoke haltingly, in no hurry to hear this or to be heard.

"You and Kenny?" Will asked.

"Me and Jennalee. This was just after we'd gotten engaged. Maybe a month or so after. Anyway we were dancing, drinking, just having some fun. And this guy I barely knew, some band geek friend of Kenny's from high school. He comes over and starts making an ass of himself. He's so shit-faced he can barely stand up. But he keeps trying to drag Jennalee out on the dance floor. She sees I'm getting kind of hot about it so she excuses herself and goes off to the lady's room. But the guy still won't leave. Suddenly I'm his best buddy in the whole damn world, and he's telling me what a lucky man I am. How she's got the hottest body he's ever laid eyes on. All that kind of crap. I'm just about ready to deck the guy when he up and asks me if Kenny's still got those nude photos of her he had in college."

"Jeezus," Will said.

"I didn't even slug the guy. I just went cold."

"So . . . what happened then?"

"Soon as Jennalee came back, I dragged her outside. We sat in the car and . . ." He tore the last of his label free. Scratched a fingernail over the rough smear of glue.

"At first she denied it," he said. "Claimed she didn't know what the hell I was talking about. So I threatened to haul that geek in the bar outside there with us and beat the truth out of him. Funny but she didn't seem to mind that idea. So then I said, 'On second thought I think there's somebody else who needs it even more.' So I started the engine and peeled out of the parking lot. I must've laid rubber for fifty yards down the road, I was so pissed."

"The somebody else being Kenny."

Another fifteen seconds passed before Harvey continued. "She made it sound like it was all so innocent, you know? Like something brothers and sisters do all the time. Just fooling around, she called it. She'd let him take pictures and maybe touch her once in a while. But she swore up and down it never went any further than that. Swore it all stopped when she went off to college herself."

Harvey looked at his bottle as if he had only then discovered it in his hands. He pulled it closer, as if to raise it for a drink, but did not, and only stared at the mouth of the bottle as he spoke.

"So I drove her home and saw Kenny's car was there too, so I said either you go in and get those photos or I will. And if it was me, I was more than likely going to turn her into an only child."

"Good for you," Will said.

"She used the cigarette lighter from the car and burned them right there along the curb. Used her bare hand to sweep the ashes down into the sewer drain."

And you probably thought that was touching, didn't you? Will thought. *Jennalee's beautiful, perfect hand sweeping away the ashes. You poor helpless sonofabitch.*

Overhead, footsteps hurried across the floor. Will knew that Laci had been awakened from her sleep, either by the police scanner or a telephone call. Now she was throwing on a pair of jeans and a shirt, making sure she had fresh batteries for her camera, sitting on the bed to tie her shoelaces.

Then the quick patter of her footsteps coming down the stairs. "I gotta turn the light on," Will whispered, speaking quickly, and reached to the wall behind him, flipped on the bar light. "Tell her you were just walking by and saw the light."

The door at the rear of the kitchen opened, then closed softly behind her, and Laci was there on the threshold. Will turned to her and smiled. "Fire or car wreck?" he asked.

"What a crazy weekend!" she said. "It's not even a full moon. I swear this job is going to kill me."

"What is it this time?"

"Break-in over at the high school. What's up with you two?"

"I couldn't sleep," Will told her. "Came down to have another look at the books. Harvey was out walking, I guess. Getting some midnight exercise. Saw the light and decided to say hello."

Laci gave Will a long look before turning her gaze on Harvey. "You couldn't sleep either?" she asked.

He shrugged. Looked down at his bottle.

"I guess it runs in the family," Laci said to Will. Her gaze was so steady, her mouth so unsmiling, that he had to look away.

"Want a Coke to go?" he asked, and before she could reply he reached down into the cooler, then brought up a dripping can of soda.

As he was drying it off on the bar towel, she said, "You have any iced tea in there?"

He lowered the can into the cooler again, looked at the other contents. "I know there's some in the kitchen."

"I'll get it," she said.

She had only stepped into the kitchen when Harvey said, "Where's that thing?"

"Shh!" Will whispered with a quick nod toward the kitchen. "What thing?"

"That pink thing. I want it."

"Shh!" Will repeated. "I already told you Stevie has it. Don't worry."

"I want it," Harvey said again.

She came back into the bar with a bottle of iced tea in hand. She said, "You lose something, Harvey?"

He said nothing. Stared down at the bar.

Will turned to her and smiled. "You really think there's anything going on at the school worth your time? Probably a couple of kids just tripped the alarm. They're long gone by now." His smile widened. "They bitch about having to be there, and then what do they do but break back in over summer vacation."

Laci smiled in return, studied his face, then slipped the bottle of tea into her bag.

"Molly still asleep?" Will asked.

"She was a minute ago." She looked at Harvey again. Then back at Will. "I shouldn't be long," she said.

"Take lots of pictures."

She gave him another look. "That's what I do." Then she turned away and headed for the door.

Will watched her go, her posture so straight, that confident stride. Now and then he would look at her, and this was one of those times, and see nothing but perfection. Her short, neat hair, that trim, compact body in jeans and a pale yellow blouse . . . even the skate shoes she called her "work boots." Perfect from the highest hair on her head to the dusty soles of her shoes. His chest ached with love for her. The one thing in his life he had done right.

"Hey," he said.

She turned at the door. He smiled, wanted to tell her then and there how he felt, wanted to somehow erase his mistakes with a confession of love. But knew the futility of it. Knew the inadequacy of anything he would ever say or do.

He pointed to the front of her blouse, sleeveless yellow cotton with a rounded collar. She looked down, saw that it was buttoned incorrectly, one side of the shirt higher than the other.

"Geez," she muttered as she yanked open the door, and unbuttoned on the run.

44

Will stood unmoving after Laci's exit, stood marveling at this turn in his emotions, from a juvenile rush of adrenaline an hour earlier to this forlorn consideration of all that he surveyed. The night was quiet inside and out, Harvey as still as a toppled statue, the ineffectual air conditioner silent. No sounds of movement upstairs, Molly asleep, dreaming sweet dreams of bright possibilities. He wondered if she would speak to him in the morning. His little girl was now gone from him too, had been for a while, he supposed. When was the last time he'd made her giggle with delight? The last time she climbed into his lap just to snuggle against him?

When she was small, every moment with her was filled with joy. Just a walk to the store was magical. She would be jabbering on about this or that, about school or her friends or something she had seen on TV, she would skip, swing her arms, sometimes walk with her small hand holding to the flap of his pocket.

Then she got older. Replaced him. And he grew small. Heavy. And weak.

Christ, it hurt. Every memory. Every loss.

He gazed down at Harvey then, only forty-three years old. He looked ancient sitting there. He looked beaten and defeated.

"What can I get for you?" Will asked.

Harvey offered no reply.

Will said nothing for a while. Then, "So? Now what?"

"Now?" Harvey said, and looked up finally, his damp eyes fierce. But he spoke in a whisper. "Now I kill him. And this time *nobody* is going to stop me."

"Hell, brother," Will answered. "I'm not going to stop you. I'm going to load the revolver and drive the getaway car."

Harvey smiled, though with not a trace of happiness in his expression. He held out a hand to Will. Will took it, gripped it hard. "But first we wait," he said.

Harvey jerked his hand away. "Wait for what?"

We wait for you to cool down, Will thought. He said, "We wait until the shit hits the fan. News gets out about the porn in Kenny's drawer, a lot of people around here are going to want his hide."

"Yeah? So?"

"So in the meantime, you don't say a word about any of this to Jennalee. Or to anybody. You think you can do that?"

"Can you? Can Stevie?"

"We have to," Will said. "We have to just stand back and see how tonight plays out. We might wait a year before we do anything. Because by then, at the least Kenny will have lost his job and be living somewhere else. Us, we're just going to go on with our lives same as always. Until that one night, a long time from now, when we pay Kenny a long-overdue visit."

Harvey turned the bottle slowly in his hands. The glass was warm now, sticky against his skin.

Will wished his brother would say something more, offer his hand again, some affirmation. Instead, Harvey set his bottle in the center of the bar, then released it, his hands slipping off the glass, knuckles against the wood. Then he slid his stool away from the bar, and stood.

Will asked, "Where you going?"

"I'm not feeling so hot. I think I'll call it a night."

"Have a ginger ale. It'll settle your stomach."

"I guess not," Harvey said.

"At least stay until Laci gets back. We can quiz her on how things went."

But Harvey was already headed for the door. "Tomorrow" was all he said.

45

Harvey walking. Unaware of his surroundings. Body stiff. Heavy. Sucking air through his mouth, hearing the animal grunts with every exhalation.

He could not remember the last time he had been awake past midnight. No, not true; it was last New Year's Eve at Will's party at the bar. But how long had it been since he'd walked these streets alone after midnight, not wanting to go home because he would feel even lonelier there?

He had done so hundreds of times as a young man. Sometimes even after a race, picking up another trophy, then banging some girl in a motel room or in the back of his Eldorado. Walking and wondering and feeling the emptiness engulf him. That had been his life back then, from childhood all the way up to his first night with Jennalee. Then he was happy for a while. Except that the gray cloud of emptiness never drifted away, but even with Jennalee seemed to hang out there on the horizon, waiting to slide over him again. And now it was here. Everywhere. Inescapable.

A dog barked somewhere. *A dog on a chain,* he thought. Poor bastard; what a life that must be, even for a dog. Chained up and howling at distant sounds, wanting to chase after them, snap his tether, revert to the dog he should have been—a hunter, meat eater, not some neutered pseudodog grateful for an occasional pat on the head and a bowl of dry kibble.

This heat, he thought, *is something strange. It's like a steam bath out here.*

Every breath was a heavy one, a soggy lump of air. Yet at his core he felt chilled. Every now and then a shiver racked through him, a quick icy rattle up his spine. His body ached with the hot heavy drag of the heat but he couldn't stop the chills from rattling through him.

He approached the high school from the long front drive, walked toward the white illumination of the lights in the windows, several rooms in a row and the lobby lit up like a jack-o'-lantern, a big brick Halloween pumpkin on a steamy August night. He counted five vehicles lined up around the circular drive. A patrol car, the sheriff's cruiser, Laci's Subaru, Kenny's Sebring, and a red Jeep Wrangler. *Probably the janitor's,* he told himself.

He cut across the circle of grass in front of the school, dragged a hand over the flagpole. The metal was cold, flaked with rust. No flag flapping in the breeze, not the slightest breath of wind. He paused there beside the naked flagpole and watched the front entrance. Could almost hear the sounds the kids make piling out of the buses every morning, the yips and laughs and moans like the ones he used to make.

If I had any kids, he wondered, *would they be happy here? Would they be popular and smart?*

I was never smart, he told himself. *I got decent grades but I was never very smart.*

From twenty yards away he could see through the window of Kenny's office, could see Laci with her back to him in there, bent toward something with her camera in hand. Kenny was there beside her, standing in profile, waving one hand in the air, gesticulating. Laci nodded and said something and took another photo. Half a minute later Deputy Walters came into the room, stood close to Kenny and told him something, finger pointing toward the hall.

Harvey watched it all as if it were a television show with the sound turned off. They were just characters in a show, nothing more. Superintendent Fulton, good-looking and well-dressed even at midnight, khakis and a red polo shirt, every hair in place. Laci the Photographer, the girl next door, cute as that girl in the movie with Tom Cruise. Renee somebody. And Deputy Walters, not the sharpest tool in the shed but wholly likable, self-deprecating, constantly trying to lose a few pounds but never able to resist just one more Big Mac, one more order of fries.

The show left Harvey cold and he soon tired of watching it. No drama, no comedy. He was not involved in any of it but felt as distant from the events in the school as a chained dog must feel when it howls at the moon. He turned his back to the building and started back down the long drive, past the darkened homes of people he knew, the lives he had no involvement in, the secrets they hid.

He had been standing a few yards from the intersection with Main Street for maybe fifteen minutes, maybe more, just standing there thinking about the possibilities to his right and to his left, when a pair of headlights lit up the road ahead of him. The car came up from behind, slowed, and stopped. Laci leaned toward the open passenger window and asked, "You lost?"

Harvey turned to look at her. He smiled. "Renee," he said.

"Excuse me?"

"Anybody ever tell you you look like that actress in that movie with Tom Cruise?" "*Jerry Maguire*," she said.

"What?"

"That's the title of the movie. With Renée Zellweger."

"You look just like her."

"Thank you," she said. "I wish I were that pretty."

"You are. Every bit," he said. "I only watched that movie because of her. Never liked Tom Cruise. He can't act for shit. And always struck me as kind of sleazy, you know?"

"That's a fairly old movie, Harvey."

"December 1999. I was twenty-three years old. Saw it at the drive-in."

She studied him for a moment. "You doing okay?"

He wondered if she could see his coldness inside. If she could feel it radiating off his flesh, a chill of refrigerated meat. "Just thought I'd walk over before heading home, see what all the fuss is about."

"Some kids broke in and trashed the place. Spray-painted the walls, tore up Kenny's office pretty good."

Harvey made a sound that was supposed to be a laugh. "Maybe Kenny did it himself. You know how he loves to redecorate."

Laci slipped the gearshift into park, then slid the whole way across the seat. "You still pissed at him?" she asked. "I mean earlier, you were mad enough to kill him, you said."

He nodded. "You know how I get. Lucky for me, Will talked me out of it. Even so . . . I can't say I'm sorry for any trouble that comes Kenny's way."

"I can understand that," she said. "He's not the world's most likable guy."

"Oh yeah?"

"He's one of those touchy-feely guys, you know? Always has to have his hand on you during a conversation. Ten minutes with him and I feel like I've been licked all over with a long, slimy tongue."

Harvey smiled, pleased with her analogy. "They leave any clues behind?" he asked. "The kids, I mean."

"A couple cans of spray paint," she said. "I think Ronnie Walters was kind of hoping they'd autographed their graffiti, but no such luck."

He nodded again.

"Apparently we're not the only ones Kenny rubs the wrong way," she told him. "From the looks of it, those kids also planted some porno stuff in Kenny's desk. Kiddie porn."

"Seriously?" Harvey said. "You sure it wasn't Kenny's?"

"It looked brand-new. Magazines and DVDs. Sheriff's going to dust them for prints. But if you ask me, it was all just too obvious. They even left the drawer hanging open so we'd be able to see inside."

Another nod. He was surprised by how detached he felt from it all. What the sheriff did or didn't find was of no consequence to him. It was all just another television show. He could watch it or turn it off. What did any of it matter?

What did matter to him was Laci. His brother's wife. Mother of his niece. Standing there looking down at her pretty face, he felt so much affection for her. Will's wife. His sister-in-law. He wished he could climb in beside her and sit with her and tell her everything he felt and believed. Wished he'd had the good sense to marry a woman like Laci, and could fall asleep every night with a woman like her in his arms. Knew it would change everything. Knew he would be a different man.

"Will really loves you," he said.

She looked surprised by his comment. "He really does," he said. "He'd be lost without you and Molly. Not worth a damn."

She let a few moments pass. "Are you sure you're okay, Harvey? You want me to give you a ride home? Does Jennalee know you're out here wandering around?"

A crooked smile came to his lips then, a twist of gathering pain.

"Thanks anyway," he said, and pulled away from the window. "I had a couple beers with Will and now I feel half sick to my stomach. It's better if I walk it off."

"It's a good night for walking, I guess. Better than for sleeping anyway."

"You need an air conditioner in that apartment."

She smiled. "Maybe next summer."

He reached for his wallet. "Why don't you let me buy you one?"

"Harvey, no. I mean thank you, but . . . you know Will would never take any money from you."

"You deserve an air conditioner," he said.

"It's sweet of you to say that. But I would really like to give you a ride home now."

"Walking," he told her, and stepped back farther and turned away, started moving down the street again. "Walking and walking."

She put the car into gear and coasted up beside him. "How about I call Jennalee? Let her come pick you up?"

"No no no," he said in a singsong voice. "No thank you, ma'am. Just me, myself and I tonight."

He kept walking but could feel the car waiting at the corner, could feel Laci watching him, wondering if he was okay. Just knowing that she cared about him made his eyes sting, made him want to turn around and tell her *Thank you*.

But he didn't, he kept walking. And finally her car pulled forward, turned to the left, and she headed toward home.

And now he turned to watch the car pulling away. Something about her departure made him feel like crying, though he did not understand why. Something about the way the red taillights looked as they shrank smaller and smaller. Something about the vast darkness ahead.

46

Will sat alone in the darkened bar with the door locked and the television off. He was ashamed of his stupidity and ashamed that he had involved Stevie and Harvey in it. Ashamed of wanting something that could never be his. He would settle now for having things the way they used to be, back when his mother still mothered and his father was still alive. Back in the innocent times. The first day of buck season, for example, between Thanksgiving and Christmas, one of the holiest of days.

Because hunting had never been about violence, not as far as Will was concerned. It had been about the tenderness of the woods and of walking tenderly through them with his brothers and father, the way the sun rose on naked trees limned with ice or hoary with frost, of black branches looking diamond crusted, the sunlight as soft as candlelight, the woods as hushed as a murmured prayer. And it had been about that almost sacred moment of coming upon a magnificent animal in the heart of those woods bathed in shafted sunlight and shadow, the breathless stillness of seeing one another in that sudden sanctified moment, hunter and hunted, the two connected by the invisible thread of the bullet about to fly.

Nor had Will ever felt violence in the ritual of gutting and skinning, nor later around the camp stove with their bellies full, mouths pleasantly numbed by the whiskey they sipped. All this had never seemed violent to him but an ancestral ceremony that strengthened and cleansed him for the other part of his life, the tedium and labor.

But all that seemed a long time gone. The woods were smaller now and there were more hunters in them. Even deep in the woods you could hear eighteen-wheelers rumbling along the highway. The stillness and the tenderness were no more. The world was not a tender place, had had all tenderness stripped away, loaded into trucks and hauled off, incinerated in huge furnaces, reduced to ash and smoke and acid rain.

47

Harvey had to pound on the door of Stevie's trailer for three solid minutes before Stevie finally appeared behind a curtained window, peeking out. Then the door creaked open and Stevie whispered, "Jesus. I thought you were the police."

Harvey pushed past him and into the kitchen. The place looked fairly clean for a change, not the way it usually did, as if a couple of suitcases and a refrigerator had exploded. Stevie looked small and frightened standing there in nothing but an old pair of gym shorts, looked as if he expected Harvey to attack him, to blame him for the awful discovery he had made. But Harvey went straight to the laptop on the kitchen table, saying before he got there, "I want that flash drive."

"It's in here," Stevie told him, and opened the hallway closet, bent down, reached inside one of his work boots. He pulled out the flash drive and took it to Harvey, who was seated at the kitchen table now, facing Stevie's laptop, its screen raised by Harvey and coming awake.

When the log-in page displayed, Harvey laid the flash drive on the keyboard, leaned to the side and said, "Log in and pull up those pictures."

"Ahh, I don't know if I need to be looking at those—"

"Don't pretend you haven't seen them more than once already. Just pull them up for me."

Leaning in beside Harvey, Stevie logged in his username and password, then plugged the flash drive into the port, opened the drive and brought up the folders. Icons for fourteen folders numbered consecutively. "Which one do you want opened?" he asked.

"Which one did you open at the school?"

"The last one."

"That one," Harvey said.

Stevie double-clicked, and the sixteen photos appeared in quick succession, lined up like erotic playing cards across the screen.

Then he turned away and went into the living room and stood there at the window, looking out into the darkness. Harvey knew that his modesty was a farce, that Stevie had certainly looked at each and every one of the photos already, all fourteen folders, had probably copied them onto his hard drive. Maybe even masturbated while looking at them. Harvey knew all this but he didn't care. He was beyond caring now, except for one last thing.

Harvey gazed intently at each of the photos. Then returned to one in particular. Leaned closer to the screen. Squinted, trying to see it better. He said, "Is there any way to make this picture bigger?"

Stevie wanted to turn away from the curtained window but didn't. "You mean the whole thing?"

"The whole thing, parts of it, I don't care. I just need it bigger."

"There's a little icon in the tool bar, up along the top of the screen. Looks like a magnifying glass. Click on it, then click on the photo you want to enlarge."

Harvey clicked on the photo. He still couldn't see what he wanted to see.

"Every time you click," Stevie told him, "it will get bigger."

Harvey clicked four more times. Then he could see it. Jennalee's hand. The wedding band on her fourth finger. Not just a golden glow on her finger anymore, not a trick of the light. Indisputable.

Calmly, too calmly, Harvey said, "So is this the most recent bunch?"

"Yeah," Stevie said.

"Any way to tell how old it is?"

"Right-click on the photo, then select Properties."

"You do it," Harvey said. He stood and made room for Stevie. Stood there watching over his shoulder. Staring at the filth in front of him.

"The sixteenth of last month," Stevie told him.

"That's when it was taken?"

"It's when it was loaded onto the drive."

"What about the other folders?" Harvey said. "You have any idea how old they are?"

Stevie sat leaning forward, shoulders hunched. Finally he said, "The oldest one's about four years old."

"Four years," Harvey repeated. For a few moments he couldn't get his thoughts straight, couldn't reason out the implication. He had to say it out loud. "Just this one bunch covers the past four years. So there's probably more. Other flash drives. Clear back to the beginning."

"Digital didn't happen till the midnineties or so," Stevie said.

Harvey wasn't listening. He pressed the palms of his hands against his eyes. Took a long deep breath through his nose. Blew it out through his mouth. Then he lowered his hands, blinked, widened his eyes and blinked again. He stood staring wide-eyed into the living room and down the short hall and out the back of the trailer and down the dark empty streets and into the nothingness of space. Kept staring and staring until he felt weightless and free falling and had to put a hand out to the back of the chair to steady himself.

A moment later he held his other hand out in front of Stevie. "I'm going to need that flash drive," he said.

48

Harvey stood on the threshold to his bedroom. The room was at once familiar and foreign to him, as if he had been away a very long time. The room looked smaller than he remembered it, and parts of it were ugly now. He had never liked that green brocaded wallpaper. The comforter on the bed, the big useless headboard, the dresser with its baroque brass handles. He had chosen none of them. Gave her everything she'd ever asked for.

Jennalee had fallen asleep with the reading light on, a magazine facedown on the bedspread, the television on with the volume turned low. A part of him wondered what magazine it was, what she might have chosen to divert her thoughts at a time like this. On the back cover was an advertisement for Absolut vodka. He thought about coming forward off the threshold and turning the magazine over, but he did not move.

Jennalee slept on her side, her knees drawn up. She was wearing only panties and a matching teddy, eggshell white. The ceiling fan turned. He could feel the slightest of breezes across his face. He could smell the refrigerated air blowing softly from the air conditioner vents. Why did she need both the fan and the air conditioner? And why had he never noticed that before?

She awoke with a start, though he had made not a sound. Her head jerked up off the pillow; legs straightened. For a moment she lay there blinking at the wall. Then she turned her head slightly, saw him there in the doorway. She said nothing. She tried out a smile.

Harvey said, "There was a break-in at the school tonight."

She tried to make her voice sound sleepy. "I know, Kenny called me. A bunch of kids apparently."

"Apparently," Harvey said. "Apparently they wrote stuff about him on the walls. Called him a pervert."

She ran a hand over her forehead. "Who told you that?"

"Laci told Will."

"Is that where you've been all this time?" she asked. "Over at Will's?"

He held the flash drive in his fist. Rubbed it with his middle finger. "You ever hear that about him?" he asked. "About him being a pervert?"

She crinkled her eyebrows, gave him a confused look. Then she reached for the comforter, drew it up over her breasts.

"If you're cold," he said, "you shouldn't run the fan and the air conditioner at the same time."

She rubbed a hand over the goose bumps on her arm. "It was so hot earlier."

"One or the other," he told her. "You don't need both. And then you sleep with a light on. And with the television running. Just burning electricity every which way you can."

"Baby," she said. "I think maybe you had a little too much to drink. Why don't you come warm me up a little bit?"

He kept looking at her and had no feelings he could identify. The love had disappeared quickly, rushed out of him like blood from a gaping wound.

"Come on," she said. "Come get me warm."

He walked to the side of the bed then. With his free hand he picked up the television remote off the bed, hit the power button and turned the TV off. Tossed the remote onto the bed. Then he went to the reading light and switched it off. Then, on his way out the door, he shut off the ceiling fan.

She called to him. "You want me to come down and watch TV with you awhile?"

He went down the stairs with eyes closed, empty hand riding the bannister rail, other hand gripping the flash drive. *Off,* he told himself. *Turn everything off.*

49

Harvey walked in shadow along the side of Kenny's house. He peered into one dark window after another, knew them all, had spent plenty of time in the house when he was younger, when he and Kenny were the best of friends. And after Kenny went off to college, Harvey still came by frequently, but to spend time with Jake, usually in either the garage or kitchen. He wondered if Kenny missed Jake too, if Louise ever thought of him, if she and Jennalee ever sat around reminiscing about him. Probably not. Jake had seemed like an outsider to the family too, an add-on sometimes included, most often not.

Still, Harvey acknowledged a kind of affection for Kenny's mother. As a boy he had had a crush on her for a while, thought her very sexy in her tennis shorts and tight tops, those smooth legs and melon breasts. He remembered all the late nights when he and Kenny had come stumbling in, trying without success to conceal their drunkenness, and she would appear in the kitchen out of nowhere in robe and slippers, chide them playfully for their behavior even as she was pouring out a glass of wine for herself, and soon she would have a skillet full of eggs and sausages ready, a mountain of toast. She used to flirt with Harvey back then, especially after a glass of wine or two. Once, when Kenny fell asleep at the table, she came up behind Harvey as he sat over his eggs and sausage and massaged his shoulders. Told him what a strong, handsome boy he was. Then she opened up her robe and laid her breasts against the back of his head. He had sat motionless, unsure of what to do. Then he carefully slid his chair away from the table, said he should probably get home now, and stood. She followed him to the door and, just as he turned the knob, put her hand on the front of his pants and squeezed his penis. If Kenny had not stirred at the table, knocking a piece of silverware to the floor, there was no telling what might have happened.

On the other hand he also remembered the scowl on Louise's face when he and Jennalee had turned away from the minister at the front of the church, turned to face friends and family for the first time as husband and wife. Louise's frown was fleeting, yes, and quickly supplanted with a phony smile. But Harvey had noticed it. He'd never resented her for it, though. Always understood her disappointment. Understood that she wanted and deserved someone better for her daughter, her perfect flower of a child.

And now, remembering all this, not with anger or resentment but a kind of melancholy acceptance, Harvey crossed to the rear of the house, and there he saw a soft light glowing at ground level, just as he'd hoped there would be. He sank low and peered through the small window and into the basement game room. Kenny was sitting on the edge of the brown leather sofa, a drink in hand, the television on.

Harvey settled onto his knees off to the side of the window, bent closer to the glass. With his free hand Kenny was bouncing a small yellow ball, a tennis ball, bouncing it up and down on the parquet tile floor. He looked too anxious to sit still. Too haunted, Harvey imagined, by all the recent possibilities suggested by the break-in. Did he know that the flash drive was missing? Probably so. Did he know that it was tucked safely in Harvey's pocket? *Not yet,* Harvey thought. *Not yet.*

Kenny took a sip from his glass, then bounced the ball five times in a row, a few seconds between each bounce. Then another sip. Meanwhile he stared at the television. Some old movie in black-and-white. Harvey watched it for a couple of minutes, then recognized the actors, Charlton Heston with a moustache, a massive Orson Welles in a fedora.

Eventually Harvey drew away from the window and pushed himself up, felt the stiffness in his knees as he stood. He crossed to the back porch and let himself into the mud room using the key he had taken from Jennalee's purse. Always when he came into the mud room he paused to remove his shoes, because that was Louise's rule. She had a maid who came at least once a week and kept the house spotlessly clean. Kenny used to joke that they had to take their shoes off because it wasn't the maid's cleaning day and his mother didn't know how to use a broom.

Harvey took his shoes off this time too. Left them beside Louise's and Kenny's on the rubber mat beside the door. Two strides later he was in the kitchen. Three recessed lights above the counter glowed softly. He crossed the floor one sliding step at a time, looking at all the familiar things. The refrigerator and gas range. The microwave and toaster oven. The coffeemaker was new, something fancy with a couple of gleaming spouts. He spotted the knife block atop the counter, was stopped by the sight of it. He knew which knife Jake had used to slice the Christmas ham. Which knives he and Kenny had used when they tried to make bows and arrows out of twigs from the apple tree.

Then Kenny's voice called up through the open basement door. "I thought you were asleep already! You want me to get you something?"

Kenny was silent for a few moments, probably waiting for a reply. Then Harvey heard the soft click of ice in the glass. *Probably scotch,* he told himself. Their favorite drink when they were young, that pleasant burn when the scotch went down, that slow scorching burn all the way into the stomach.

Kenny called out again. "You looking for a Valium or what, Mom?"

A moment later Harvey descended the last carpeted step and stood on the game room floor. Between him and Kenny was a load-bearing, four-sided white pillar. He looked for the marks he and Kenny and

Jennalee had made as kids, back when they had measured themselves, Kenny and Harvey always in a friendly competition of who was growing the fastest. But the marks were gone now, painted over. No evidence remained of the children they used to be.

When Harvey took a step past the pillar, Kenny jerked upright, and sucked in a sudden breath. Some of his drink splashed onto his trousers.

Harvey said, "Looks like maybe you're the one could use the Valium."

"Harvey, for Christ's sake," Kenny said. "I thought you were . . ."

Harvey approached him slowly. "You thought I was what—your friend? Is that what you thought?"

Kenny's smile was pale and thin. To Harvey the smile looked tight. The way Jake's smile had looked at his funeral service. Harvey's smile, on the other hand, felt comfortable and real to him. Felt calm. As if he were watching a humorous movie. A movie about a guilty man sitting on a leather couch, pretending to smile and be unconcerned even as he cast about with his eyes, looking for something with which to defend himself from an intruder. The intruder had the only exit blocked and looked to be a strong man, a man who had used his muscles all his life, not like Kenny who, though he had managed to keep his weight down by walking on a treadmill three times a week, was soft inside and out, had always been soft, always needed somebody else to take the first risk, always needed to feed off somebody else's boldness and daring, a weak man on his own, but a man who liked to control others in every way he could.

Harvey had the only exit blocked and the billiard table to Kenny's right was too far away, the rack of cues on the farthest wall. To Kenny's left, a little over a yard away, was the fireplace with its andirons and tools, the poker and the shovel and the fireplace brush, none ever used, never dirtied by ashes because the logs in the fireplace were made of ceramic, they glowed but never burned. And the mantel was lined with Kenny's and Jennalee's trophies, hers for tennis, his for debate and state band.

Kenny let the tennis ball drop. It bounced three times, then rolled across the floor. He held up his empty hand, palm out, a gesture of surrender as he slowly rose to his feet. "If this were the middle of the day, Harvey, I wouldn't mind you coming into my house without knocking. But seeing as how it's, what, nearly twenty minutes before two in the morning . . ."

"Stand still," Harvey told him.

Kenny forced his smile wider. "I'm not going anywhere."

"I saw that same smile on Jennalee not long ago," Harvey said. And reached into his pocket.

And Kenny flinched, a full-body flinch in reaction to Harvey's movement. *He thinks I have a weapon,* Harvey thought, amused, and made his hand bigger in his pocket, as if he were pulling out a pistol or a knife.

But then Kenny lunged in a ducking sidestep toward the fireplace, tossing his drink at Harvey, then seized the set of fireplace tools in both hands, pivoted and swung them in a heaving arc at Harvey's face. Kenny held on to only the gold-handled shovel, and let everything else fly.

Harvey turned away, covered his face. The tools sailed past him to bang against the wall, but the heavy metal base of the holder caught him in the chest, a sharp corner stabbing in hard, knocking him breathless. The thing he had been holding in his hand, the weapon he had reached for earlier, now fell to the floor, didn't even bounce when it hit the carpet. A flash drive. Pink. A small, harmless thing.

A part of Kenny must have recognized the object, recognized that it was not a weapon, at least not of the conventional kind. Harvey was the weapon. But Kenny was already in motion and did not stop himself, did not freeze the movement of the shovel in his hand or attempt to stop its momentum. The flat side of the shovel slammed against the side of Harvey's head.

Harvey staggered and went down on one knee as everything turned black and filled with streaking white sparks. With one arm twisted over his head he waited for another blow, but it did not come. He heard Kenny's huffing breath, turned his head just enough to look at him, saw him standing there with the little shovel raised like a baseball bat, Kenny poised like a boy ready to step out of the batter's box, afraid of the speeding pitch, too timid to swing.

And in that moment when Harvey turned his dazed eyes on Kenny, in that moment when the clouds in Harvey's eyes seemed suddenly to ignite, that moment when his face went scarlet with rage, some recognition or fear must have ignited Kenny as well, for he put his arms in motion again, drew back and stepped forward and swung.

Harvey ducked under the swing and dove forward and up, plunged into Kenny with arms outstretched. Together he and Kenny went back over the arm of the leather sofa, Kenny twisting as they fell, and landing atop Harvey on the floor, his knees squeezed together between Harvey's outstretched legs.

Kenny drew back the shovel for another swing, but an instant before the blade could make contact, Harvey seized Kenny's wrist and yanked the shovel free. And then the blade reversed its direction and was slammed against the side of Kenny's skull, and he fell to the side.

Harvey pushed away and stood over Kenny as he struggled onto his knees. "You're a disgusting man," Harvey said, and was about to toss the shovel aside when Kenny wrapped both arms around Harvey's legs and tried to pull him down. So Harvey swung the shovel again, this time putting all of his weight and strength behind the blow. The vibration rattled through his hand and up his arm like something alive, a snake in his veins, so to shake it free he swung again, and again, and again, until finally the blade broke off and Harvey was left holding only the handle itself, gold-plated and shining wet with blood, slippery in his hands.

Harvey stood over Kenny and did not understand what had happened here. The room was suffocatingly warm; his lungs burned with every breath. His pulse was a hammer inside his head and his heart hammered at his chest. His right arm was numb from the fingertips to shoulder. In the distance the television played, the characters mere shadows, mumbled words, a strain of dark music.

Harvey dropped to his knees beside Kenny and thought he heard a woman screaming somewhere. He thought he heard a dog barking. He thought he would like to turn off that god-awful television once and for all, would like to put his fist through the screen. He thought about Will and wished Will were there to explain all this to him, wished he had the strength to find his cell phone in his pocket.

Even when Harvey looked up to see Kenny's mother coming toward him, saw at once the savage horror in her eyes and the small dog yipping behind her, cowering at her heels, even as he watched her stoop to pick up the fireplace poker, he was moving away from all this, walking away in his own mind, strolling down the street in front of Will's place, heading for the front door, going inside to have a beer with his brother.

And everything else that happened was the work of somebody else, a man he did not know. Harvey watched it all as if from across the street, as if watching a television screen through a shop window. While now and then a pleasant scent drifted by. The smell of the bakery down the street from Will's place, of doughnuts and fresh bread. He was able to enjoy the fragrance in a detached kind of way, the way a man who doesn't eat might enjoy it, with longing and regret, a man who had never tasted sweetness because he possessed no mouth, no tongue, no stomach for this life.

And when Harvey stumbled out of Kenny's house a quarter of an hour later, the woman was no longer screaming. The dog no longer barked. The television was silent. A bone was broken just below his left wrist where he had raised it to block the poker that the woman swung at his face, and the flesh was swollen and pulsing, the splintered bone pulsing too. Otherwise as he walked back through town he was as quiet inside as the night itself, no thunder in his head. And the only thought he would permit himself was a wish deep and aching that Will's place were still open, because he could really use a cold one now.

50

Nowhere to go but home. Harvey required no lights in order to see those dark rooms clearly; the details were emblazoned on his mind. The kitchen with its painted cupboards, the noisy ice maker in the refrigerator. The living room with the rose-colored sofa Jennalee had begged him to let her buy, nearly two thousand dollars. He did not regret the expense anymore. He regretted nothing. He settled into his recliner facing the television set, gazed at the gun cabinet against the rear wall, thought of all those seasons of hunting deer and turkey with his father and brothers. Even as he eased himself back and let his arms fall limp beside him, he could recall the scent of autumn leaves kicked up beneath his boots, the fragrance of pine woods in those minutes before dawn when the fog is lifting and the air is chill. It all came back to him then, all the happy moments unfettered by desire, by need, and he understood that everything was slipping away from him now, and it was nearly out of his reach already.

As he sat there, wanting to sleep yet reluctant to close his eyes, the numbness faded too, all the wounds he had been ignoring, the blows to his head and body, the broken forearm, the heated, throbbing heaviness of something broken in his chest. His hands were stiff with dried blood, his forehead was stiff with it. He tasted blood in the back of his throat. He did not regret the blood because you cannot regret the inevitable, but he was nostalgic for all that he had lost this night, and all he had never possessed.

He was not startled when the light flared on overhead. There was an inevitability to revelation too. Just as there was to Jennalee's sharp intake of breath at the sight of him, the abrasive sound of the inhalation in her throat. He could only imagine how he must look to her, as if he had dipped his head in blood, his torn shirt splattered with it and sticking to his chest. He smiled to tell her it's not as bad as it looks. The pain was there but far away. *Everything is leaving me now,* he wanted to say. *Everything is going.*

"My God!" she said, and stepped as near as the television set, no closer. "What happened to you?"

He held out his hand, opened his stiff fingers to reveal the pink flash drive in his palm. Then with a tired flick of his wrist he shook it free, sent it falling toward her feet.

She stared down at it, pink and bloody against the tan nap of the carpet. Within seconds, tears were sliding down her cheeks. Her head moved back and forth in a slow, repetitious denial, *no no no* as her mouth twisted into a grotesque frown, her forehead tightening, hands sliding up her arms to hold herself, to pull herself inward.

Her voice was hoarse and weak. Harvey was surprised by how small it sounded, how lacking in confidence. "Did you hurt him?" she said. "Harvey, please. Please tell me you didn't hurt him."

He had no desire to move, to say anything. But knew she would keep talking if he did not speak. "He isn't hurt anymore," he told her. His voice was hoarse too, a low rumble from the back of his throat.

Her response was an explosion, too loud, it blasted and ricocheted inside his head. "What did you do to him?" she screamed. "*What did you do?*"

His voice, in comparison, was thick and soft and slow. "What would any man do?"

Her legs buckled, and she dropped to one knee. Then, slowly tilting, she clung to the side of the television cabinet until she was sitting on the floor. Each sob struck him like a nail of glass fired into his brain.

He looked away from her face, so twisted and ugly, and noticed that she was wearing only her panties and teddy, that she looked so inelegant there, naked knees spread apart. The soles of her feet were dirty.

She sobbed, every moan followed by a gasp, the side of her head against the cabinet. Then her eyes fell on the white telephone standing up in its white base on the end table beside the sofa, and she pushed herself up, lunged for the phone and hit the speed dial button and listened to the ring.

He could hear the ringing too, hollow and distant, again and again. When the voice recording began, she punched the Off button and placed the call again.

Again the ringing. He said, "Nobody to answer it." He was about to say, *Not even the dog,* but she responded with a prolonged scream of "Nooo!" and flung the phone at him. When it struck him on the shoulder and bounced away and he merely smiled lazily, she grabbed the closest, heaviest object she could find, the candy dish filled with M&M'S, the Imperial Carnival bowl on a fluted stem and pedestal base. She seized it by the lip of the bowl, yanked it off the coffee table and sent the colored candies flying, and strode over to him and swung it at his head again and then again, screaming all the while. He sat tilted away from her, his right arm raised to protect his head, but did nothing else to defend himself, only absorbed the distant blows and the distant pain, and thought, as if he were watching the scene from far away, *She's just like her mother.*

When the bowl slipped from her hand and fell heavily to the floor, she stopped screaming finally, was too breathless to continue, and leaned away from him moaning, a kind of whimpering sound he had never before heard.

He lifted his eyes to hers, could scarcely recognize her now. His voice was whisper soft. "Tell me the truth, Jennalee. Why did you ever marry me?"

She was as quick as a snake, lunged forward and hit him in the face, three times before his hand came up and shoved her away. She dropped to the floor, where she curled into a fetal position and sobbed. He had not known he was going to shove her. Never intended to do so.

Seconds passed, maybe more. Every sound she made stabbed at him. Again and again he winced, one jagged shard after another. Finally he leaned forward in his chair and with one good hand pushed himself up. She backed away from him, huddled tighter.

He stepped around her to the gun cabinet, felt for the key along the top of the cabinet. Found it and unlocked the door. Looked at the guns hanging from their racks, thought of all the good times he had had with them, the .30-06, the 12 gauge and the over-and-under. The single-shot .22 he had owned since he was a boy.

He wished she would be quiet now. Wished he could close his eyes and go back to the woods.

But she was leaning up against the coffee table. Banging the heel of her fist on the glass top. Rattling the cherry-scented candle.

The 12 gauge, he told himself. And lifted it free.

Boxes of ammunition waited below the guns. He leaned the 12 gauge against the cabinet, took out a handful of shells. Awkwardly hooked an arm around the shotgun and returned to his chair.

It took him a while to get the shotgun loaded. Because of the pain in his wrist he had to pause several times to catch his breath. All the while Jennalee sat huddled against the coffee table, half turned from him as she whimpered and sobbed.

Again he stood. Crossed to Jennalee. Touched her arm with the butt of the shotgun. She jerked away as if shocked.

He laid the gun at her side, the barrel against her naked leg. Returned to his chair. Leaned back and closed his eyes.

After a while, her whimpering stopped. He knew without seeing that she was looking at him now. He said, "You know how to use it. I'm the one taught you."

It felt like a long time before she moved. Time was slowing for him now, and pleasantly. That was one of the things he liked best about the woods. If you take things slowly in the woods, don't try to force them or rush, you can hear every click and rustle. You can hear the breeze whispering in the treetops. You can feel the woods breathing.

He could hear her movements, tentative at first, still frightened. Once a doe and her fawn had come out of a stand of red pines to see him standing against a tree, and he had remained perfectly still, breathed softly and quietly. She came into the hardwoods first, left her fawn to stay behind and watch. She came to within ten yards and paused. Sniffed the air. Waited for him to separate himself from the tree. If he had, she would have wheeled around and run leaping back to the pines, her fawn bolting too. But he held his place, became a part of the trunk, a thick growth of bark. And soon she came closer, indifferent, and nibbled at the ground.

She was standing in front of him now, he could feel her heat. Slowly, so as not to frighten her, he raised his good arm, palm open, and moved his hand through the air until it bumped against the barrel.

He wrapped his fingers around the cold metal. Drew it closer, until the tip of the barrel pressed against his chest. Then he said, as softly as he could, smiling, "It's nice."

"What is?" she said.

"Being here like this. Where I don't need you anymore."

51

She thought the gunshot was the loudest sound she'd ever heard.

And after a while she laid the shotgun across the arms of his chair. There was not as much blood as she had expected. A round, dark hole in his shirt. He didn't look real. Maybe he had never been real.

She went to the kitchen, trembling, the entire house was trembling, a frozen place, so cold. And soon she returned dragging a kitchen chair, which she pulled in front of his. She sat facing him with her bare feet straddling his legs, their knees touching. She leaned forward and picked up the shotgun, ejected the empty shell, rammed another one home. Then she wedged the shotgun's stock into Harvey's crotch. Rested the barrel between her breasts. Held it there with her left hand. Now she leaned toward her husband, bent her head and shoulders toward him as the barrel pushed hard against her chest, and her right hand reached out, fingers stretching. Finally she found the trigger, that scimitar moon of metal. Laid her thumb inside its curve. And pushed. And this time she heard no sound at all.

III

52

The bodies were still warm when Laci got the call. Neighbors had reported gunshots. Only two, several minutes apart.

Ronnie Walters told her, "I don't know if you want to do this one. It's family."

And suddenly she understood the nature of the peculiar feeling that had washed through her less than two hours earlier, when she had encountered Harvey on the street. She had felt something sinister hovering around him. Something hungry and resolute. And now she knew, without being told, without hearing a name, that Harvey was dead. But that was all she knew.

She turned to look at Will sleeping with his back to her. She wanted to reach out and lay a hand on his naked shoulder. Wanted contact. The reassurance of flesh.

"It's a mess," Ronnie told her.

"Who?" she said, though what she meant by it was, *Who else?*

"Harvey and Jennalee."

"Ahh," she said, an involuntarily moan, and doubled forward as if stabbed in the chest. Then three more *ahh*s before she could ask, whispering hoarsely, as if she were choking on the words, "How did he do it?"

"What it looks like," Ronnie told her, "is that she shot him first. Then turned the gun on herself. Shotgun. Like I said, it's a real mess. I can call somebody else if you want me to."

But she did not. Did not want anyone else taking pictures of them. Harvey deserved somebody who cared. Jennalee too, she supposed. But was unable to muster much emotion for her. Not while her heart was breaking for Harvey. For Harvey and Stevie and Will.

"Give me a few minutes," she said. "I need to tell my husband."

"Take your time," he told her. "The coroner hasn't shown up yet. Just be ready for what you're going to see. If that's even possible."

She wanted to say something but found herself unable to speak. Found herself wanting to lay the phone aside, to lie down against her husband's back, wrap an arm around his chest.

"I'm sorry, Laci," the deputy said. "What a god-awful thing."

53

Leaving Molly alone in the apartment, still sound asleep, was not an easy decision. If they woke her, she would have to be told about her uncle and aunt. And they weren't ready yet to share that information with her. So Laci wrote a note in blue ink and taped it to the inside of her daughter's bedroom door:

We had to go to Harvey and JL's place. Be back soon. Call if you need us. Love you, Mom & Dad.

They felt certain that at least one of them would return to the apartment before their daughter awoke.

Outside, at the car, Will handed her the keys. "You better drive," he said.

He wasn't sure he was even awake. It felt like a dream. His body was heavy and resisted all movement. He didn't remember pulling on his trousers or the T-shirt, didn't remember slipping his sockless feet into shoes. He thought he remembered Laci gently shaking him awake, leaning down close, saying whatever she had said, whatever words. Now all he remembered clearly was *Harvey and Jennalee both.*

"You're shivering," she said as she pulled away from the curb. "You want me to turn the air-conditioning off?"

He shook his head no, but continued to sit leaning forward, hunched over, hands holding his elbows. When he turned to look out the window he could see only shadows upon shadows, the car's movement too quiet, everything too hushed. He told himself, *I think I'm still asleep.*

"We better talk about this," she said. "We're going to be questioned. Especially you. He was at the bar tonight."

"He was," Will said.

"Did he say he was going to do anything?"

"Like what?"

"Like anything."

Will stared out through the windshield.

"Did he say anything about going over to the school after he left? I still don't understand why he went over there."

"He did?" Will said.

"I already told you that."

"Okay," he said.

"What time was it when he came to the bar?"

"I don't know," Will said. "I can't remember."

"It was just after midnight when I saw him there. And then what—forty minutes or so later he was walking out by the school. And sometime between then and now"—she glanced at the clock on the instrument panel—"two forty-four . . . and now they're both dead."

He turned his head to look at her. Her face was dark. Everything was dark but her hands on the steering wheel, illuminated by the lights from the instrument panel, fingers thin and small and eerily blue.

"Are they dead for real?" he said. "Is this happening for real?"

She lifted one blue hand from the steering wheel, laid it atop his thigh. "I'm sorry, babe, but it is."

"He said he was going home," Will told her.

"You mean when he left the bar?"

Will nodded.

"What was so important that he had to walk over to the school in the middle of the night? And then to go home and . . . have this happen?"

"I don't know," Will said. "I don't know."

Parked in Harvey's driveway were the town's patrol car and the sheriff's car, their light bars strobing, making shadows jerk and dart. An ambulance at the curb, four-ways blinking. And twenty feet behind it, a black Kia Sportage, dark.

"The coroner's here," she said.

She pulled up behind the Sportage, powered down all the windows, then turned off the car. As she reached into the back seat for her camera, Will popped open his door.

"They're not going to let you in there," she told him. "Not yet anyway."

"He's my brother," Will said.

"You can't go in. It's a crime scene."

Will shook his head. Now the tears came. Now it was real. Lights shining all through the house. Lights on in the neighbors' homes. Porch lights burning, vehicle lights stinging his eyes. People standing in their yards. A figure in the doorway of his brother's house. Police tape across the front of the yard.

"After they bring the bodies out," she told him. "Maybe then you can see him. Just sit tight until then, okay?"

He looked past her out through the windshield. "Everybody's watching," he said. "Like it's some kind of fucking show."

He never swore in front of her. Didn't even seem to realize that he had.

"I'll be back as soon as I can," she told him. "Please don't try to come inside."

He turned to look at her then, his face wet. A tear fell off his chin. "He's my brother," he said.

And she started crying too. Allowed it for a few moments as her hand reached for his, squeezed his fingers, squeezed them as tightly as she could.

54

The coroner met her at the door, a slight man of medium height, bald, a horseshoe of graying red hair around the sides of his head. "You sure you want to do this?" he asked. "I can probably get somebody else here."

She looked up into his eyes. Blue. She had always thought of them as nice eyes, not icy like some blue eyes, but warm, not pale like his complexion, his round soft face, but kind and summery. Baby blues. "I'm okay," she said.

"The sheriff doesn't think you should do this. You being related and all. I had to talk him into it. Told them there's nobody else half as good."

"Thank you," she said.

"It's not pretty, Laci. Something like this is going to stay with you a good long while."

As it should, she told herself. And that was why she could not let somebody else take the pictures. Somebody who would refer to her brother and sister-in-law as the victims. The deceased. Somebody who would go home afterward and shower and sleep for a few hours then wake up feeling nothing. Somebody who would tell his friends about what he had seen, maybe even make a joke about it. Keep copies of the shots on his hard drive. Do who knew what with them.

"I'm good," she said. "Where do you want to start?"

He handed her a pair of paper booties and a surgical mask.

55

For a while after Harvey had left the trailer, pink flash drive in hand, Stevie had felt too restless for sleep. He had wanted to do something for Harvey, comfort him somehow, but as always in such moments, he had sat silently, feeling awkward and unsure.

After a while he had dragged himself to bed and listened to the last hour of a late-night talk show on his laptop, something about a Planet X that was going to enter the solar system, cause a pole shift and earthquakes and floods, fulfill the prophecy in Revelations of global chaos and destruction.

For him the destruction seemed to have already begun, and he wondered if maybe he had had a role in it. If they had not broken into the school, Harvey might never have learned what his wife had been doing. Was not knowing a good thing or a bad thing? *Ignorance is bliss,* his mother used to say, especially after she started drinking too much. Then she found a man who liked to drink as much as she did, and off they went to Florida. That was the beginning of the destruction. Or maybe jumping off the porch roof was the beginning. In any case, the pictures on that flash drive weren't going to do Harvey a damn bit of good. The marriage was surely over now. What would Harvey do? Would he quit his job and move away too? Stevie thought he should call Harvey later in the day, offer to take him in. *You can have the bed,* he'd tell him. *I don't mind sleeping on the couch.*

He drank a beer and swallowed an extra ten-milligram tablet of melatonin and finally drifted off to the fading but frantic voice of the radio show's guest. He had been asleep less than an hour when the ringtone on his cell phone woke him, accompanied by the female voice saying *Call from Will.* He rolled over quickly, grabbed the phone, and said, "Hey. What's up?"

And Will, sobbing, told him. "She killed him with his own shotgun, Stevie. The lying bitch shot him."

He jerked away from the phone. Looked at it. Put it back to his ear. "What are you talking about?"

"I'm outside his house right now," Will said. "Laci's inside taking pictures."

"Of what?"

"I just told you. Jennalee shot Harvey. Killed him. And then she shot herself."

And for the next few minutes Stevie had no idea where he was, whether in a dream or somewhere else. The darkness and confusion was just like when he had landed on his back in the yard, head banging down hard. A strangely deep and vast and confounding darkness in which he felt both light and heavy, both there and not there.

Time passed but he had no idea how much. And at some point he realized that Will was still talking. ". . . that you don't say anything to anyone about the school thing. Don't even answer your phone unless it's from me . . . must've told her or something . . . went to sleep and then she did it . . . just can't believe it, Stevie. Just can't get my head around it."

Stevie was still confused when the conversation ended. Still uncertain. He knew the word that seemed to apply, though. *Hypnagogia.* He wasn't really awake, nor wholly asleep. Caught in the interstice between the two. Or maybe only dreaming that he was. He laid the phone aside and reminded himself to check the call log in the morning. If it included this call from Will, the call was real. Except that it wasn't. Couldn't be.

Ignorance is bliss, he heard his mother say.

56

To sit and do nothing was excruciating. Every time Will's thoughts turned to what was inside that house, what Laci must be looking at, photographing, he wanted to tear at his skin. He had always been jealous of that house, its spaciousness and stolidity. A normal house on a normal street. Two floors, an attic, a basement, a garage. Two people who loved each other.

Except that Harvey was always angry. Always simmering just under the surface.

Will leaned forward and thudded his forehead against the dash. "Fuck fuck fuck fuck fuck fuck *fuck.*"

He must have known, Will thought. Must *have known. But didn't want to know. Wouldn't let himself.*

It would have been like a cancer in the brain. A tumor. You know it's there but you ignore it. You have to live, have to go to work, have to sleep at night. Have to find some way to keep from tearing your skin off and clawing out your veins.

Will was torn between wanting to rush inside the house and needing to run off into the darkness. To just keep running until he collapsed.

When he sat up and leaned back, he saw Deputy Chris Landers coming down off the porch. Without thinking he was going to do it, Will found himself climbing out of the car and hurrying toward the deputy. Landers saw him coming and paused, ready to block Will's path.

Eight long strides and Will was standing in front of him. "Jesus, Chris," Will said. "What's going on in there? Why haven't they brought him out? Get him to the hospital or somewhere. Wherever they're going to take him."

"As soon as the coroner's finished, Will. It takes time to process the scene."

"He's not going to cut him up, is he? Harvey would hate that. He would absolutely hate it."

"Cause of death is pretty much cut-and-dried," Landers said. "An autopsy shouldn't be necessary. He's just getting some pictures with Laci, is all. The sheriff has to write up a report."

Will nodded, but remained agitated. He held both hands tight against his sternum, fingers hooked together, arms tense and shaking, as if he wanted to pull his hands apart but couldn't.

And then he had a thought. Looked around, peered up and down the street. "Where's Kenny?" he said. "Where's that sonofabitch at?"

"They're not answering the phone," Landers told him. "I'm headed over there now. See if I can shake them out of bed."

And Will stopped pulling at his hands. His hands relaxed, fell limp at his sides. Because he knew. Not specifically. But sufficiently. *They're not answering the phone.* He knew what his brother had done. And had to ask himself, *Wouldn't you do the same?*

57

The coroner, wearing white latex gloves, booties and a surgical mask, picked Harvey's hand out of his lap, turned it over, and studied the palm. His movements were delicate, never abrupt. He was always reverent when handling a body, and seemed especially so tonight. Laci was reminded of the first time she had worked with him, and his soft-spoken admonition, *Always remember, Laci. Don't let yourself forget. This is a human being.*

He had been in attendance at Harvey's and Jennalee's reception, both he and his wife. They had shoved their dollar bills into the money bag and thrown back their shots of Jack and schnapps and danced with the happy bride and groom.

And that, Laci told herself, *is one of the problems with small-town life. You grow up with people, get to know them and like them, have to watch them suffer and mourn, see some of them turn into drunks or druggies, people who beat their children, cheat on their spouses. You have to handle their bodies sometimes, put those bodies into the ground.*

The coroner pressed his fingers atop Harvey's to flatten the palm. "Close-ups of both hands," he said.

She spread her feet to straddle Harvey's outstretched leg. Leaned in close. Focused. Five quick shots of the right hand, each shot at a slightly different angle. Five quick shots of the left.

They had the same hands, Harvey and Will. Big hands. Strong. Always working, those four hands. Lifting, pulling, toting hands. Fingernails clipped short. Sturdy, comforting, loving hands. They could have been her husband's except for the abrasions down each palm. The blood like a rash of scarlet freckles all over the top of his fingers, but none on his palms.

She had already taken dozens of shots of the room, the open door of the gun cabinet, the position of the shotgun at Harvey's feet, Jennalee's body lying on its side as if she had drifted to sleep and fallen off the chair. Every splatter of blood, every angle and object that might add context to the scene. Entrance and exit wounds for both bodies, front, back and profile. Medium-range two-person shots to establish their positions and proximity to one another. She didn't focus on the faces, kept her eye on the center of the frame.

The coroner spoke softly into his cell phone's recorder as Laci photographed the bodies, as he moved and positioned the bodies so that Laci could do her work. "Male victim shot in the chest, point blank. Exit wound several inches lower. Approximately forty-five-degree angle. Victim sitting, possibly sleeping, shooter probably standing . . . Bruise on female victim's shoulder compatible with shotgun recoil. Female victim shot in the chest, again point blank. Exit wound . . . approximately twenty, twenty-five degrees higher. Might have used male victim's body to stabilize the weapon. Female victim was originally seated, as indicated by damage to chair, then toppled by the force of the blast. Position might be confirmed by examining male victim for recoil bruising of thighs and genitals."

Every now and then a brief dizziness would assail Laci, and she would feel on the verge of weakening, dropping to her knees. She tried to breathe without taking in any scents, and the mask helped, muted but did not cancel out the scents of two exploded bodies. She could hear the soft whimper that emanated from behind her mask now and then, was aware that the coroner looked up at her each time it happened. His name was Ted but she never thought of him as that, always as "coroner," or sometimes as "Donaldson." Always wanted to keep her distance from him when he was working. Separate herself from the grisly intimacy that was part of his job, not hers. But now when he heard the whimper and his voice paused and he looked her way, she saw in his baby blues an understanding, a kinship, and suddenly felt close to him, grateful for his soft voice and kind eyes.

The smell was what she had a hard time with. Even with a surgical mask, the smell always got to her. That same dirty penny smell, and the stink of an unflushed toilet, and the dry, sulfurous scent of gunpowder. She hoped she would not associate that scent with her brother-in-law from now on. Would not see this scene in her mind's eye for a month or more of nights to come.

She breathed shallowly through her mouth, concentrated on the *click click click*, did her best to ignore the nausea and the tightening of her throat.

And then the coroner stepped away from Harvey's chair and peeled off a glove, slipped the cell phone into a pocket. "You know the rest," he told her. "I'm going to grab a smoke outside. Compare notes with the sheriff."

She was finishing up with a few more midrange shots from the front wall of the house, squatting low, Harvey on the left side of the frame, Jennalee on the right, when she noticed, through the camera, a spot of pink beneath Jennalee's naked calf. Jennalee's toenails were red. The blood was a darker red. But pink?

M&M'S were scattered everywhere. But pink? Were M&M'S sometimes pink?

Yes, she remembered now. It had been at a wedding, or maybe a baby shower. No, a 5K. Somebody was handing them out at the finish line. Bags of pink and white M&M'S. A 5K walk for breast cancer research.

What about that thing? Harvey had said at the bar. *That pink thing.*

She zoomed in on it. Just a short line of pink, maybe two inches in length. Half-buried in the carpet beneath Jennalee's leg. Definitely not an M&M.

What in the world? she thought. Whatever the thing was, it didn't belong there. Wasn't natural to this scene. Unless it was. Unless it was integral to it. Unless it *explained* this scene.

What about that pink thing?

A cell phone rang not far outside the front door. Then a mumbling of voices. Deputy Walters stepped closer to the door but remained in the room with her.

She stared at the sliver of pink. Had anybody else seen it? The EMTs? The sheriff and his deputies? The coroner hadn't pointed it out to her, hadn't lifted Jennalee's leg for a photograph.

She lowered the camera and looked around the room. The sheriff's broad back was filling the front doorway now, his voice a rumble as he talked on the phone. Ronnie Walters stood just behind the sheriff, listening in on the conversation.

Quickly she reviewed her previous photos, paused to squint at every shot of Jennalee. No pink visible.

She blinked, cleared her eyes. Peered again through the camera. Still there.

Stevie has it, Will had said. And Harvey said, *I want it.*

What did Will know about this? Was he involved somehow? *Oh God*, she thought. *Oh God.*

She moved closer to Jennalee, clicking continuously, head and shoulders only. Kept an eye on Deputy Walters, who, though his face was half-turned toward her, head cocked, ear toward the door, could see her only peripherally at best, a photographer doing her job.

She squatted close to the body, kept clicking, clicking. Then used her left hand to push at the flesh of Jennalee's calf, expose the thing in the carpet. A USB drive. *The pink thing.* She didn't even know she was going to pick it up until her fingers covered it, pulled it into her palm, tucked it into her fist.

She stood, shaky, thinking she might stumble and fall. Clicked a few more shots of Jennalee. Turned and took a few more of Harvey. Then stood there breathing through the mask, sucking in the scent of cotton, the taste of blood in her mouth.

When she thought she could move in a straight line, she crossed to the door. "Excuse me," she said, and squeezed past the deputy, who gave her a quick glance and then a smile, and pushed himself against the wall. The sheriff looked back from the porch, saw her and stepped aside.

She pulled the mask down off her mouth, let it hang around her neck. To the coroner she said, "I'll get these to you within the hour."

"Appreciate it," he said. He took a drag from his cigarette, then flicked it into the yard and blew out a smoky breath. "If you want, we can take Harvey down to my place. While we have the ambulance here."

"Oh," she said, and worried for a moment that the pink drive was not completely concealed in her hand, but did not want to look down and draw attention to it. "For Harvey, yeah," she said. "But you should ask Kenny where he wants Jennalee to go."

The coroner looked to the sheriff, who returned the look with a tiny nod.

The sheriff said, "Kenny and his mom are gone too, Laci. Deputy Landers is over there now. I'm on my way."

"Gone where?" she said. But the confusion lasted only a moment. "Oh my God no. No."

The coroner said, "I thought we could take Jennalee and her family to Murphy's. He's got a bigger operation than I do. Unless you want Harvey and Jennalee together. It's your call. Yours and Will's."

"I can't believe it," she said, and squeezed her fist tighter. "How did they die?"

"According to the deputy," the sheriff said, "it looks like they were beaten to death."

"By Harvey?" she said.

"We don't know that yet. To be honest with you, we don't know diddly-squat. I'm hoping you and Will can fill me in a little on what was going on with them all."

"Nothing was going on," she said. "I had coffee with Jennalee yesterday. My God. I just can't believe all this."

The coroner gave her a few moments. Then he asked, "You up for another batch tonight? I know it's asking a lot of you."

She said nothing. Was watching the cigarette ember in the yard. It looked like a dying firefly. Its soul a wisp of smoke clinging to the grass.

The coroner said, "I'm going to call somebody else. You don't have to do anything more tonight."

"No," she said. "No. I'm all right. I want to do it."

"If this is too much for you . . ." the sheriff said. "Hell, it's too much for me."

"I'm good," Laci said. "Just let me do my job."

The coroner said, "Why don't you ride over with me, then? You can send Will back home."

The sheriff said, "Ask him to come talk to me in the morning. See if we can't figure this whole thing out."

She nodded. Then looked toward the curb, where Will was sitting with his car door open, feet atop the concrete, gazing her way. She said, "Does he know about Kenny and Louise?"

"We haven't talked to him yet," the sheriff said.

She held the camera in her right hand, pressed her fist against her hip. "I need to tell him." And she moved away from the two men. Across the wide porch. Down the steps. Heard the paper booties making a hissing sound through the grass.

"I'll see you over at Kenny's place," the coroner said. "No need to rush."

58

Laci walked to the car as if she were in a hurry but didn't really want to get there. One bootie peeled away from her, dragged for a few steps, then lay atop the grass.

She climbed into the car and set her camera between her legs and without buckling her seat belt turned the ignition key to start the engine. Her left hand remained closed in a fist, held tight against her belly. Will swung his feet back inside the car and closed the door just as she was pulling away from the curb.

He said, "I didn't get to see Harvey."

"They're taking him to Donaldson's."

"Is that where we're going?"

"Not yet," she said.

She drove for another minute, then pulled over on a dark street and put the gearshift in park. "Kenny's dead too," she told him. "So's his mother. Both beaten to death."

He took a shallow breath. Another. And nodded.

"You knew?" she said, her voice louder now.

"Chris Landers told me."

"How could he tell you? He's over at their house."

"Before he went there. He said they weren't answering the phone."

"So you knew what Harvey was going to do?"

"No," he said. "No, I . . . I just had a feeling."

She brought her fist away from her body then, held it open to him. And said, her voice louder than she intended, "Is this why he killed them?"

He flinched. "Please don't yell."

"And now you've dragged me into it!"

He winced again. Then asked, "How did you get it?"

"I picked it up. It was under Jennalee's leg. Do you know what it is—what's on it?"

"Why did you do that?"

"Because of you! I heard you and Harvey at the bar. How are you involved in this?"

"I'm not," he said. "I just . . ."

"Do you know what's on it?"

He nodded. "Pictures."

"Of what?"

"Jennalee. And Kenny. And other men."

Her head drew back a little. She looked down at her hand. Then lowered her hand to the seat, turned her hand over, reclaimed it, empty, and laid it against her throat. She said, "Jennalee *with* Kenny?"

"Yep," he said.

Both of them were looking down at it now. *The pink thing.* Its color muted by the darkness.

"Harvey said he wanted it," she said. "At the bar. And you said Stevie had it."

"He must've gone to Stevie's after leaving the bar."

"So Stevie's seen it too."

"I'm sure."

"Did Harvey know she was doing that?"

"No. I mean . . . He told me tonight—last night, I guess—that back before they got married, he had some suspicions. But never wanted to believe it."

"So what's on here," she said, and touched the seat beside the flash drive, "this was all a surprise to him?"

"Absolutely," he said. "I mean . . . it was proof. Probably the first time he had any proof."

"And where did it come from?" she asked. "How did it end up with Stevie?"

Now he looked up at her, eyes full of sorrow. "It was in Kenny's desk at school."

"That was you at the school?" she asked, again so loud that he winced, kept his eyes closed for several seconds. "The three of you?"

"I'm sorry," he said. "We didn't know it was there. We just wanted . . ."

"You wanted to act like children? You wanted to behave like a bunch of *idiots*?"

"Please," he said. "I'm sorry. It was stupid, I know."

She tapped her fingertip atop the seat. The flash drive bounced with every jab. "I committed a crime here, Will. Because I knew this had something to do with you. I knew it did!"

He said, "We should just get rid of it. Nobody will ever know."

She leaned away from him. Sat with her back against the door. Breathed loudly through her nose, long sucking breaths and quick exhalations.

He put his hand over top of the flash drive. "I'll get rid of it," he said.

And she put her hand atop his. "No."

He waited. Made no attempt to move.

She took two of his fingers in her hand, and lifted his hand off the flash drive. "The way things are going to look now," she said, her voice soft, words measured and slow, "this was all Harvey's fault. First he beat Kenny and Louise to death, and then he went home and . . . maybe told Jennalee what he'd done. Because the way the bodies are, the way it looks, he sat down, maybe fell asleep, and she took the shotgun and killed him. And then shot herself."

"So she really did it? She really shot him?"

"That's how it looks, yes. People will say she had a right to. They'll say he deserved it. But I *knew* she was cheating on him, Will. She as much as admitted it to me. And I don't want Harvey taking the blame for everything. I don't want Molly spending the next four years in this town hearing about how awful her uncle was."

He kept his eyes on hers. Could not look away. She said, "Harvey's hands had fresh marks on them, right across the center of his palms."

"What kind of marks?"

"If you stood one hand on top of the other, the marks would match up perfectly. Like it was a rope burn, you know? Like he was holding on to a rope and somebody pulled it through his hands."

"That's how we got into the school. Through the skylight."

She nodded. Said nothing more for a while. He knew that she was thinking now, faster and better than he ever could, keeping her anger and disappointment at bay while she thought things through. So he said nothing. He waited.

Finally she said, "I'm going to take you home. You need to get your head straight on this. Because the sheriff wants to talk to you in the morning."

"He wants to talk to me?"

"He's looking for why Harvey did this, that's all."

"They know he did it? Killed Kenny and Louise?"

"Who else would have done it? And why else would Jennalee have killed him?"

He crumpled forward again, hands and forehead against the dashboard. She laid a hand against his back.

"We're the ones who have to live with this," she told him. "You and me and Molly. But we both know what a prick Kenny was, and what a bitch his mother could be. And I know what I know about Jennalee too. So if there's anybody's reputation we have to protect, it's not theirs. You understand?"

He remained motionless; said nothing. He could feel the car's vibration in his head and hands; could feel it in his eyeballs and teeth. And there was a second kind of rumbling too, a low and rolling rumble located somewhere in the back of his brain, not at all like the engine noise with its staccato vibration but more fluid, smoother, like the thunder of a huge wave rolling in, building from the back of his brain, getting ready to slam forward and wipe out everything in its path.

"Will!" Laci said.

Another wince. "Take me home," he told her.

59

A state policeman was stationed on the front porch of Kenny's house. He recognized Laci and directed her to the basement game room. Just inside the house, Deputy Chris Landers sat on the foyer floor, wedged into an empty corner where the stairs to the second floor descended, his knees drawn up, one hand splayed against the slate tile, his eyes heavy, face drawn and pale.

"You doing okay?" she asked.

"Two in one night," he said. "All people I know. People I grew up with."

She nodded. "I hear you," she said.

"There's gloves and booties for you in the kitchen," he told her.

"Thanks, Chris. Hang in there."

"I don't know how you do it," he said.

"On autopilot, I guess."

In the kitchen she donned a fresh pair of booties. She had not worn gloves in Harvey's house and disliked using them. Sensitivity in her fingertips was important when working with the camera. Besides, she was always very careful to touch nothing but the camera when doing her work. But this time was different. This time she had the flash drive to contend with.

The basement door stood open and the voices of two men drifted up the carpeted stairs. The coroner and the sheriff. She knew they would have processed the scene by now and were waiting for her to finish up. It was going to be difficult to plant the flash drive with the two men just standing around and watching. She had been thinking about it ever since dropping Will off in front of the bar. She had wiped the device clean of her own fingerprints, plus Will's and Stevie's, and consequently Kenny's and Harvey's too. It was going to look fishy if not a single print was found on it. She had hoped to be able to rub the plastic case over Kenny's fingertips, but now doubted it would be possible. But maybe they wouldn't even bother to check it for prints. Not after they viewed the contents.

She slipped on one glove, then extracted the flash drive from her pocket and tucked it into the collar of her high-top skate shoe, then pulled the top of the paper bootie up as far as it would reach. Then heard footsteps coming up from the game room. She hurried to stand erect and reached for the other glove, her heart racing.

The sheriff appeared at the top of the stairs. He said, "I'm not sure I want you down here, Laci. You're related to these people."

"I was related to Harvey and Jennalee too."

"That was a murder-suicide. It was clear who did what."

"I know my work," she told him. "Who are you going to get that's better?"

"Coroner already made that argument for you. I still have to ask you some questions."

"Go ahead," she said.

"Where were you last night from between . . . let's say ten and two?"

"Home with my daughter," she said. "Until I got the call to go to the school. Where you saw me."

"And after that?"

"Home. In bed with my husband."

"How about your husband?"

"What about him?"

"Where was he during the same time?"

"Before being in bed with me? Downstairs in the bar. Working on the books. Harvey was there with him when I left to go to the school."

"Was he there when you got back from the school?"

"Will was. But I saw Harvey on the street just down from the school when I left."

"You saw Harvey there? Just after the break-in?"

"He said he was walking home from the bar, decided to swing by the school and see what was going on."

"So you stopped and talked to him?"

"I asked him what he was doing. Then I offered him a ride home."

"Did he take you up on it?"

"No."

"How did he seem to you?"

"Same way he did in the bar. Like he had a lot on his mind."

"Did he seem angry?"

"Not particularly. More sad than angry. He didn't say much at all at the bar."

"Is that typical of him? To show up at the bar on a Sunday night?"

"The bar is part of our lives," she said. "An extension of our home. They come and they go, Harvey and Stevie both."

"You have any idea where Stevie was last night?"

"None whatsoever."

He nodded. "When was the last time you saw Jennalee?"

"Yesterday afternoon. We had coffee together at the mall and shopped for shoes. She bought some, I didn't."

"Did she talk at all about her marriage? Say it was in trouble or anything like that?"

"Not that I can recall, Sheriff. Little other than the normal pleasantries. Mostly she talked about shoes."

"She didn't seem angry or depressed about anything?"

"Just the opposite."

She waited for him to respond, to nod or ask another question. But he stood motionless on the stairs, left hand on the rail, eyes gazing downward.

She said, "Anything else you want to know?"

A few more moments passed before he looked up. "Harvey didn't say anything about being ticked off at Kenny over something? Either last night or any other time?"

"Not last night," she said. "But before? Yes. There was a thing about a motorcycle."

"What kind of thing?"

"Harvey and Jake had restored an old motorcycle together. And Jake had promised to leave it to Harvey in his will. Except that after Jake died, Kenny and Louise said there wasn't any will. So Harvey tried to buy the motorcycle, but Kenny kept raising the price on him. And yes, Harvey was ticked off about that. But enough to beat two people to death? Over a motorcycle? I just can't believe that's true."

"I'd hate to believe it myself," the sheriff said. Then he made a slow turn and started down the steps again. "Come on down when you're ready," he said.

She remained at the table a couple minutes longer. A chill rattled through her. Then her body flushed with heat. Her hands trembled as she pulled on the second glove.

60

After checking on his daughter, still sleeping soundly, beautiful little princess, heartbreaking just to look at, Will tried standing at the window but kept feeling like he was going to tumble forward into it, out into the darkness stretching away like a squared-off tunnel of some kind, telescoping into the distance. In fact he wanted to fall into it. Could envision himself leaning forward, head and shoulders silently pushing out the screen, body in slow-motion free fall just like in that movie *Inception*, or like George Clooney in *Gravity*, not a bad thing at all, just drifting into the blackness, thinking nothing, becoming nothing . . .

But Molly. Laci. They had to come first. Before he could disappear into nothingness. *Get your head straight,* he told himself.

He went downstairs so that Molly would not hear him on the phone. Stood in the kitchen, leaning against the upright cooler. For some reason he did not want to go out into the barroom, the last place he had seen his brother. Afraid he might see him standing there at the corner of the bar, his chest a ragged, gaping hole. *Great plan you had there, Will,* Harvey would say. *Way to go, brother.*

On the fifth ring the call went to voice mail, so Will hit End Call and tried again. This time Stevie answered. "We need to get our stories straight," Will said.

He could hear Stevie sitting up in bed, heard the squeak of bed-springs, the headboard thumping once against the wall.

Still groggy, Stevie asked, "Did you call me a while ago?"

"Of course I did."

"I thought maybe it was a dream."

"I wish it was, Stevie. Are you awake now? We need to talk about this."

"She really shot him, Will?"

"She really did. But that's not all of it. First he went over to Kenny's place and killed him and his mother. All four of them are gone now."

"Holy shit," Stevie said. And then his voice became muffled. "What the hell happened? Why would he do such a thing?"

"You need to get the phone out of your mouth, Stevie. I can't understand you."

"I said why would he do such a thing?"

"You know why. You saw the photos. More than I did probably."

"Okay. But why Kenny's mother? What did she have to do with anything?"

"For Christ's sake, Stevie, I don't know! That's not what matters now. We need to get our stories straight. Sheriff wants to talk to me in a little while. He's going to want to talk to you too."

"What are we supposed to say?"

"What you don't say," Will told him, "is that you saw Harvey tonight. You haven't seen him since . . . when? Since we had pizza and watched that movie with Nicolas Cage in it. But whatever you do, don't mention Harvey asking to use my revolver. Just say he dropped by but didn't stay long. You could maybe say he seemed antsy, restless, but you don't know why."

"Where am I supposed to say I was tonight? Can I say I was with you?"

"No! Laci knows you weren't."

"I'll just say I was home by myself all night."

"That's not good enough. They'll think you were with Harvey breaking into the school. You need to get yourself an alibi of some kind. Get one of your buddies to say you were out spotting for deer or something."

"It's too early to be spotting."

"For God's sake, Stevie. Just think of something. You don't know anything about the stuff you bought or about Harvey breaking into the school."

"I'm not a very good liar, Will. I'm terrible at poker. You know that."

"Because that's a bad kind of lie. When you're trying to take advantage of somebody. I'm asking you to tell the good kind of lie. It will help Harvey if you do. It will make people think better of him. You can lie to help Harvey, can't you?"

"I'd do anything for Harvey. Or for you. Or for Laci or Molly or . . . any of my family."

"Good. Then all you have to say is that Harvey never talked to you about him and Jennalee. You never knew a thing about her screwing other men or anything like that. Laci has that flash drive you found—"

"She what? What the hell, Will?"

"She found it at Harvey's place and picked it up for some crazy reason. I guess she thought she was protecting me, I don't know. But we don't know anything about a flash drive. That's all you need to remember. Just play dumb on everything. And if he asks if you and me talked about this, you're going to have to say yes, we talked, because if he wants to he can pull the phone records and see I called you twice. Just don't tell him what we talked about, other than we talked about Harvey. You understand?"

"Give me a little credit, Will. When are you ever going to do that?"

"I'm sorry, I'm just . . . You're going to do fine. Better than me probably."

Stevie was silent for a few moments. Then he asked, "What happens now? To Harvey, I mean."

"They're taking him down to Donaldson's tonight. How about you meet me at the sheriff's office at nine in the morning. Afterward we'll go to the funeral home together and get things figured out."

"He going to let us see Harvey?"

"Doesn't matter if he wants to let us or not," Will said. "We're going to."

"Okay," Stevie said.

"You all right, then? Going to be okay?"

"I'm going to say a prayer for Harvey now."

"That's not a bad idea," Will said. "Say one for all of us."

61

Both men were standing near the bottom of the stairs as Laci descended. "There's our girl," the coroner said, looking up, smiling.

Halfway down she could detect the odor, not nearly as strong as in Harvey's house. Vague behind the mask, but recognizable. Blood and urine and defecation. All the ignominy of violent death.

She paused on the bottom step and surveyed the room. Louise nearby in a blue velveteen house robe and matching slippers, belly and left cheek to the floor, legs spread wide, one knee hooked. Her face was unrecognizable, hair and skin painted with blood. Thighs fat and white, exposed up to her thick support panties. Laci felt sorry for her, revulsion and pity.

A yellow tennis ball. Broken glass. A set of andirons, pieces scattered.

Across the room, Kenny lay on his side with his back to her, forehead up against the paneled wall, his body bent around the corner of the sofa, arms twisted beneath his chest. She would have to squeeze in behind the sofa to photograph his face.

She could feel the flash drive against her ankle. And in Kenny's posture, saw an opportunity.

The sheriff asked, "How's Will handling all this?"

"He's in a fog," she said. "I told him you wanted to talk in the morning, and he'll be there. Just don't expect a lot." Then she turned to the coroner. "Okay if I get in behind the sofa?"

"If there's room," he said. "If not, just shoot a few close-ups from above. We both checked him out already. It's pretty clear what happened here."

"The final result is clear," the sheriff said. "Not the sequence."

She nodded. She started by walking to her left around the perimeter of the room, recording the scene in full. When she came to Kenny's body near the opposite wall, she turned back toward the sheriff and coroner, walking slowly in front of the sofa, and continued with the long-range shots. She knew that she was breathing too shallowly, thinking too much about the flash drive in her shoe, and concentrated on regulating her breath. Sometimes her eyes watered but she kept clicking anyway.

She walked carefully, blood everywhere, streaks and splotches all over the carpet, a few splatters on the walls. But at the end of the sofa, where the padded arm rested barely a foot and a half from the wall, she pulled up short. Louise's little dog lay curled and still against the corner of the room, head and chest bloody, back end caked with its own waste. She realized what she was breathing and tasting, and gagged twice before getting herself under control again.

"Crawled back there to die probably," the sheriff said.

She had to step over and to the right of the dog, swinging her body to put her back to the wall. When she brought her left foot over the dog too, she saw that everything was going to be all right. This was going to work. Keep inching behind the sofa to the other end. Take several shots down at Kenny's face while standing erect. Then a few while easing into a squat. Not much space to maneuver. Keep easing down, body twisting. Camera dipping below the top of the sofa. Hands hidden as she went down on one knee. If she were any bigger, this would be impossible. Left hand letting go of the camera, hand dipping toward her foot. Fingers searching beneath the papery bootie.

There. Plastic. She worked it out with finger and thumb. Gave it a soft flick under the sofa.

Looked toward the men. Both smiled. The sheriff said, "It's not worth pulling a muscle over, Laci."

The coroner said, "She'll get it done. One way or the other, she always does."

A few minutes later she started to back away from the corpse, camera and hands invisible behind the sofa. Then stopped suddenly. Cocked her head. Looked toward the men again, her eyebrows knitted.

"You stuck?" the sheriff said.

"My hand touched something. Underneath the sofa. Did you check under here already?"

"I had a look," the sheriff said, but was crossing toward her now.

"I'm pretty sure I touched something."

He reached for the flashlight on his belt. Flicked it on and dropped to his knees. Lowered his head to the floor.

"I'll keep my hand here," Laci said. "Whatever I touched is just a few inches away."

The sheriff checked the carpet for blood, repositioned himself, touched his head to the floor. Laid the flashlight close to his chin. Shined the light into the darkness. "I got it," he said. "It's pink."

"From blood?" the coroner asked.

"Nope."

Laci said, "Do you want me to pick it up?"

The sheriff said, "Not before you shoot it."

"I doubt I can get a camera on it from here."

The sheriff did not reply, so she set the camera on the floor, aimed it underneath the sofa, and clicked off several shots, subtly redirecting the camera's aim each time.

When satisfied that she had captured the drive's location, she clicked off twenty or so close-ups of Kenny's face, then worked her way out from behind the sofa, took more photos of Kenny, then more shots underneath the sofa from the front.

When the clicking stopped, the sheriff said, "Go ahead and pull that thing out now."

She stuck her arm under the sofa, reached toward the back, pulled her arm back out. "I can't reach it," she told him. "My arm's too short."

The sheriff came forward, lay on his side in front of the sofa, slid his arm underneath. He had to flatten himself against the sofa and stretch his fingers to their limit to reach the flash drive. He pulled it out, sat up, looked at the drive, then laid it atop the sofa cushion before standing.

"A couple close-ups ought to do it," he told Laci.

She clicked off half a dozen. Then, to calm herself, to keep busy, she said, "I still need to do medium range and the rest of the close-ups."

"Have at it," he told her.

She photographed everything, every body, every object in the room. The ball and broken glass and fireplace tools and the flash drive again. Close-ups, medium shots, wall-to-wall shots. A headful of clicks. Each seemed to go into her ears like the snap from a string of firecrackers, then bounced and ricocheted and echoed through her skull.

When she finished she could feel the pressure behind her eyes, all those clicks crowded on top of each other. She blinked. Looked around the room. Saw the men watching her. "I'm satisfied if you are," she said.

"Thanks again, Laci," the coroner told her. "I know it's been a hard night for you."

She nodded. "There's a lot of hardness ahead, I think."

The sheriff touched her shoulder as she started up the stairs. "Do me a favor and tell the deputy he can start bagging now."

She turned to face him. Even from the first step she had to look up. "Any chance you could tell me how it looks to you?"

"It looks ugly," he said. "But I'm betting you already know that."

His eyes were soft. Understanding. She held his gaze and took a chance. "There's nothing here to prove it was Harvey," she said. "Nothing I could see."

"Hmm," he said, a deep quick growl in the back of his throat. He looked about to say more, to contradict her. But then he smiled, and his smile made her feel small, a child. "We'll piece it all together," he said.

"Even if it was him," she said. "You know Harvey. He was rough-spoken, sure, but he didn't hurt people. He loved Jennalee and he loved this town. How do you know he wasn't just defending himself?"

The sheriff held his smile. "You go on back and be with your own family now, okay? Try to get some sleep. I'll talk to Will in the morning. As close to nine as he can make it."

She went up the stairs and out through the kitchen and into the foyer. At the door she removed her gloves and booties and mask and left them on the floor.

The state policeman and Deputy Landers were standing together on the porch, talking softly. It seemed a long way across the street from where she stood. The neighbors in their yards and on their own porches seemed far away and small. All around the large house was empty space. She had a fleeting sensation of standing on a floating island in a vast sea of tiny, distant lights.

To the deputy, she said, "Sheriff needs you to start bagging the evidence now."

"I hate to even go back down into that room," he told her.

"It's okay," she told him. "You'll be okay."

62

They lay awake for a long time, exhausted, holding hands, speaking in whispers.

"He'll probably look at it as soon as he gets back to his office," Laci said. "Maybe sooner if he has a laptop in his car. And that will explain why Harvey did it. What I'm worried about is you and Stevie and what you did at the school."

"Hardly anything," Will told her. "Some graffiti on the walls is all."

"Breaking and entering," she said. "Trespassing."

"We were all wearing gloves. All except Harvey."

"And you're sure you didn't leave anything behind? Nothing that can be traced to you?"

He remembered the cans of spray paint. "Stevie said he got everything."

"And you trust him?"

"What choice do I have?"

She blew out a breath. "I can't believe you were that stupid, Will. I really can't believe it."

"You and me both," he said.

They lay side by side on their backs, only their hands touching. Even so he could feel the stiffness of her body, as rigid with tension as his.

She said, "Let's just go through it all again. Get it straight in your head for morning. So you know what not to say."

"Do it," he said.

"You guys went into the school around midnight."

"Earlier than that," he said. "We were out before midnight." And now he remembered looking at the bar clock when he and Harvey came through the door. He said, "It was eleven fifty-four when Harvey and I got back to the bar."

"Okay," she said. "And almost one-thirty when I got the call about Harvey and Jennalee. So all you have to tell the sheriff is that you were working on the books until Harvey showed up. Then not long after I left for the school, Harvey left too. Said he was going to go see what was happening over there. You were at the bar the whole time."

"I wish I had been able to see him at his house," Will said.

"No you don't."

"I should have been allowed in."

"Trust me," she said. "You wouldn't want to see him like that."

"He's my brother," Will told her. "My brother."

"But what good would it have done? Why would you want to see him looking like that?"

Ten seconds passed before he spoke. "You have the pictures you took, right? Still on your camera?"

He was already moving, preparing to rise from the bed. She reached out, touched his back. And lied. "I gave the memory card to the coroner."

"Before I could see them?" he said.

"Not because of that. Because he asked for it. Needed to study them, he said. They're police property anyway."

He remained motionless, leaning on one elbow.

"Lie back down," she told him. "You'll see him soon."

Half a minute passed before he acquiesced and eased down beside her again. "What if his . . . What if his soul was still there in the house for a while? What if he didn't even realize what had happened to him?"

She heard the catch in his throat, knew that tears were sliding down his cheeks in the darkness. She put out her hand, felt for his. Held it and said nothing for a while. Felt the trembling of his body as he silently wept.

Only when he was still again did she speak. "The sheriff's probably going to ask you if you knew about what was going on with Jennalee and Kenny. He'll ask you about the flash drive."

"What do I say?"

"I keep going back and forth on that," she said. "Is it better to say you knew about it, or better to say you didn't?"

"Better for who?"

"For you. First you have to protect yourself. Keep yourself out of the whole thing."

"I don't want people thinking Harvey just went berserk or something. Like he was some kind of crazy man. Jennalee's the one responsible for all this."

"It matters what people think about you too."

"No it doesn't. I don't give a damn about that."

"You better," she said. "If you love Molly and me, you better care."

"All right," he said.

"Besides, you're in the best position of all for deciding what people think and what they don't."

"What are you talking about?"

"The bar," she told him. "Sooner or later you're going to be asked why Harvey did what he did."

"I'll tell them to mind their own damn business."

"No you won't. You'll tell them what Jennalee was doing. What Harvey told you he found out she and Kenny were doing. You won't have to tell more than one or two people. And within thirty-six hours the whole town will know. They'll probably know anyway, because somebody in the police department is going to whisper it to somebody else. You think Chris Landers will keep his mouth shut about what was on the flash drive? You think Ronnie Walters won't tell his wife?"

"Then why do I have to tell it?"

"Corroboration. You're closer to the source. And don't forget, you said there were other men in those photos with Jennalee. Did you recognize any of them?"

"Yes," he said, his mouth tight.

"All right then," she said. "I don't want to know any names. Kenny and Jennalee are the ones at fault here. Her especially. She's the one who lied, not Harvey. She's the one who cheated. He found out, did something about it, and she killed him for it."

"That's how it happened," he said.

"And that's all anybody needs to know."

63

"So as far as you know," the sheriff said, and drank the last sip of coffee in his mug, his third of the morning, "that's the only reason he was upset? Because of that deal with the motorcycle?"

Will rubbed his forehead, looked at the photograph on the wall behind the sheriff's chair. It was a picture of somewhere out west, a wide green valley with snowcapped mountains in the background. Five brown and black horses were grazing in the valley, everything green below the frozen gray and white. He could feel the coroner's presence behind him, a silent man seated against the opposite wall, listening.

The photo seemed oddly out of place in the sheriff's office. Everything else had an official air to it—the heavy black desk, the sheriff's black leather swivel chair, the cracked brown leather chair Will was in, the black deacon's bench against the wall where the coroner sat. Even with a shaft of morning light streaming in through the high window behind the sheriff, the room felt dark and heavy with the solemnity of the office. The framed photograph was like another kind of window, one that opened onto a distant green and airy place.

"Will?" the sheriff said. "He didn't have any other reason to be upset?"

"It was just a rumor he said he'd heard. I have no idea about the truth of it."

"What rumor was that?"

"He wouldn't tell me anything specific."

"Well, what did he tell you?"

"That Kenny was into something . . . I don't know. *Perverted* is the word he used."

"Harvey heard a rumor that Kenny was into something perverted."

"Right," Will said.

"That's it?"

"Pretty much."

Beside the sheriff's left hand was a yellow legal pad. In his right hand he now held a blue pen, which he tapped atop the paper, leaving an erratic trail of blue dots. "And you have no idea what kind of perversion it was?"

"Only that Harvey was pretty fired up about it. I asked him, I said something like, 'What are we talking about here? You mean he's fooling around with the kids at school?'"

"And why would you come up with that out of the blue? Why would you assume Kenny was fooling around with kids?"

"I don't know. I guess because . . . we'd been talking earlier about kids. About my Molly first. About how hard it is knowing what to do, what to say to them. She's been wanting to start dating an older guy, and I . . . I still can't figure out how to handle that right. And then Harvey was saying how he didn't know if Jennalee was ever going to want kids or not. But he did. He'd always wanted kids. And I said something to the effect that it seemed sort of odd, her being a teacher and not wanting any kids of her own. So I guess that's what had me thinking about kids."

"And what did he say in response?"

"He didn't say anything. Just stood there and looked at me."

"And you took that as a confirmation?"

"I guess I did," Will answered.

"You ever hear anything like that about Kenny yourself? Other people talking?"

Will continued to look at the horses. He wondered if they were wild. What would it be like to ride a wild horse? He bet it would be a blast, if he could do it without breaking his neck.

Then he returned his gaze to the sheriff. "I run a bar," Will said.

"What is that supposed to mean?"

"People have a few drinks, they talk. I overhear stuff."

"And you overheard people talking about Kenny molesting schoolkids? When did this happen?"

"When did I hear it?" He shook his head. "Too long ago to remember. I guess I figured it was just some loudmouth exaggerating, making jokes."

"So you didn't believe any of it?"

"I wouldn't say that, Sheriff. I mean a guy that age, never married and still living with his mother? People are going to wonder."

"Sounds as if you didn't like Kenny much."

"I won't lie and say I loved him like a brother. I didn't. He just wasn't a well-liked person, you know? There always seemed to be something a little too slick about him. Reminded me of a lawyer."

"You have something against lawyers?" the sheriff asked with a small smile.

"Doesn't everybody?"

Behind him, the coroner chuckled.

The sheriff said, "And you think that's why Harvey killed him? Because of that rumor? Or because of the motorcycle?"

"It wasn't the motorcycle. That wouldn't have done it."

"The kids then," the sheriff said. "Were they supposed to be boys or girls?"

Will went silent for a moment, then said, "Boys, I think."

"You think?" the sheriff said.

"Sorry. My brain is like, shutting on and off right now. Like I said, Harvey didn't get specific about any of it. So it must've been because of that earlier time. When I overheard that guy in the bar. That must be why I'm thinking it was boys."

The sheriff drew a small blue circle. Then another one overlapping it. And a third. He said, "So there's the rumor you heard in the bar a while back. And the rumor Harvey says he heard, but which might not even have been about the same thing. Is that it?"

Will put a hand to his face, squeezed the bridge of his nose. Five seconds later he lowered his hand. "There's also this thing he said to me at Jake's funeral."

"And what was that?" the sheriff asked.

"It was during that part at the gravesite. The minister said a few words, then they let the casket down, and then everybody walked back to the cars. Except for Harvey. He didn't seem to want to leave. And I didn't want him standing there alone, so . . . Anyway, there was just the two of us there. But the thing is, Harvey wasn't looking down at the casket, he was watching Kenny out by the cars. They were standing out there, Kenny and Jennalee and her mom, and Kenny was laughing about something. Which ticked off Harvey, I guess. He had this look on his face. Like he hated the sight of him. And he said, looking at Kenny, 'He's not even a man.' And I said, 'What do you mean?' And he said something like, 'Jake knew what he was like. That's why they never got along.' I tried to get more out of him, but it was no use. But it was clear to me then and there how Harvey felt about him."

"I thought they were good friends," the sheriff said.

"Years back," Will told him. "Something happened between them, though. Right before Harvey got married. Kenny was supposed to be his best man, but at the last minute Harvey asked me instead. Kenny wasn't in the wedding party at all."

"And why do you think that happened?"

"I don't know anything definite."

"But you suspect something."

Will shrugged. "I brought it up last night when he was at the bar. All he would say is, he saw something. Back before he got married."

"Meaning what?"

"That's what I asked. I said, 'What did you see?'"

"And?"

"He just said he planned to find out if it was true or not. Once and for all, he said. Said he had to know."

"So these rumors he told you about," the sheriff said. "The recent ones. How recent were they?"

"I got the impression it was very recent. Like yesterday or the day before."

"Was it kids he was talking to when he heard these rumors? Teenagers? Full-grown men?"

"Again, Sheriff, I'm sorry. I wish I had asked him more. I mean he was my brother and all, but we never had that kind of relationship. Never probed into each other's private lives. We just sort of danced around everything. The way we were raised, we all pretty much just kept stuff to ourselves."

The sheriff puckered his lips, drew circles on the tablet. "Kenny's been here at the school for what—fifteen years or so?"

"Sounds right. Started out as assistant principal. Then principal. Then superintendent."

The sheriff nodded. Drew a few more circles. "And what about Harvey's relationship with Jennalee?"

"He loved her. More than anything in the world."

"Did she feel the same way?"

"I thought she did. Until Saturday afternoon anyway."

"What happened then?"

"Laci had coffee with her. Out at the mall. And apparently something Jennalee said made Laci think Jennalee was cheating on Harvey."

"Do you know what was said?"

Will shook his head. "She might have told me, but I can't recall it. It would be better if you get it from her."

The sheriff kept drawing concentric circles on his tablet, extending the circles into a tube slowly rising toward the top of the paper. "And you're sure Harvey never mentioned having been at the school earlier last night? Before he came to the bar?"

"No sir, he did not."

Now, for the first time, the coroner spoke. "Any chance you noticed wounds on his hands? While he was at the bar?"

Will turned halfway in his seat to look at him. "Wounds?" he said.

"Cuts, scratches, abrasions—anything at all?"

"I didn't," Will said. "As far as I recall, he had one hand wrapped around a beer bottle most of the time. Kept the other one below the bar."

The sheriff said, "Is it usual for him to show up at your bar around midnight? Especially when the bar's supposed to be closed?"

"He said he was walking around town and saw the light on. Knew I was in there doing something."

"So is it usual for him to be walking around town at midnight?"

"Sheriff, I don't see *anything* usual about what happened last night. All I know is that he said he was having a hard time sleeping and went out for a walk. I couldn't sleep either. That's why I was downstairs going through my books. It's not usual for me to do that at midnight either."

The sheriff did not nod or even look up. He continued drawing his tube of circles. From where Will sat, it looked like a Slinky. His favorite toy when he was a boy was a Slinky dog. He would set it at the top of the stairs, give it a nudge, and the dog would tumble, red plastic head over red plastic butt, over and over down the stairs. Sometimes it would land on its feet and sometimes it wouldn't.

After a while the sheriff laid his pen down and looked over Will's shoulder to the coroner. The coroner said nothing, but Will imagined that the man shrugged.

The sheriff said, "Harvey ever mention anything to you about a USB drive?"

"A what?" Will said.

"One of those little removable drives you plug into a computer. For storing files on. Reports, pictures, whatever. He ever mention anything about him or Kenny having one of those?"

"Not that I can remember, he didn't. Neither one of us is very handy with computers."

The sheriff leaned back, away from the desk. Laid the pen atop the tablet. "What can you tell me about Harvey's relationship with his mother-in-law?"

"I can tell you they weren't close. Not like he was with Jake."

"You think he was the kind of man who'd take a hand to her?"

Will sat there looking at the sheriff, blinking but silent.

"Will?" the sheriff said.

"I'm sorry. You just reminded me of something."

"And what's that?"

"It must've been a good two weeks ago," Will told him. "I guess Harvey went to Louise about the motorcycle. Said he thought he could convince her that Jake promised it to him."

"And?" the sheriff said.

"She didn't want to hear it. Apparently called Harvey a liar. Said the bike belonged to Kenny and he could do whatever he wanted with it."

"This is what Harvey told you?"

Will nodded. He didn't know what to do, what to say. There was always the chance of saying or doing the wrong thing. A better-than-average chance. But he had to take it.

"I guess they got into it pretty good," he said. "Harvey told her how Jake was embarrassed by the way she babied Kenny and treated him like he was made of gold. Said that's why Kenny turned out the way he did."

"Harvey said that?"

"Harvey said Jake said that."

"And what did he mean by that—'turned out the way he did'?"

"What did Jake mean by it? I have no idea. Soft, I guess. You knew Jake—he was a tough old bird. He wanted his son to be like that too. Instead he got a mama's boy."

"And that was the end of their argument?" the sheriff asked. "Harvey and Louise?"

Will shook his head. "That was when she went batshit crazy on him, Harvey said. Said she threw the glass she was holding, threw it right at his head. He ducked and it smashed against the sink. Then she grabbed a broom that was up against the wall and started beating him over the head with it, and screaming at him to get out of her house and never come back."

"Louise took after him with a broom?"

"I'm just telling you what Harvey told me. Said she chased him outside and off the porch."

"Any chance anybody else saw this happen?"

"I have no way of knowing that," Will said.

The sheriff looked past Will again and toward the coroner. Will watched the sheriff's eyes, the way his frown twitched at the corner of his mouth.

Then the sheriff asked, "You have any idea what your other brother was doing earlier last night? Say ten to one or so?"

"Stevie? No idea whatsoever."

"You haven't talked to him about it?"

"I talked to him twice last night by phone. And I did ask if he knew anything about the break-in at the school. He said he didn't. The rest of the time we just . . ."

The sheriff and coroner remained silent.

"He cried and I cried," Will said. "None of it makes any sense to either one of us."

Another long silence followed.

Finally the sheriff tore the top sheet of paper off his tablet, not angrily or noisily but with one long, smooth tug on the paper. Then he folded the sheet in half, then did the same a second and third time. Then he leaned to the side and dropped the paper into his wastebasket.

He said, "You want to ask your brother to come in for a minute?"

"Will do," Will told him. He stood, wondered if he should shake the sheriff's hand or not. Decided no. Then started to turn but stopped for a last look at the photograph on the wall. "Was that taken somewhere out in the Rockies?" he asked.

"Outside of Grand Junction, Colorado," the sheriff said.

"Looks like Heaven."

"Probably the closest thing we have to it."

Will kept looking. He felt his eyes filling with tears but couldn't stop them. "Harvey was always talking about the three of us going out there together. Mule deer. Elk. Maybe even bear if we could get a tag for one."

The sheriff said, "I brought home a bull elk with a fifty-four-inch beam. Plus a decent bighorn ram. Full curve. One of the best weeks of my life."

"I can't even imagine," Will said.

The sheriff stood then and put out his hand. "I'm sorry, Will. My sympathies to your family."

Will held the sheriff's hand for a long time, squeezing hard, did not want to let it go. Then did, abruptly, and strode to the door.

64

"You on something right now, Stevie?" the sheriff asked. "You wouldn't be high by any chance, would you?"

"Mrs. Wilson gave me an Ativan. From back when her husband passed away."

"I saw her sitting out there in the hallway with you. She drive you over here?"

"Yes sir, she's a very nice lady. Very nice. Voluptuous."

The sheriff's eyebrows went up. "Do I want to know how you know that?"

Stevie smiled. "Like pillows," he said.

The coroner said, "How long have you been taking that drug, Stevie?"

"Just this once. It's nice."

"It's also very addictive. You need to be careful with that."

"Mrs. Wilson is very careful," Stevie said.

The sheriff said, "You know about your brother Harvey, and Jennalee, and the Fultons?"

"Yes sir. Will told me. Mrs. Wilson gave me an Ativan because I couldn't stop crying."

"You loved your brother a lot."

"Yes sir. We're all we have."

"When was the last time you spoke to Harvey?"

"That would be . . . last week sometime. We had pizza and beer at Will's place. We watched a movie on TV. Will doesn't have HBO or Cinemax. Even I have that."

"Do you remember what the movie was?"

"Nicolas Cage was in it. I don't remember the title. He was an angel in a trench coat. He was in *Bobby Sue Got Married* too. You remember that? He talked funny in that one."

"I believe that was *Peggy Sue Got Married*," the coroner said. "With Kathleen Turner."

"That's right!" Stevie said. "And now *she* talks funny! Like she swallowed Darth Vader or something."

The coroner stifled a chuckle.

"Let's get back to Harvey for a minute," the sheriff said. "So you didn't see him at all last night?"

"Last night? What night was that?"

"That was Sunday night. The night the high school got broken into."

"It did, didn't it? I remember hearing about that."

"Any chance you were involved in it?"

"In what, sir?"

"Breaking into the school with your brother Harvey."

"Harvey did that? Why would he do that?"

"Can you tell me where you were last night?"

"Yes sir."

"How about you tell me, then?"

"I was with Mrs. Wilson."

"And where was that?"

"At her place."

"And what were you doing there?"

Stevie smiled. "She told me to be a gentleman. And gentlemen don't kiss and tell."

The coroner and sheriff looked at each other, both with eyebrows raised. The sheriff said, "We're talking about the same Mrs. Wilson sitting out there in the hallway?"

"Only one I know," Stevie said.

"And you were with her last night?"

"All night long."

"Is she going to verify that if I ask her?"

"I'm pretty sure she will," Stevie said.

The sheriff stood and walked out of his office. His footsteps echoed down the long hallway with its marble floors and high, rounded ceiling.

Stevie smiled and gazed at the large framed photo hanging behind the sheriff's desk. "That sure looks nice," he said to no one in particular.

The coroner said, "You brother Will thought so too. I guess we all think so."

Stevie turned in his chair to smile at him. "It's nice to agree," he said.

Moments later the sheriff's footsteps echoed again, growing louder with every step. Then he was standing beside his desk, looking down at Stevie. He said, "Mrs. Wilson's going to take you back to her place now, Stevie. She says you're going to be staying with her a while."

Stevie nodded. "We're going to take care of each other." Then he stood and shook the sheriff's hand. Then the coroner's hand. Then he looked out the empty doorway, and felt confused for a moment.

The sheriff laid a hand on Stevie's back. "Make a right out the door," he said. "Then straight down the hall."

Stevie stepped into the hallway, looked right; Mrs. Wilson, seeming a mile away, waved to him. He wanted to run but remembered that he was inside the courthouse, the same place he paid his driving violations and bought his concealed-carry permit and once a long time ago a dog license for the mixed-breed husky pup that chased after a kid on a bike and got itself crushed by a Chevy Cobalt. So he walked instead. His body felt light, though in the back of his head somewhere was the knowledge that his brother Harvey was dead, and pretty Jennalee was dead, and he would never again see either one of them standing up. And that knowledge was very heavy and very black. And though the sight of Mrs. Wilson standing up to meet him made him happy enough to laugh, the thing in the back of his head made him want to cry instead.

Mrs. Wilson took his hand, leaned close and whispered to him. "Do you promise me you had nothing to do with breaking into that school?"

"Yes ma'am," he said, and told himself, *This is the good kind of lie.* "I promise."

She squeezed his hand, then started them walking toward the exit.

65

"Okay," the coroner said, he and the sheriff alone now in the sheriff's office. "Let's say Laci did put the flash drive under the couch. Why not just hand it over to you? Why not say, 'Here, Sheriff. This might shed some light on why Harvey did what he did'?"

"Didn't want me to know she knows. Embarrassed by the whole thing. But still wants to get the truth out."

"In other words, she provided you with evidence."

"Planted evidence."

"I think it's open to interpretation."

The sheriff chose not to respond to that. "Let's run through what we do know and don't know. Facts only."

"Well," the coroner said, "we have Harvey's blood on the carpet in Kenny's game room, and on three of the fireplace tools. Plus he has defensive wounds, showing that he was struck by at least two of those tools. He has Kenny's and Louise's blood on his clothes. Their blood is on the little shovel."

"So Harvey got into it with Kenny's mother, and maybe she laid into him with the fireplace poker. It's hard to say if she was killed first or Kenny was."

"Could be Kenny attacked him, then Louise joined in, and Harvey found himself fighting for his life. Or Louise started it, and Kenny joined in."

"It's pretty clear whose side you're on here," the sheriff said.

"I'm not on anybody's side. I'm talking science. Everybody's got defensive wounds. It all happened within a matter of minutes. And unless you can say whose wounds came first, you can't say if it was murder or self-defense."

"So there was a fight," the sheriff conceded. "No way of telling who started it."

"Only who survived it. Who killed whom. The flash drive is hard evidence of motivation."

"And far more credible than the kiddie porn story. I think Harvey planted that stuff."

"The question is, Why? When he apparently knew the real reason."

"That's the thing," the sheriff said. "Did he really know? Before breaking into the school, I mean? 'Cause if he did know, why would he need a kiddie porn excuse to go after Kenny?"

"Maybe he wanted to keep the truth to himself about what his wife and brother-in-law were doing. Figured if he got away with killing Kenny, maybe he and Jennalee could get back on track again."

"You think he'd be willing to forgive her that stuff?"

"You ever been in love?" the coroner asked. "Blind stupid crazy in love?"

"Dozens of times," the sheriff said. "Then I got married."

The coroner smiled. Then let the smile fade. "He plants the evidence that will make the entire town despise Kenny Fulton. Then waits around the school afterward to see when Kenny goes home.

"Follows him home. Uses the key in his pocket to sneak inside. Confronts him. Things go south, the old lady wakes up, he ends up fighting for his life, Kenny and his mother end up dead."

"And the little dog too. Three against one, is that what you're saying?"

The coroner shrugged. "The dog was collateral damage. Harvey goes home afterward, pretty well beaten-up himself, I might add, where he tells Jennalee what happened. She puts a shotgun round into his chest, then does the same thing to herself."

"The thing I don't get," the sheriff said, "is when did Laci get hold of the flash drive?"

The coroner thought for a moment. "Harvey was at the bar after the school break-in. But apparently before going to Kenny's house."

"You think he went to the bar to give the flash drive to his brother?"

"Maybe asked him just to hold on to it for a while."

"As evidence. In case Harvey needed it later."

"You think Will knew that much?"

"Maybe not. Not until Laci took the phone call about Harvey being dead. They probably looked at it then."

"If that's the case, why didn't she give it to you at Harvey's place?"

"I'm not sure it was needed then. It would just make Harvey look like an even bigger fool."

"But then she found out that Kenny and Louise were dead too. And what did she do before she went over to their place?"

"Took Will home," the sheriff said. "And grabbed the flash drive. Then pretended to find it underneath the sofa. I *knew* it wasn't there when I looked the first time. Goddamn, I knew it. I looked under every piece of furniture in that room."

"Well then," the coroner said, "let me give you another scenario. A bunch of kids break into the school and trash Kenny's office. One of them finds the flash drive. They all look at what's on it. And decide Harvey needs to see it. So they give it to him. He's stunned. Just absolutely coldcocked by it. Who can he talk to? His brother Will. So he goes over to the bar and gives the flash drive to Will for safekeeping. Maybe he tells him what's on it and maybe he doesn't. Then he walks over to the school to have it out with Kenny, but can't till the police leave, which means he ends up going to Kenny's house later. He confronts Kenny, probably threatens him with exposure. There's a fight, Kenny and Louise get killed. Harvey goes home and tells his wife. Shows her he has the evidence. She shoots him and then herself."

The sheriff blew out a long breath. Sat there leaning over the edge of his desk, hands clasped between his knees, shaking his head back and forth. "We're not ever going to know the truth of it, are we?"

"Not unless you can raise the dead and get them to talk," the coroner said.

The sheriff turned his head to the side again, stared at an uneven square of light cast down on the floor. All of the dirt and ancient filth between the floorboards was made clear by the light. All of the soiled comings and goings of the years.

"You want another thing to worry about?" the coroner asked.

And the sheriff said, "No."

"Who else was at the scene of the crime? Who else maybe had the opportunity to toss that flash drive under the couch?"

"Don't even go there," the sheriff said. "Neither one of my deputies would ever do such a thing."

"Just stirring the pot," the coroner said.

The sheriff offered no response. A few moments later he leaned back in his chair.

The coroner asked, "What about the other men in those photos?"

"What about them?"

"You going to charge them with anything?"

"For Christ's sake," the sheriff said. "If people could be charged for stupidity, we'd have to build three or four more jails."

"You at least going to have a talk with them? Maybe put the fear of God in them?"

"Do I look like a preacher to you?"

"They need to know what they were a part of. The consequences of their behavior."

The sheriff thought it over, then said, "Might not hurt to round them up for a little conversation, I guess. Let them know we know what they've been up to."

"A good dose of humility never harmed anyone."

The sheriff nodded. Pursed his lips. Glanced at the square of light again. Then he swiveled around so as to gaze up at the photo on the wall. "I need to get back into those mountains," he said.

And the coroner, rising to his feet, said, "Haven't you seen enough senseless violence for a while? Why don't you just leave those poor animals alone?"

66

In his only suit, dark blue and a little tight under the armpits, Will swept the sidewalk in front of the bar. He knew he was getting his shoes dirty; even though no wind was blowing, the dust drifted back and settled over his shoes and cuffs. But he was not able to sit still and do nothing; even on this day he lacked the capacity.

Usually when he swept the sidewalk or the interior of the bar he moved with a brisk and calculating purpose, breaking the floor or sidewalk into grids, sweeping one pile of dirt into another so as to ensure that he missed nothing and achieved cleanliness from corner to corner. He did not think about how quickly the area would become soiled again. Did not think of the job as merely a temporary stay against the endless encroachment of dirt.

This afternoon he moved with the briskness and purpose of a somnambulist. Often he swept the same spot twice, missed others completely. He noticed all this with a vague detachment. He was killing time, nothing more. Any minute now Laci and Molly would come downstairs and outside and he would walk with them to the funeral home to say his last goodbye to his brother.

The day's heat was already suffocating, the air still and heavy and thick. He wanted to rip off his tie and coat. Wanted to sit in front of a giant fan that would blow his hair back and dry his face. Wanted to sit alone atop a snowy mountain and feel the cold slow his blood and freeze his brain silent.

Instead he swept.

He didn't even hear Laci and Molly emerge from the bar, didn't know they had arrived until Laci tapped him on the shoulder. He turned and saw them there, looking so pretty and fragile in their dresses, their legs and arms bare, their faces so clean and pretty and sad that his throat thickened and eyes stung and a terrible ache blossomed in his chest.

"You ready?" Laci asked.

He nodded. Stepped back to the wall and propped the broom against the door, against a sign he had taped to the wood: CLOSED FOR FUNERAL.

"You just want to leave it there?" she said.

He answered with a crooked smile. As if a broom leaning against a closed door mattered. As if anything did.

The next thirty minutes seemed to last half a day, one long unbroken drone. He reacted numbly to the hands that shook his. He heard little of the funeral service. The buzz of a fly. The shuffling of feet.

He was supposed to go to the back of the room then for more handshaking; supposed to stand there with Laci and Molly and Stevie, accepting consoling clichés as everybody filed out the door. It seemed such an unnatural custom, even, as he contemplated it, a nauseating one, as if grief could be shared or somehow assuaged. Just the thought of touching all those hands sickened him. The fraudulence. The lie. He dared not look his neighbors and customers in the eye, not with guilt plastered all over his face the way it was.

He told Laci, "Give me a couple of minutes," then went straight to the casket before she could react.

Harvey looked like himself but didn't. Looked like a wax replica of himself. Like a prop in a haunted house in broad daylight. Pitiful but not scary.

Donaldson came up to him and laid a hand on Will's shoulder. Said, "I'll get the other pallbearers rounded up. We'll need to close the casket soon."

Will said nothing, could not even nod. Held to the chrome handle on the side of the casket. Kept staring at his brother's waxy cheeks. The paleness of his lips.

It wasn't long before he felt somebody else at his side. Someone smaller, probably Laci. But if he turned now to look at her he might collapse, might need to grab hold of her to stay on his feet. He gripped the cold handle. Felt the coldness bleeding into him.

"You ever see the play *Our Town?*" the person said. Will turned his head just enough to see out the corner of his eye. Merle, of all people.

"It's fairly simple on the surface," Merle said. "Act 1, youth and innocence, the trivialities of daily life. Act 2, love and marriage. Again, fairly routine. Something everybody can identify with. Act 3, death. Bam, it hits you out of the blue. A cruel reminder. People die, and they forget all about us. They have to."

Will turned his head, looked down. What was he talking about?

"Thing is," Merle said, "life's a lot messier than a three-act play, isn't it, Will? People make stupid choices and don't realize until too late how stupid they were."

And there was something in Merle's tone, something knowing, damning, that set Will back on his heels, made him feel that if he did not hold tight to the casket's handle he was going to tumble over backward for sure. The entire weight of his body was leaning backward, pulling on the casket, threatening to slide it off its pedestal.

"People die," Merle said, "and then they're out of this mess. The rest of us have to keep dealing with it, though. The best way we know how. That's Act 4. It all takes place behind the curtain."

Will felt his knees weakening, his body sagging. To take his weight off the casket he held to the handle but sank down on his knees, laid his head against the shiny hull, heard his own frantic breath.

Merle's hand on his shoulder.

Then nothing. A long moment of contact, then the hand moved away. Merle moved away. And Will remained kneeling, motionless, breathing fast and shallow, waiting for Laci to come and help him to stand.

67

Will and Stevie and four men from the Jimmy Dean plant in Gallatin lifted and shouldered the casket outside to the hearse. Harvey's weight pressed hard and sharp on Will's clavicle, dug deep into his chest, tightened around his lungs. He felt that his spine was being crushed, was about to crumple like a straw.

Every shift of Harvey's body made Will wince, every tilt and scrape. His ear was pressed against the hull, heard everything, absorbed every whisper. He thought for a moment about dropping his corner, ducking under the casket and letting it crash atop him, crush him flat, put an end to all this heaviness, this burden that would never leave him now, never lift away.

Then the casket was in the hearse but the heaviness remained. Heavy in every breath. Every heartbeat a dull and labored thud.

He and Laci and Molly and Stevie rode in Donaldson's long black Cadillac as it made its way to the cemetery on the northern edge of town. The irony of the vehicle's luxury did not escape Will: there is more comfort in death than in life.

68

At the cemetery the air was a little cooler beneath the scattered oaks and maples. The sky had darkened to the color of ash, and Will hoped for rain. None came.

After a while Will found that he was standing alone at the gravesite with Laci and Molly. Cars were pulling away from the curb, on their way to the bar, where foil pans of lasagna and cold cuts and desserts would materialize on the tables as if out of thin air.

"Sweetie?" Laci said, and took his hand. "We should go now."

He looked down at her. "What are people going to eat off of?" he said.

"What?"

"Was I supposed to get plates for everybody? I have glasses but not enough plates."

"It's okay," she told him. "It's been taken care of."

He stared at her. "What am I supposed to do?"

"Nothing," she said. "Just come and be there with us."

Laci took his hand, led him back toward the waiting car. Deputy Walters and Donaldson were standing at the rear of the car. As Will and his family approached, the deputy came forward to meet them halfway.

He smiled at Molly first, then at Laci. "Any chance I could speak with your husband for a minute?"

She turned to look up at Will, whose eyes were on Walters, Will's expression pinched, eyes squinting. To Molly she said, "Why don't you wait in the car with Uncle Stevie, okay? It's cooler there."

She watched Molly turn away, saw Donaldson open the car door for her. Then, to Walters, Laci said, "What's it about, Ronnie?"

The deputy gave her a crooked smile. "I'm supposed to give you this," he said.

Reached into his pocket and withdrew a business card, which he held toward Will. Laci took it from his hand, read the glossy face.

"This here's a company out of New Castle that cleans up houses after situations such as these," Ronnie told her. "You'll probably want to get them taken care of ASAP. Send the bill to the address I wrote on the back. It will all get deducted from the estates."

Laci looked up. "Why do we have to do this?"

"It's just the one room in each house. This company will clean them up so that nobody will even know what happened there."

"But Ronnie," she said, still looking at the address he had written, "why are we responsible for having this done?"

"The sheriff's putting the incident at Kenny's house down to a mutual combatant situation."

"Okay," Laci said. "And what does that mean?"

"It's just impossible to pin down timewise," Walters said. "So unless he gets pushback from the community or the town council or somebody . . . If that happens, the DA might or might not insist on a more specific charge."

She was beginning to understand. No criminal charges against Harvey. "Do you think that's going to happen?" she asked.

The deputy shrugged. "I think everybody's dead and there's nobody left to punish. Sheriff said so himself."

She looked up at her husband. Wondered what he was thinking. If he was following any of this.

"There's just no way to attribute intent," Walters told her. "Not with the defensive wounds Harvey incurred. And no way to say who struck the first blow."

Will released a breath through his nose, a small moan from the back of his throat.

Walters gave him a look, then addressed Laci again. "That lawyer on the back of the card I gave you is handling the disposition of the estates. The way it looks is, since Kenny and his mother died first, minutes apart, their estates would go to Jennalee and become part of her marital assets. But then she shot Harvey, which means that even if she had lived, she couldn't accrue any profit or benefit from killing him. Which means he inherits her share of marital assets, along with his own. Where it gets tricky is that Harvey was involved in a double homicide too. If he were to be charged criminally for that, he couldn't benefit either. Except does he really benefit if the assets go to his next of kin?"

Will spoke, surprising both of them. "I, uh . . . I don't know. I'm sorry."

"No, that's okay," the deputy said. "I wasn't asking you to answer that question. I'm just saying it's a tricky situation. But in all likelihood, it's all going to end up with the two of you. You guys and Stevie."

Laci looked from Walters to her husband. Then down at the card. "Why would anybody want either one of the houses?"

"You might be surprised," the deputy said. "Two of the nicest houses in town? I bet Stevie would love to get out of that little trailer of his. I know I would if I was him."

Laci regarded her husband. He looked as limp as a scarecrow, one arm hanging at his side, the other held outward only by Laci's hand in his.

"Of course, the state's going to take its chunk," Walters said. "But what's left won't be insignificant. The land, two houses and everything in them, insurance policies, savings accounts, the whole shebang. The lawyer will contact you when he's got it all straightened out."

Will said nothing, motionless but for his head moving back and forth by a few degrees. He stood as he had at his brother's grave, eyes on the ground, head shaking almost imperceptibly. His hand tightened around Laci's.

"If you and your family need anything," the deputy said, "you just let me know. Anything at all."

Laci nodded, thanked him with a small smile. Then looked up at her husband again. The deputy nodded in return, then walked away.

Laci reached up with her free hand and slipped the business card into the breast pocket of Will's suit coat. "Did you get all that?" she asked.

Will nodded, but his eyes looked glazed. He seemed to be having a hard time looking at even her. Or maybe having a hard time being looked at.

69

After Deputy Walters's departure, only one vehicle remained in the cemetery. Donaldson's Cadillac. It sat with the engine and air conditioner running. Behind the tinted windows, Donaldson sat at the wheel, Stevie in the passenger seat, Molly in the rear seat, all waiting for Laci and Will.

Will had moved away from the grave, had walked a couple of yards beyond it and stood facing the woods in the distance, his back to the car, leaving Laci beside the grave.

"You doing okay?" she asked.

He said, "I feel like I can't get any air into my lungs."

She crossed to stand beside him, and laid her hand against the small of his back. "What do you want to do?"

After a few moments he reached into his pocket, took out the key to the bar's front door, handed it to her. "Just open the place up. I'll be there in a while."

"You want me to stay here with you? I can give the key to Stevie."

"I need to walk," he said.

"Alone?"

"I think so," he said.

She stood on her toes and kissed his cheek. "Don't be too long, babe. Don't make us worry about you."

She turned and headed toward the car, but paused midway to look back. He was already walking, a brisk, angry stride, yet anything but straight, staggering toward the trees.

70

Ten minutes into the shade and a semblance of calm finally descended. Movement and shade were all Will had needed, just like as a boy. This was the only place he had ever felt comfortable. Maybe there was something wrong with him, some flaw that made him uneasy around people, made him too conscious of himself. Not a good trait in a barman. But in the woods he felt wholly different. Enveloped in something. Cloaked. Not a man standing conspicuous and alone and exposed in his uncertainty.

Harvey had loved the woods too. How many times had they walked through these woods together, ten yards apart but tethered by their silence and blood? Tethered by their love, which was never spoken aloud, never even by allusion. To be felt was enough.

Even their father, for all his rough talk and apparent disdain for them, despite the quickness of his hands when he felt disobeyed or ignored, even he had loved the woods and been changed inside them.

Will thought back to their last hunting trip together, all four of them in their canvas jackets and orange vests. There had been a fine powdered snow on the dry leaves that morning, a light breeze blowing through bare branches, long shafts of low, golden sunlight glinting on ice-encrusted limbs. Every movement crackled. Every breath vaporous and warming on the face.

It was Stevie who spotted the big buck behind a thick shrub, its antlers looking like a trophy rack, thick hindquarter showing clearly once you knew where to look. Harvey had said, because his father had been ill for a while now, everyone aware of what lay ahead, "It's yours, Pops. Go on and take it."

Their ailing father raised the rifle, squinted into the scope. Used his teeth to pull off a glove, let it fall to the ground. He flicked off the safety. Slipped a finger through the trigger housing. And his sons stood frozen in place, eyes on the buck, and waited for the loud crack of the bullet.

But then their father had lowered the rifle. Said, "What do you say we just look at him this time, boys? Give him another year to enjoy all this."

Remembering that day—remembering the love he had felt for his father at that moment, the release of fear and resentment, and the consequent swell of affinity with his brothers as well, for the woods and all they held—Will sagged, knees buckling, and he stumbled forward, braced himself against a tree, right palm and forehead against the rough bark as he wept. He was either going to be sick or pass out. He hoped for the latter.

But neither happened. For even as he wept, each inhalation took in the scent of the woods, the leaf-matted ground and the shaded moss. And each breath filled his lungs and emptied them, the clean, cooling air going in, the dark, heavy air going out.

He had been silent for a few moments, yet still braced against the tree, when a hand pressed lightly against his back. It did not startle him. He half expected to turn and see Harvey standing there. Or else Laci. But it was Molly. Beautiful sweet Molly.

He smiled. "What are you doing out here?"

"Following you," she said.

He turned fully, leaned back against the tree. "I thought you were still mad at me."

"I am. I just wanted to make sure you don't get lost."

He kept smiling, felt the warming ache in his chest, felt tears of a different kind wanting to come to his eyes. "I know these woods pretty good," he told her.

"What makes you think I don't?"

"You've been out here before?"

"Lots of times," she said. Then, "A couple anyway. Maybe not lots."

He said, "You feel like walking with me awhile?"

"Might as well," she said.

And they walked side by side for a while. He tried to match his stride to hers. Wanted to reach out and guide her each time they encountered a scraggly vine or deadfall, but resisted, kept his hands to himself.

Until he stopped and raised a hand in front of her. "Look up there," he said, and pointed midway up a medium-size oak.

"Look where?" she said.

"About twelve feet up. In that fork."

A ball of gray. Motionless. Black nose and small dark eyes.

She reached for his hand. "What is it?"

"Groundhog," he said. "It's not dangerous." Then wished he hadn't said it, didn't want her to reclaim her hand.

She didn't. "A groundhog in a tree?"

"They do that sometimes."

"I thought they lived underground."

"They do. But you live in a building and you used to climb trees."

"What's he doing up there?"

"Hard to say. Maybe he heard us coming but was too far from his burrow. So he scampered up there."

"It looks like a koala bear."

"It sort of does," he said.

Her hand was small in his, her skin warm. He wished he could raise her hand to his lips as he had when she was small; could kiss her fingers and palm and lay her hand against his cheek; could bring her face close so that he could kiss her forehead and eyes and nose and let the flood of emotion wash over her again, let it bind them inextricably as it had in previous years, the only form of communication either one needed.

But she was too old for that now. He didn't know how to throw open the floodgates anymore. All that love dammed up inside.

Then her hand slipped out of his. He felt reduced by that; made less than he had briefly been.

She started walking again, and he stepped forward, a long stride to stay beside her.

A few minutes later, she spoke. "Did you really see him making out with another girl?"

He did not understand. Was she talking about the groundhog? Harvey? But then it dawned on him—the older boy she liked. "I'm afraid I did. And smoking weed."

"You and Mom used to smoke it."

He was surprised she knew that. "Used to," he said.

"What did she look like?"

"Your mother?"

"The girl he was making out with."

"Older than you," he told her. "But not half as beautiful."

"I bet," she said. Then, a few moments later, "Anyway, it's no big deal if he was kissing somebody."

"Really?" Will said.

"We don't get freaked out by things like that the way your generation does."

Interesting, he thought, and wasn't sure if her statement troubled him or not.

She said, "That still doesn't make what you did okay."

"I know, sweetie. And I'm sorry I embarrassed you. I really am."

She looked down at her feet as she walked. "Are you going to let me look at the video? Mom said it was up to you."

"You can look at anything you want," he told her. "Just promise that you'll try to see things from my point of view. You mean everything to me. I will never be willing to let somebody break your heart."

"You broke it," she said.

"I'd rather die than do that."

She said nothing.

"If anything bad ever happened to you or your mother," he told her, "I couldn't live anymore. I would need to stop living just to shut off the pain."

She lifted her head, looked up at him. He could see surprise in her eyes. Realized that maybe she had never before considered it—this awful side of love.

"You're a beautiful young woman," he told her, "and from here on in, boys are going to try to take advantage of you. Once the testosterone starts flowing, they can get pretty selfish sometimes. You know about testosterone, right?"

"Of course, Daddy. We learned about it in health class. *Years* ago."

"It's always a problem with guys. Some of them learn to control it; some don't even try."

"Is that what happened with Uncle Kenny and Aunt Jennalee?"

"How much do you know about that?"

"Everything. Mom said what they did was wrong."

"Most people would agree."

"But what do you think?"

"I don't know, honey. I think maybe they were both very lonely people inside. Or they felt they couldn't trust anybody else besides each other. I honestly don't know what to think."

"Heather says the royal families used to do incest all the time back in the olden days. It was because they thought they were special and better than everybody else."

"So your friends are talking about it now?"

"They say that's why Uncle Harvey beat them up and killed them."

"Deputy Walters said it's impossible to know who started that fight. It might have been Kenny. It might even have been Louise."

"Who do you think started it?"

"All I know is that I never once saw my brother start a fight. I saw him finish a lot of them, though."

They walked in silence, moving without hurry. Will matched his stride to hers. Felt that he could walk like this forever.

"Testosterone also makes men aggressive," Molly said.

"It certainly can."

"I think that's what happened at Uncle Kenny's house."

"You're probably right."

"Why do you think *she* did it, Daddy?"

"Jennalee, you mean?"

She nodded. Sniffed. They walked a few steps.

He said, "I guess she's the only one who knows that, sweetheart. Maybe Harvey knew too. But I sure don't."

He heard the hoarseness and the quiver in his voice and knew that she had heard it too, for now she looked up at him. A tear slid off his cheek but he did nothing to wipe it away. And then she too began to cry and leaned into him and he wrapped both arms around her and pulled her close. The scent of her hair made him cry even harder, and his cheek bucked against the side of her head. And for a while he felt that if he loosened his grip on her he would go sliding off into oblivion.

But soon she pulled away, not fully at first, then more, until she was standing apart from him, looking at the ground.

He said, "You think we ought to turn around and head back?"

She said, "Let's go a little farther," and started walking again.

He caught up to her. Thought about reaching for her hand. Did not know if he should.

She said, "Are you going to the funeral tomorrow? For Uncle Kenny and Jennalee and her mother?"

"We'll all go," he said. "It won't be easy, but we'll go."

They continued walking. She paused to look at a patch of small ferns. Bent down close to them, laid her palm beneath a frond, the tiny leaves bright and delicate against her skin.

He wished he knew the name of the fern. Wished he had something instructive to say. He should have learned more when he was a boy, a young man. Should have paid closer attention.

She lifted away from the fern, pressed her hands together and looked ahead, slightly to the right, then slightly to the left. "Is this where you always go hunting?" she asked.

"Since I was a boy," he said.

"Are you going to do it this year? You and Uncle Stevie?"

He thought for a moment. "It's funny," he told her, "but now that I think about it, Stevie never shot at anything. I don't know if he ever once fired his gun."

"He doesn't like to hurt things. Unless they're dangerous or causing problems."

"How do you know that?"

"He told me."

"When did this happen?"

She shrugged. "When we talk. I do talk to him, you know. Just because you guys never talk to each other about things doesn't mean he doesn't talk to Mom and me."

He couldn't help but smile; she was so much smarter than him. Better than him. Just like Laci. He and Stevie were so lucky to have them in their lives.

"You can go hunting with Stevie and me this fall if you want," he said. "You're old enough."

"I'm not shooting anything either," she said.

"That's okay. We don't need to hunt."

"I mean I'll come out in the woods with you. But I'm not going to shoot anything. It's too pretty here for that."

And then he knew that he was done with hunting too. All he needed was to walk with her. With Molly and Laci and Stevie. He would walk with them wherever they wanted to go. Summer spring winter fall, as many seasons as he was allowed. He would walk and walk and never stop walking with them. Around the world and back again.

71

Presiding behind the bar, Laci poured drafts and shots of whiskey and lined them up near the outer edge. She tried not to think about how much money she was giving away. Each time the worry formed, she pushed it down. *This isn't the time for that,* she thought.

When not pouring drinks or thanking somebody for coming, she watched the people milling around, a dozen or so still standing in line to fill their plates from the buffet table. Stevie moved from one pocket of conversation to the next, Mrs. Wilson at his side as he nodded somberly and returned one handshake after another.

It was nice to see the room so full. Several of Molly's friends had turned out too, all of them seated around the big table at the back of the room, waiting for Molly to return. Laci looked at their young faces and felt a pang of sadness. So much misery ahead for them. So much uncertainty and regret.

Nobody ever prepares you for that, she told herself. *They tell you the future is bright and full of promise, but nobody ever mentions the other side.*

Now and then the door swung open and suddenly the room would fill with a silent explosion of blinding afternoon light. Laci would squint into the light, unable to identify the individual or couple approaching until the door fell closed again. And sometimes Laci would shiver when the light was cut off, because she knew that something else was out there too, menace and foreboding out there hiding behind the light, waiting for the chance to pounce and enter.

But this family, she told herself, and leaned into the bar, gripping it hard with both hands, *this family is not going to fall apart. This family will survive.* She would make sure of that. With vigilance and resolve, she would make damn sure of that.

A few minutes later Stevie made his way to the bar alone. His eyes were wet and shining. "What are we going to do, Laci?" he said.

She said, "You're going to go get yourself and Mrs. Wilson something to eat. And you're going to remember all the good things Harvey did. And we're all going to live our lives the best way we can."

He nodded, but said, "I'm going to need some help getting through all this."

She handed him two cans of soda. "You know where to find it."

Again he nodded, then turned to walk away.

"Stevie," she said, and motioned for him to lean close so that she could whisper in his ear. "When you're eating, honey?" she told him. "Make sure you chew with your mouth closed. Women like a man with good manners."

ACKNOWLEDGMENTS

My thanks, as always, go out to Sandy Lu, literary agent par excellence, and to Jessica Tribble, Charlotte Herscher, and the entire team at Thomas & Mercer, and, of course, to the unnumbered but never forgotten readers who give this story and every story their reason for being.

ABOUT THE AUTHOR

Photo © 2016 Maddison Hodge

Randall Silvis is the internationally acclaimed author of sixteen novels, a story collection, and a book of narrative nonfiction. He is also a prize-winning playwright, a produced screenwriter, and a prolific essayist who has been published and produced in virtually every field and genre of creative writing. His essays, articles, poems, and short stories have appeared in *Discovery Channel Magazine*, the *Writer*, *Prism International*, *Short Story International*, *Manoa*, and numerous other online and print magazines. His work has been translated into ten languages.

Silvis's literary awards include two writing fellowships from the National Endowment for the Arts; the Drue Heinz Literature Prize; a Fulbright Senior Scholar research award; six fellowships for his fiction, drama, and screenwriting from the Pennsylvania Council on the Arts; and an honorary doctor of letters degree for "distinguished literary achievement."

Learn more about Silvis's work at www.randallsilvis.com.